"Don't be afraid, Roslynn,"

he whispered, his voice husky, his Welsh accent stronger. "I told you I could be patient and gentle. See, very patient, me."

He angled closer to her, and although she felt his arousal, he made no effort to hold her any tighter, his excitement held in check by his undoubtedly powerful will. Nevertheless, she could sense his desire lurking like an animal only temporarily tamed.

As her fears kept her passion caged.

Until now. Until she had married this man who could set her free and release her from the chains of her past.

Holding him tight, she relaxed against him, her passion burning hotter as she parted her lips and pushed her tongue into Madoc's warm, wet mouth.

MARGARET MOORE

The Warlord's Bride

HQN™

Recycling programs
for this product may
not exist in your area.

ISBN-13: 978-0-373-77348-0
ISBN-10:   0-373-77348-X

THE WARLORD'S BRIDE

Copyright © 2009 by Margaret Wilkins

This edition published by arrangement with Harlequin Books S.A.

® and TM are trademarks of the publisher. Trademarks indicated with
® are registered in the United States Patent and Trademark Office, the
Canadian Trade Marks Office and in other countries.

www.HQNBooks.com

Printed in U.S.A.

Also by

MARGARET MOORE

Knave's Honor
The Notorious Knight
My Lord's Desire
Hers To Desire
Hers To Command
The Unwilling Bride
Lord of Dunkeathe
Bride of Lochbarr

For those who share my affection for men with broadswords, with my thanks.

The Warlord's Bride

CHAPTER ONE

Wales, 1205

LORD ALFRED DE GARLEBOINE drew his dappled palfrey to a halt and peered through the water dripping from his coif. More rain fell from the pine trees beside the road and roused their heavy scent, while the verge was a mess of mud and running water. The drizzle rendered the sky a leaden gray and the rest of the landscape all mucky brown and dull green, the few exposed rocks like hunched little men trying to keep dry.

"God be praised, Llanpowell at last," the middle-aged nobleman muttered as his mount refooted, its hooves churning up mud and pebbles.

From under the sodden hood of her cloak lined with fox fur, the young lady riding beside him followed his gaze to what was most definitely a castle and not just another stony outcropping in the south of Wales.

"My lord!"

At the alarmed cry, Lord Alfred and Lady Roslynn de Werre looked back to see a heavy wooden cart stuck in a rut and tilting precariously. The toothless carter leaned to one side, whipping the pair of draft horses and exhorting them to move. The horses snorted and pulled against the harness, but the wheel only sank deeper into the mud.

"Don't just sit there like a lump of dung," Lord Alfred ordered. "Get off and make those stupid beasts move!" He pointed at six of the soldiers in the escort. "Stay with the wagon until it's at the castle. The rest of us will continue."

He shifted forward, then turned his steely, gray-eyed gaze onto Lady Roslynn. "Do you have any objection to leaving the wagon and going on to the castle, my lady?"

"You are in command here," she said with a beatific smile quite at odds with her internal turmoil. In truth, she would rather sit in a downpour than reach Llanpowell. "Are six men really necessary to guard the wagon when we're so close to a nobleman's castle, and in such inclement weather?"

"I'll not take any chances," Lord Alfred replied before raising his hand and shouting for the rest of the cortege to move on.

Lady Roslynn suppressed a sigh. She didn't

know why King John's courtier had even bothered to ask her opinion. No doubt she shouldn't have bothered to answer.

The cortege continued on its way, the silence broken only by the falling rain, the jingle of accoutrements and soldiers' chain mail, and the slap of hooves on the muddy road, every step bringing them closer to the castle of the lord of Llanpowell. Like the rocks, it seemed to be a natural feature of the landscape, exposed by time and the weather, not an edifice built by men.

This entire land was a rough contrast to Roslynn's familiar Lincolnshire, where the flat fens stretched out for miles and the sky seemed endless. Here, there were hills and valleys, unexpected streams and wet bracken, scree and rocks. It was wild and untamed, strange and breathtaking, despite the presence of the colossal fortress looming ahead.

Roslynn tried to stifle her dread as they neared the massive, bossed gates of thick oak. Whatever happened here, at least she was away from the king's court, and the accommodations should be better than those they'd had along the way.

A voice called out from the top of the barbican, speaking Norman French, albeit with a noticeable Welsh accent. "Who are you and what do you want at Llanpowell?"

"I am Lord Alfred de Garleboine, on the king's business," the nobleman shouted back.

"The king's business?" the man on the wall walk repeated. "Which one?"

"Is the man a simpleton?" Lord Alfred muttered. He raised his voice. "John, by the grace of God, king of England, lord of Ireland, duke of Normandy and Aquitaine, count of Anjou."

"Oh, the Plantagenet usurper who killed his nephew."

Although the man on the wall had said only what many believed was true, this didn't bode well for a pleasant reception.

Three others, likewise bareheaded and wearing tunics, not chain mail, joined the man on the wall.

"What does John want?" one of them called out.

"I will discuss that with your overlord," Lord Alfred replied.

"Maybe you've come to attack," the first man called back.

Lord Alfred shifted impatiently in his ornately gilded saddle. "Do we look like a band of brigands?"

"Can't be too sure these days," the first man replied, apparently quite unconcerned by the nobleman's growing impatience. "Seen some well-dressed Norman thieves in our time, we Welsh have."

"Open these gates or the king shall hear of this, as well as your master!"

It seemed that while the sentries were content to make sport of Norman visitors and their king, the lord of Llanpowell was not likely to be amused by their insolence, for the massive gates slowly began to open.

What did that say about the lord of Llanpowell? That he ruled by fear and harsh punishment? Or was he simply not to be trifled with, but respected and obeyed?

Whatever Madoc ap Gruffydd was like, there was no turning back or running away now.

"About bloody time. Insolent savages," Lord Alfred growled as he flicked his gauntleted hand and gestured for their party to enter the castle.

Inside the outer wall was a large area, grassy and perhaps fifty yards long. Beyond the outer ward was the inner curtain wall, taller than the first, with another gate and a less elaborate gatehouse.

The inner gates were open, and a large wooden cart pulled by two thick-chested oxen rumbled toward them, followed by a group of twenty men, all wearing sword belts, with bows in their hands and quivers at their hips. They wore only leather tunics, breeches and boots, however, not chain mail or helmets. Their hair was almost uniformly dark brown or black, and most sported thick beards.

Despite their attire, they must be part of the garrison, for they briskly formed two rows lining the road leading through the studded gate to the inner ward.

Lord Alfred's jaw clenched. "The king shall hear of this insult, as well."

"I believe it's a guard of honor, my lord," Roslynn quietly offered. "See how they're arranged and how still they stand?"

Lord Alfred's only response to her observation was a noncommittal grunt.

Nevertheless, she was sure she was right, for the men remained where they were, staring stoically ahead, as the cortege continued into the courtyard.

Here the buildings were of several sizes and materials. Some were made of stone, with slate roofs. Others, like the stables, were half-timbered and wattle-and-daub, and some looked like little more than wooden lean-tos attached to any available wall. At least the yard was cobblestoned, so while there were several large and growing puddles, it was not a sea of mud.

Unfortunately, there were also several armed soldiers around the perimeter, standing beneath the eaves of buildings and watching them warily.

Before they could dismount, or a groom or stable boy arrived to take the horses, the door to the largest of the stone buildings flew open as if caught by a strong wind. A rotund, gray-haired fellow clad in a dusky green tunic, plain breeches and scuffed boots, with a dark brown woolen cloak thrown about his shoulders, came hurrying down the steps. Like the others, his hair was long and his beard full. Unlike the others, he wore only a simple belt, with no obvious weapon at his side, and a smile lit his round face. He also carried a huge mug in his hands, despite the continuing rain.

"Welcome, my lord, my lady!" he called out in Welsh-tinged French, ignoring the puddles as he splashed his way toward them. "Welcome to Llanpowell! Welcome to my home. An honor it is to have you here!"

It felt as if a stone had settled into Roslynn's stomach as she realized this must be Madoc ap Gruffydd, the lord of Llanpowell.

She had—foolishly, it now seemed—assumed the Bear of Brecon would be a younger man. She'd also assumed he was called the Bear because of his fierceness in battle, not for wild gray hair that fell to his shoulders, his bushy beard or the size of his belly.

Or perhaps that name had been given to him in his youth.

The Welshman called out a few orders in his

native tongue, and immediately grooms and boys appeared from the stables to take hold of their horses.

Apparently the lord of Llanpowell's servants were as well trained as his soldiers, in spite of his jovial appearance and friendly manner.

"Come inside and get dry!" the Welshman cried as he waved his hand toward the large stone building that must be the hall, paying no heed to the drink that spilled from his mug.

Roslynn sincerely hoped Madoc ap Gruffydd wasn't a drunkard.

His expression grim, Lord Alfred swung down from his saddle and came to help her dismount. Once on the ground, she took a deep breath and shook out the full gored skirt of her gown of perse, while Lord Alfred stiffly held out his arm to lead her into the hall behind their host.

The soldiers in the yard remained where they were, watchful and suspicious.

The hall was rather small, and close, and old, the beams dark with age and smoke. Unlike more recently built halls, it had a central hearth and the roof was held up not by pillars of stone, but wood, some plain, some carved with vines and leaves and faces of animals. Rushes covered the floor, and three large hunting dogs, as shaggy as their master, lumbered to their feet, sniffing at the Normans as they passed.

Several servants waited by the walls, watching like the soldiers in the yard, as their host led them toward the hearth and the benches and single wooden chair arranged around it.

After seeing the castle's fortifications, Roslynn had assumed that the living quarters of Llanpowell would be more modern and comfortable. It was disappointing to discover they were not, but at least they would be dry.

And no matter how primitive the accommodations, this was still better than being at King John's court, where she had to fend off the advances of the king and every other lascivious courtier who believed, given her recent history, that she should be grateful for his attention.

"Sit you down by the fire, my lady," their host said as he threw off his cloak, goblet still in hand. He didn't seem to notice or care that his cloak fell to the rush-covered floor before a servant had time to grab it.

"Bron, what are you about, girl?" he demanded of another maidservant standing by the wall, who looked about eighteen years old. "Take her ladyship's cloak."

The young woman darted forward and waited while Roslynn removed the rain-soaked garment. The servant, just as quickly, hurried to hang it on a peg on the wall before returning to her post.

It was warmer near the fire, and Roslynn was well dressed in a thick woolen gown and heavy boots, but she shivered nonetheless and wrapped her arms about herself as she took a seat on the bench.

Smiling expansively, the Welshman settled his bulk in the chair and grinned at Lord Alfred, who stood so stiffly, one might conclude he was incapable of bending at the waist.

"No doubt you're wondering what has brought us here," he began just as stiffly.

"Aye, I do, but sit down, man!" the Welsh nobleman commanded with a deep chuckle. "Drink and food before business. Can't think of important matters when my belly rumbles. Bron, some mulled wine for our guests, and barley bread and the soft cheese, not the hard. No *braggot*. Not yet, anyway."

As the young woman disappeared into what was likely the corridor to the kitchen, the Welshman turned to Roslynn with a wink. "*Braggot*'s Welsh mead, my lady, and strong, so we best stay with the wine for now."

She managed to return his smile. Madoc ap Gruffydd was neither young nor handsome, but that was surely all to the good. Had she not learned how deceptive youth and a comely face and form could be? Besides, a man of his age could well be past greed and ambition, happy to live out his days in quiet contentment on his estate. That could explain why Madoc ap Gruffydd was so cheerful and welcoming: he had no reason not to be.

"So, my lord, how does the king fare these days?" he inquired as he tossed his now-empty goblet at another of the servants, who caught it so deftly, she assumed this happened often. "Still happy with his little French wife?"

"King John is quite well and, yes, happily wed. We have every hope an heir to the throne will soon be forthcoming," Lord Alfred coldly replied. "Now, if you will permit me to introduce myself, my lord. I am Lord Alfred de Garleboine and this is—"

"Lord Alfred de Garleboine? There's a mouthful. Can't say I've heard of you, but then, I don't pay much attention to the English court and the mischief they get up to." The Welshman patted Roslynn's hand. "Much more pleasant to tell stories round the fire and sing songs of brave deeds, eh, my lady?"

"A nobleman must pay heed to what transpires at court if he is to assist the king and protect his family," she replied, not impressed by his apparently lackadaisical attitude, especially in such times, and with such a king upon the throne.

"Oh, I know enough, I know enough. Not quite at the end of the world, us," Lord Madoc replied, be-

fore raising his voice to shout for Bron. She immediately reappeared in the doorway, a distinctly har-
ried expression on her pretty face. "Where's the
food, girl? And the drink? Our guests are starving!
Fine thing if they can't get a bite to eat after riding
in the wet!"

The maidservant said something in rapid Welsh,
then disappeared again.

"It's not that we don't have plenty in the larder,
my lady," the lord of Llanpowell explained as if it
was a matter of grave concern. "It's just you
caught us between meals while we wait for the
patrols to come back. Had a bit of bother with
them over the mountain."

As Roslynn smiled to show him she wasn't disturbed by the delay, she wondered what he meant
by "bit of bother" and who "them over the mountain" might be. Enemies, clearly, but how many and
how powerful? She'd been told almost nothing
about the lord of Llanpowell and even less about
any potential enemies he might have.

"My lord," Lord Alfred began again, his exasperation obvious. "We have come—"

"Ah, here's the food now!" the Welshman interrupted as the serving girl arrived carrying a large
tray bearing three unexpectedly fine silver goblets,
a carafe of steaming wine, whose spicy scent filled

the air and a beechwood platter covered with a napkin. One of the other male servants hurried forward with a small bench, which he put in front of Madoc ap Gruffydd. After Bron set the tray on it, the Welshman whisked off the napkin to reveal two sliced loaves of fresh, brown bread and several slices of thick cheese, as well as honey cakes.

As the aroma from the warm bread and spiced wine filled her nostrils, Roslynn's stomach growled loudly.

She blushed with embarrassment, but the lord of Llanpowell laughed and handed her one of the goblets before pouring her some wine. "What did I tell you? Hungry you are, and no mistake. I could see that by the look of you, and a little more flesh on your bones might not be amiss."

"Perhaps *now* we could discuss the purpose of our visit," Lord Alfred said through clenched teeth.

The Welshman's merry expression disappeared in an instant, replaced by cold disapproval. "You may have come from the Plantagenet king, my lord, and with no invitation I'm aware of, but it's hospitality first in this household, business after."

Lord Alfred's narrow face reddened before he finally, slowly, sat down across the fire from Roslynn and accepted a goblet of mulled wine.

"There now, eat and talk after," the Welshman

said, his anger disappearing as swiftly as the steam from the carafe.

The wine was surprisingly good and did indeed warm her. In spite of its taste and comforting effect, however, she was careful not to drink too much. She didn't want anything clouding her ability to think.

"Isn't that better?" the Welshman said after the platters were nearly empty and Roslynn couldn't eat another bite. "And now to business. So, Lord Alfred de Garleboine, what brings you and your lovely daughter to Llanpowell?"

Roslynn nearly spit out her wine, although it was an innocent mistake. Lord Alfred *was* old enough to be her father.

"Lady Roslynn is not my daughter," Lord Alfred sternly replied. "She is—"

"Your pretty wife then, is it?" the Welshman cried, grinning. "What a fortunate fellow you are!"

Lord Alfred couldn't look more appalled, while Roslynn felt the most unexpected urge to giggle, despite her circumstances. "No, she most certainly is not my wife. She is—"

"Saints preserve us," Lord Madoc cried as if torn between scandal and admiration, "you don't mean to say she's your lehman?"

"No!" Roslynn gasped, breaking into the conversation. "I am *not* his mistress!"

"Well, thanks be to heaven for that," the Welsh-man said with genuine relief as Lord Alfred's face went from red to purple, "or I'd be thinking you were lacking in taste."

"My lord," Lord Alfred ground out, "Lady Ros-lynn is here at the behest of King John."

"He has women ambassadors now, does he?" the Welshman replied with amazement, not the least upset by Lord Alfred's anger and addressing Ros-lynn instead of the Norman. "Interesting, I must say, and clever, too. I'll gladly listen to anything a beautiful woman has to say."

"If you will allow me to explain, my lord," Lord Alfred said, his hands gripping the stem of his goblet as if he were wringing a chicken's neck, "Lady Roslynn de Werre has recently been widowed—"

"Oh, there's a pity," Lord Madoc exclaimed, re-garding her with sympathy as he patted her arm again. "So young, too."

"Widowed," Lord Alfred forcefully continued, "and the king has—"

The door to the hall banged open and a tall, clean-shaven young man with dark hair to his broad shoulders strode into the room.

He was dressed like the other men in a plain leather tunic over a light shirt that laced at the neck, with woolen breeches tucked into scuffed leather boots. Unlike Lord Madoc, he wore a swordbelt, old and supple, and the hilt of the weapon in the sheath was of iron wrapped in leather strips darkened with age and wear.

Also unlike Lord Madoc, he was unexpectedly, astonishingly handsome. Curling dark hair framed a face of sharp planes and strong angles. A wide forehead and brown brows overshadowed equally dark eyes that seemed to glow with inner light. His nose was straight and narrow above full, well-cut lips.

As he returned her scrutiny, she began to tremble. Yet it was not from fear or lust, but from the sudden certainty that he could see her beating heart thudding with dread.

She was just as surprised to realize, from the wrinkle that formed between those penetrating eyes, that he was not pleased that it was so.

The lord of Llanpowell hoisted himself to his feet and hurried forward to meet the man, mercifully taking his disconcerting attention away from her. They conversed in rapid Welsh, the older man seemingly trying to placate the younger.

Their stances similar, they could be relatives. Father and son, perhaps?

She hadn't been informed that the lord of Llanpowell had been married before, or had a son or other children, but then, she'd been told almost nothing about Madoc ap Gruffydd. All John had told her was that the Bear of Brecon was to be rewarded with a wife and rich dowry for helping to end her late husband's rebellious schemes, and she was to be the bride.

What if he was his son? A grown son made a second wife's position much more precarious—if she were to marry the lord of Llanpowell.

"We're being rude," the older man suddenly declared in Norman French, turning toward his guests. "Come and meet our visitors."

Lord Alfred was already on his feet, and Roslynn slowly joined him, sliding her hands into the long cuffs of her gown and gripping her forearms to still their trembling as they approached.

"This is Lord Alfred de Garleboine come from King John," the older man said, "and this is Lady Roslynn. Not his daughter or wife or anything else to him, apparently, and recently widowed, poor thing."

The young man planted his feet and crossed his arms as he regarded her warily.

He didn't mask his feelings, his thoughts or his reactions, as so many did. Because he didn't have to? Because he had the power and confidence to reveal exactly what he thought and felt, to everyone?

Power and confidence—yes, he fairly exuded

those qualities. His manner made Lord Alfred seem a model of gentle courtesy, and his father hospitality personified.

As quickly as the heat of desire had rushed over her at that first glance, it died. He wasn't some untamed warrior prince to be admired and desired, but an arrogant, powerful man who might do her harm.

She had vowed that she would never again allow a man to hurt her, whatever King John ordered.

Her determination and pride roused, she raised her chin and met his suspicious scrutiny steadily. "I am Lady Roslynn de Werre."

"De Werre?" the younger man repeated, his eyes narrowing. "Like the traitor?"

"Yes. I was Wimarc de Werre's wife, and since the king is grateful for your father's recent—"

"My father?" the younger Welshman interrupted. "My father's been dead these past three years."

Roslynn's startled gaze flew from the younger man to the older one behind him and back again. "Isn't your father Lord Madoc ap Gruffydd?"

"No," the young man replied. "*I* am the lord of Llanpowell."

CHAPTER TWO

HE WAS MADOC AP GRUFFYDD? This young, strong, arrogant fellow was the man King John expected her to marry?

She felt for the bench and sat heavily. She could reconcile herself to a marriage to an older man, especially a friendly and generous one. But marriage to an arrogant, virile warrior, who could prove to be as violent and cruel as her first husband? That she could never accept.

"Uncle, what have you been doing?" the young Welshman asked of the man they'd assumed was Madoc ap Gruffydd.

"Welcoming your guests, since you weren't here yourself," the older man replied without a hint of remorse. "Proper introductions must have slipped my mind, what with the surprise and the lady's beauty." He smiled at Roslynn. "I'm Lloyd ap Iolo, Madoc's uncle. I'm in charge of Llanpowell when Madoc's on patrol."

Lord Alfred glared at the man who'd welcomed them. "What sort of Welsh trickery is this?"

The real Lord Madoc regarded Lord Alfred with undisguised scorn. "There was no trickery or deceit. My uncle is in command of Llanpowell when I'm absent, and I count on him to act as host in my stead. If he says he forgot to introduce himself, that is the truth. No insult was intended."

"Aye, a mistake, that's all, what with the unexpectedness of your arrival, you see," the older man assured them.

"Uncle, will you be so good as to pour the lady a drink?" the young lord of Llanpowell ordered. "She looks a little faint."

Roslynn was not weak or dizzy. If anything, she had never felt more alive—with furious indignation. Once again, a man had deceived her, and although the explanation seemed harmless and plausible, it nevertheless implied disrespect.

Unfortunately, because she was a woman and a guest, and considering the reason she was here, she was in no position to voice her true feelings, so she silently accepted the goblet of wine Lloyd ap Iolo held out to her.

The young man walked to the chair and sat upon it as if he were a king upon his throne. "I apologize for any distress this mistake may have caused you," he said, not looking the least bit sorry. "Perhaps you'll be so kind as to explain why you've come to Llanpowell, Lord Alfred."

"I've been trying to," the Norman nobleman snarled.

"I'm at your disposal, my lord," Madoc ap Gruffydd replied with exaggerated politeness.

Again she felt as if they were being treated with contempt, and her indignation increased.

Lord Alfred clearly felt that way, too, but he answered with the civility of a man used to the hypocrisy of the court. "King John is grateful for your help defeating the rebellion planned by Wimarc de Werre."

Lord Alfred then paused, as if giving Lord Madoc time to appreciate the king's magnanimity.

"His gratitude I can do without," Lord Madoc remarked instead. "What about the payment I was promised?" His glance flicked to Roslynn and his lips jerked up into a disdainful smile. "Are you about to tell me Lady Roslynn is my reward?"

Roslynn flushed, but met his scornful gaze steadily. "As a matter of fact, my lord, I am."

She had the brief satisfaction of seeing the arrogant lord of Llanpowell look as stunned as she'd felt when she found out who he was.

"Lady Roslynn and her dowry are indeed your reward," Lord Alfred clarified.

"Dowry? Did he say dowry?" Lloyd ap Iolo asked as his nephew stared at Roslynn like a man who'd been struck over the head with a heavy object.

"Her dowry consists of eight hundred marks in silver and jewels, as well as many fine household goods," Lord Alfred added.

Madoc ap Gruffydd launched himself out of his chair as if he'd been set ablaze. "I was promised money for my aid, not a wife! I want no wife, especially one chosen by another man."

Hope surged through Roslynn. He was going to refuse! She would be spared another terrible marriage and the king couldn't blame her.

Lord Alfred rose, nearly apoplectic with ire. "How dare you reject—?"

He took a deep breath and got his rage under control. "Think wisely, Welshman, before you reject what King John so generously offers. It is Lady Roslynn and her dowry, or nothing."

"Be reasonable, Madoc," his uncle urged. "That's a lot of money, that dowry, and it's time you married again."

Again?

"And although you've got one son already, more would be better."

He had a son?

"I don't marry at any man's command, or to

breed children," Lord Madoc replied, "and I won't have any woman forced to marry me, either."

As if a woman's wishes could possibly matter to a man like him.

"Lady Roslynn is not being forced," Lord Alfred said, turning toward her. "Tell him, my lady. Tell him that you came here of your own free will and you'll marry him of your own free will."

Roslynn would much rather have kept silent and let them argue, but since she had been appealed to, she answered truthfully. "I was not threatened or starved or tortured until I agreed to this proposal. However, it was do as the king bid, or stay at his court, and I was very keen to leave it."

"My lady!" Lord Alfred gasped, as if no one had ever wished to be away from the king and his court before.

She ignored the Norman who had brought her here, treating her as little better than a box or barrel, and addressed the Welsh lord and his uncle. "I would have agreed to anything if it meant I could leave the court.

"I am also still a young woman and I desire a home and children. I'm well aware that as a traitor's widow, I will be no man's first choice, so I acquiesced to the king's command and hoped for the best.

"But you should know, my lord, that this offer costs John nothing. The dowry is not even as much as I brought into my first marriage. All that money and property became my husband's, and thus forfeit to the crown when he was convicted and executed for treason. John adds nothing of his own. The king sends me to you as he would a worn gown to a beggar."

Lord Alfred looked as if he might explode. "My lady! That's not—"

"It *is* the truth, my lord, and we both know it," she firmly interrupted. She folded her hands in her lap, feigning a serenity she certainly didn't feel. "I would have Lord Madoc know it, too."

As the Welsh nobleman studied her, she grew warm, and it was not from embarrassment. He was an attractive, handsome man, even if he had a hot temper, hair to his shoulders like a savage and dressed little better than one of his men-at-arms.

In that, he was the opposite of Wimarc, who had worn the finest silks and expensive fabrics and kept his hair in the smooth Norman fashion. Wimarc never looked as if he'd just returned from riding hell-bent across the open moor.

"I appreciate your honesty, my lady," Lord Madoc said, his lips curving up a little, his tone somewhat conciliatory, "although you underestimate yourself. You are a far cry from a worn garment."

That little hint of a smile and his compliment could not touch her. His deep voice could not affect her. She would not be tempted by this man, no matter how he looked or spoke. She would fight the arousal that bloomed within her, the same weakness that had led her eagerly into an evil man's arms. Nor would she respond to his flattery.

"What will happen to the lady if we don't marry?" Lord Madoc asked Lord Alfred.

"We shall both return to court to inform John of your refusal," the Norman tensely answered.

"No, we will not, my lord."

Roslynn had foreseen this eventuality and had already decided what she must and would do, whether Lord Alfred approved or not. "You and my dowry may return, Lord Alfred, but I would rather give myself to the church than go back to the king's court."

Lord Alfred stared at her as if this was the most outrageous proposal in the world. "But the king—"

"Should have no cause to complain. I have done what he commanded. If Lord Madoc rejects me, the king cannot say I disobeyed. If you fear to return without me, tell John I fell into melancholy and only the promise of a life as a bride of Christ could revive my spirits. No doubt the return of my dowry will help to ease any other disappointment he may feel."

The lord of Llanpowell resumed his seat. "It appears the lady and I are in agreement, at least on this point. We will neither of us marry simply because King John wishes it."

Lord Alfred's hands balled into fists at his sides. "May I remind you both it is never wise to antagonize a king?"

"Perhaps it isn't wise of John to antagonize *me*," Lord Madoc retorted. "I doubt he can afford to lose the friendship of any man who has alliances in the Marches.

"Fortunately, I have not yet refused the king's gift. She's a beautiful woman, after all. Bold, too, and while some men like their women placid, I don't. I prefer a woman who speaks her mind, as this lady so obviously does. So I may yet accept her."

Surely he didn't mean that! How could he be so adamantly opposed to the king's offer one moment, then acquiesce the next—unless the thought of the dowry was too appealing to decline.

"However, as I said, the lady must be willing."

Which she was not and never would be, no matter how handsome he was.

He must be trying to put the responsibility—and the blame—for thwarting John's plans back onto her.

"This is ridiculous! She's only a woman!" Lord Alfred protested. "She has no right to an opinion."

"In my hall she does," Lord Madoc replied. "Well, my lady? What say you?"

She would not be caught in his trap, so if he expected her to say yea or nay, he was mistaken. "We have only just arrived," she said instead. "Must I give my answer now?"

"No," Lord Madoc said at once. "We should both take time to decide whether or not we'll suit."

She already knew the answer to that, and unless she was mistaken, he did, too.

"I should return to the king without delay," Lord Alfred declared. "He is most anxious to have this settled."

"He's had months to fulfill his bargain, so I think he can wait a few more days," the lord of Llanpowell replied as he got to his feet. "You can blame the Welsh weather if you need a reason, my lord. Now, if you'll excuse me, I should find my steward and tell him important guests have arrived. Uncle, please see to the accommodations for Lord Alfred and his men."

"Aye, nephew, gladly!" the older man said with a broad grin.

"Bron," Lord Madoc continued, "show Lady Roslynn to the bedchamber in the south tower. She'll want to rest until the evening meal."

ALTHOUGH DISPLEASED by Madoc of Llanpowell's arrogant dismissal and subsequent swift exit,

Roslynn was glad to be alone. She needed solitude and quiet to consider all that had happened since arriving in this place.

The upper chamber the maidservant took her to was surprisingly comfortable, if a little dusty. The furnishings—curtained bed, small wooden table, stool and washstand—were old, but well polished. The linen bed curtains, dyed a vibrant blue, hung from bronze rings. No ewer or linen were on the washstand, suggesting this room had not been used recently.

Perhaps it was kept only for guests, and the lord had a finer chamber in another part of the castle.

She strolled toward the narrow window and looked outside. She could see only the inner wall—hardly an inspiring view.

On the other hand, perhaps she had seen all she needed to of this castle and estate, since she probably wouldn't be staying here much longer.

Although she didn't want to anger the king by a direct refusal, she would if she must. She would rather face John's wrath than marry a hot-tempered, possibly violent man who would make her miserable. She had lived that life once; she wouldn't again.

She heard the sound of heavy boots coming quickly up the stairs and turned toward the door just as Lord Alfred barged inside.

"By the saints, my lady," he declared as he strode uninvited into the chamber, "to think I ever felt sorry for you!"

He came to a halt, arms akimbo, glaring at her. "Who do you think you are?"

"I am Lady Roslynn de Werre, the daughter of Lady Eloise and Lord James de Briston," she answered, not afraid of Lord Alfred or his anger. He had very little real power over her here, so far from the king.

Her calm response didn't ease Lord Alfred's aggravation. "What sort of tricks are you playing at, my lady? You made nary a squeak in protest the whole way here!"

"I play no tricks. As I said, I'm not averse to the marriage—only to returning to court if Lord Madoc doesn't want me. You know the sort of men John has about him. Is it any wonder I'm loath to return?"

Lord Alfred didn't answer directly, no doubt because he did know the sort of men John had about him. "You should have told the king of your feelings."

As if John would care. But she didn't say that. Instead, she said, "As he should have told me more about Madoc ap Gruffydd."

"So you could find excuses not to do as the king wills?"

"To know what manner of man I was expected

to marry. He appears to be a hot-tempered savage who finds it amusing to make us look like fools. I especially should have been told he already had a son, as any sons I would bear him wouldn't inherit his estate, but only a portion of it."

"Any children I have will inherit equally, except for the title," the savage himself declared from the doorway.

Both Roslynn and Lord Alfred wheeled around to see Lord Madoc standing on the threshold, his arms crossed.

God help her, how much had he heard?

"That's a decision I made before I had any children at all and I'll stand by it, should I be blessed to have more," he continued as he sauntered into the chamber. He raised an inquisitive black brow. "Might I ask what you're doing in the lady's chamber, my lord?"

Lord Alfred drew himself up to his full height. "As the king's representative, I have every right to speak to her in private."

"Not in my castle you don't."

The Norman couldn't look more offended if he'd been struck across the face. "I'm an honorable man!"

"So you say, but words are cheap."

"Then hear me," Roslynn declared, her own anger rising. "Whatever my late husband was, I'm an

honorable woman and there is nothing unseemly
between Lord Alfred and me!"

"So I should hope."

"Lord Madoc," she snapped, "if you have only
come here to insult us—"

"I came here to speak with you, my lady, prefer-
ably without the king's lackey present."

"My lord!" Lord Alfred huffed, his hand going
to the hilt of his sword, "I am the king's *representative* and so responsible for Lady Roslynn. Unless and until you are wed, you may not be alone
with her."

The Welshman's brows lowered menacingly.
"Do you think I'll force myself upon her?"

Fighting the fear his words engendered, the vi-
sions and memories they roused, Roslynn began to
back away, reaching for the dagger she had tucked
into her belt. It was small, but lethally sharp, and she
would use it if she had to. Never again would she
let a man use her as he would. Never.

"She is under the king's protection!" Lord Alfred
exclaimed, likewise reaching for his blade.

"Who, I gather, forces himself on women all the
time, even the wives and daughters of his own courtiers," the Welshman replied. "And why should I not
risk it, if you would have us wed? The lady would
surely not refuse me if I did."

God help her! He might be even worse than Wimarc.

Lord Alfred drew his sword and moved in front of her. "You touch her at your peril, Welshman. She is in my care, and I will protect her honor with my life."

For one breathtaking moment, she feared they would come to blows, until the lord of Llanpowell slowly let out his breath and shook himself, not unlike a great shaggy bear, as his anger seemed to dissipate. "Your defense of the lady does you credit, Lord Alfred. You can put up your sword, for her virtue is quite safe with me. I've never forced myself upon a woman and I never will.

"Unfortunately, I find it almost impossible to tell if a Norman's honorable or not. Now I'm sure *you* are."

Roslynn shoved Lord Alfred aside. "Was this some sort of trial, you Welsh oaf, to determine Lord Alfred's honor—or mine?" she demanded, her whole body quivering with rage. "Perhaps you hoped to find me in Lord Alfred's arms, the better to reject me and seek a different reward from the king? How unfortunate for you that your plan was doomed to fail, for I value my honor as much as any man." She pointed at the door. "Get out!"

He raised a brow, but otherwise didn't move.

"Get out!" she forcefully repeated, and when he still didn't move, she pulled the dagger from her belt.

In two strides the lord of Llanpowell crossed the floor and grabbed her forearm. He looked like an enraged god, angrier than she'd ever seen any man, even Wimarc when he was captured. Terrified, she cried out and twisted away, protecting her head with her other arm as she anticipated the hard blow, the curses and the kicks that would come.

Instead, she heard his voice, quiet yet strained, firm but steady, as he let go of her. "I'm not going to strike you, my lady, although you drew a blade and I have every right to defend myself, even from a woman."

Although she had never met him before, he sounded sincere and she choked back her fear. "I drew my knife because I will never again allow a man to take me against my will."

Lord Madoc's eyes flared with surprise, then what had to be pity, as if she were a poor, pathetic thing.

"I wasn't raped by a stranger," she hurried to explain. "It was no thief or outlaw who outraged me. It was my husband. Our bed was only for his pleasure, never mine."

Lord Alfred flushed. "If he was your husband, it was his right to—"

"Leave us, my lord," Lord Madoc ordered. "I will speak to this lady alone and I will not touch her."

Roslynn saw the truth of his promise in those deep brown eyes that seemed to reveal every flicker of emotion. This might also be her one and only chance to secure her freedom. Therefore, she would take it, and if she was wrong to trust those eyes, she still had her dagger.

Lord Alfred wasn't willing to acquiesce. "It is most—"

"My lord, please," Roslynn insisted.

Lord Alfred sheathed his sword. "Very well, I shall go, but know you this, my lord. I will not be kept waiting like a dog on a leash. In two days, I return to court with Lady Roslynn, or without her. However, if this marriage does *not* take place, rest assured that *I* shall not be held responsible!"

CHAPTER THREE

AFTER LORD ALFRED had left the room, Lord Madoc turned to Roslynn and studied her as if he'd never seen a woman before. "You were ready to kill me if I tried to force you, weren't you?"

She saw no reason to dissemble. "I was. I meant what I said."

"I meant what I said, too. I've never taken a woman against her will, and never shall. I never hit women or beat my servants. Those are the acts of a brute and a coward."

Words could be meaningless and as insubstantial as air. How could a man of his temperament not strike out in anger?

He walked past her to the window, where he stared at the wall and spoke without facing her. "Your marriage to Wimarc—were you forced into that?"

"No, my lord," she said, although it both shamed and pained her to admit it. "I thought he loved me, only to discover I was nothing more to Wimarc than a dowry and a woman to abuse whenever he felt the need. Worse, he was a traitor and although I was innocent, I could have faced a traitor's death, too, if not for intercession of friends. Kings are suspicious men, and my fate could easily have been otherwise."

"So the king let you live to use you as his tool, his gift."

What could she say to that? It was the truth.

The Welshman turned at last, resting his narrow hips on the sill and crossing his powerful arms. "I've heard about your husband. Quite the smooth otter he was, and handsome and clever. Older and wiser heads than yours were turned by him. And love can make a fool of anyone."

"I don't believe now that I did truly love him. I was flattered by his attention and swayed by his outward appearance."

God have mercy, what had compelled her to make that confession, and to a stranger, too, especially one she was supposed to marry?

"So you were deceived and married a traitor and now the king thinks to use you," Lord Madoc mused aloud. "Yet you have family and friends. Surely the convent is not your only alternative if we don't marry."

"I've disgraced my parents, and I have imposed upon my friends long enough, so if I don't marry you, it will be the church for me."

"Then you will never be able to have children."

"Since I'm not a simpleton, I'm well aware of that."

He walked around her and she felt his gaze upon her, but didn't move. Let him stare all he liked. She had been the object of men's scrutiny before, especially at court.

"I think you're no more keen to enter the church than I am to make enemies," he said at last. "Despite what I said to Lord Alfred, I would prefer not to have John for an enemy. Even so, as I said before, I won't marry an unwilling woman."

He halted behind her and when he spoke again, his voice was low and soft, like a lover's, or as she'd always imagined a lover's should be. "But you need not lock yourself away in a convent, my lady. Excuses could be found to explain why we won't marry. An illness perhaps, or I could claim I've gotten betrothed since I made my bargain with John. Or that our grandparents were too closely related. Meanwhile, you're welcome to remain my guest for as long as you like, and whether we marry or not."

Whether they marry? He was actually considering agreeing to the king's proposal?

She turned to face him and tried to gauge his true feelings. Did he want *her,* or only the dowry? Was he hoping to use her, as Wimarc had? As a bedmate, or political pawn, or both? What did he really want?

What she saw in his eyes was not greed or lust or ambition, but a speculation that matched her own, as if he was just as curious to know what *she* wanted.

As their gazes met and held, however, she saw and felt something more.

Desire.

Yes, he was a man to tempt her, but what then? Madoc ap Gruffydd was no boy, no green lad playing at love. He was no courtier, used to smooth banter and games of seduction.

Madoc of Llanpowell was something else altogether—more elemental, more primitive. More virile and more arousing than any man—*any* man— she'd ever met.

As that realization struck her, so did another—that he was, therefore, even more dangerous to her than Wimarc. Wanting him, she might weaken and make another terrible mistake that would result in misery.

She wet her suddenly dry lips. "I thought you were offended by the proposal."

To her even greater surprise, his mouth curved up in a genuine smile that made him look like a juvenile version of his uncle, and just as harmless. "I was angry because John didn't send what he promised. Aye, and shocked at what he did send, too, but I'm beginning to think I was too hasty in my temper."

This was not what she wanted to hear. Not now, not ever.

Not from him.

If he saw her dismay, he wasn't upset by it. "There's no need to decide about this marriage today," he said genially, holding out his arm. "I don't mind making Lord Alfred wait. Do you?"

It was on the tip of her tongue to tell this man that her decision was already made and she would never be his wife, until caution warned her to say nothing. However Lord Madoc behaved now, he was a stranger to her and he could still be planning to put the blame on her if they didn't wed. It would be much better for her, her friends and her family if Madoc ap Gruffydd thwarted the king's will.

So she lightly placed her hand on his muscular arm and ignored the little thrill of desire that seemed to snake its way from that touch to her heart. "Not at all, my lord," she said. "Whatever you decide, I'm delighted by the prospect of a sojourn in Wales."

His eyes narrowed, but she simply smiled that bland, meaningless smile she had used so effectively at court.

ACUTELY AWARE OF the beautiful woman seated on his right in the torch-lit hall, Madoc tried to eat as if he had not a care in the world. Unfortunately, he did, not the least of which was hoping that his desire for Lady Roslynn wasn't completely obvious.

He had felt it the moment he'd first laid eyes on her, and even after he'd learned why she and the Norman nobleman had come to Llanpowell, although that should have stemmed his passion immediately and permanently. To his chagrin, it had only seemed to make his lust grow stronger. How else to explain his request to be alone with her, and the almost overwhelming urge to take her in his arms when she spoke of her brute of a husband?

Yet he had been around beautiful women before. He had made love to more than one. What was it, then, about Lady Roslynn that seemed to cast such a spell over him?

Her beauty, to be sure. Her bold spirit, as he'd said. But there was something else, a challenge in her shining eyes that made him think being chosen by her would be no little accomplishment.

Unfortunately, if he agreed to marry her, it would also mean accepting a permanent bond with a woman he didn't know, and a stronger alliance with the Plantagenet king.

He set down his silver wine goblet, careful not to so much as brush his arm against Lady Roslynn's. He didn't want to imbibe too much, lest he say more

than he should—about her, about himself, or what
he really thought of King John.

Uncle Lloyd obviously had no such concerns as
he finished yet another cup of *braggot*. Interest-
ingly, and although he'd likely rue it tomorrow, Lord
Alfred was keeping up with him, goblet for goblet.

If his hall wasn't the biggest or the most luxurious,
at least he need not be ashamed of the food and drink
his larder and buttery provided, Madoc reflected.

His cook, Hywel, had learned his trade in the
kitchen of the Earl of Pembroke himself and was
well versed not just in ordinary fare, but cream
soups and cheese tarts, baked apples, pastries, salmon, trout and even swans, curlews and blackbirds,
although the latter were too expensive to be served
at Llanpowell. Farmers and fishermen came to
Llanpowell with their best, freshest produce, and
what wasn't roasted, Hywel turned into savory
stews, pottages and soups. His bread was the best
to be had in Wales and his sweets and custards as
fine as anything in England.

Even though these visitors had come upon
them unexpectedly, Hywel had risen to the
occasion and admirably so, with six courses, including a beef stew, roasted mutton, pike with a
green sauce made with vinegar and parsley,
chicken stuffed with eggs and onions and ending

with pears served in a wine syrup, as well as his speciality, baked apples, spiced with his own secret recipe.

Lloyd caught Madoc's eye and raised his goblet in salute. "Quite a beauty John sent you, nephew," he crowed in Welsh. "Like the first flowers of spring she is!"

Madoc didn't need reminding that Lady Roslynn was a beauty, with her pale smooth skin, bright blue eyes and lips as red as holly berries, or that she was young. Her manners were impeccable, and she ate and drank with the delicate daintiness one would expect from a highborn lady.

Her dress was likewise demure and modest. Her gown was of deep blue wool with a square-necked bodice, without trim or other embellishment. Even so, there was no disguising her shapely figure.

The tooled-leather belt that sat on her slender hips had accentuated the graceful sensuality of her walk. Most of her hair was covered by a white veil, but that seemed meant to tease him with the hint of thick chestnut-brown hair beneath.

What man in this hall wouldn't envy him the chance for such a bride? What man here wouldn't want her for his own?

Ivor, his friend and his steward, no doubt.

He glanced at Ivor, seated nearby. Simply attired

in a long, belted woolen tunic, the steward was as watchful as always. Nothing escaped his shrewd hazel eyes, and while his crippled left leg made it impossible for him to hope for military glory, his cleverness and loyalty had made him indispensable at Llanpowell.

Yet Ivor had been the first to speak against helping the Plantagenet king round up traitors who were planning a rebellion, until Madoc, seeing little risk for greater gain, had overruled him.

Madoc had been right, for he'd not lost a single man in the effort. And then John had sent him not silver as promised, but a bride, although her dowry was considerable.

What kind of woman was Lady Roslynn de Werre? How would she run his household and raise their children? What would she be like in his bed? He'd already had one weeping bride; he didn't want another.

"I hear you paid Lady Roslynn a little private visit before the evening meal," Uncle Lloyd remarked in Welsh, his eyes twinkling with a mischievous grin. "Having a little chat, were you?"

Madoc forced himself to smile and tried not to notice that Lady Roslynn was listening, even if she couldn't understand the language. "As a matter of fact, we were," he replied. "Don't you think I should get to know her first if we're to marry? And she should get to know me?"

Uncle Lloyd frowned. "What, you just talked?"

"She's an honorable woman and I'm an honorable man, so what else?"

"What's to talk about?" Uncle Lloyd replied. "She's a lovely woman and you're the best catch in the country. And it's time you married again, nephew. You can't live like a monk forever. It's not natural."

Madoc reached for the heel of a loaf of barley bread in the basket in front of him. "I'm not celibate and you know it."

"As good as," Uncle Lloyd charged. "How long has it been? And you in the prime of life, too! Why, if I was your age and had your looks—"

"Yes, Uncle," Madoc said, hoping to cut the conversation short. Even if the lady didn't know their language, several of the household nearby, including Ivor seated at the Norman's left, did. Most of them were snickering, or trying not to.

Except the slender, thoughtful Ivor. He looked as grim as death, no doubt because he was considering what this marriage would mean politically, as well as financially.

"Your uncle seems to be a very amusing fellow," Lady Roslynn noted in the ensuing moment of silence. "It's a pity I can't understand what he's saying."

Uncle Lloyd's eyes fairly danced with glee. "Will you tell her, Madoc, or shall I?"

"He says you're very beautiful and I'm a lucky man," Madoc replied.

Uncle Lloyd laughed and patted Lady Roslynn's arm. "Isn't that the truth! I hope you aren't upset by my nephew's temper. He's a passionate fellow, is Madoc."

Lady Roslynn's eyes were as enigmatic as eyes could be. "Yes, so I've noticed."

Uncle Lloyd's bushy gray brows furrowed with a frown. "Nothing to worry about there, my lady. Madoc flares up quick as lightning and cools down just as fast. Not one to hold a grudge, either—well, not often, anyway, and not without good cause."

Madoc shot his uncle a warning look. Lloyd was venturing into dangerous territory.

"He's a fine bowman, too," his uncle said, wisely changing the subject. "He can hit the bull's-eye from a hundred feet easy as you please."

"You, a nobleman, use a bow?" Lord Alfred asked with disdain.

Madoc didn't care what the Norman thought of him, so he answered without rancor. "I do. Whatever the Normans think, it's a valuable weapon. Puts the enemy at a disadvantage when they're still far away. A good volley, and they'll run before you've struck a single blow."

"Hardly chivalrous," Lord Alfred sniffed.

"So says a man who wears sixty pounds of armor," Uncle Lloyd noted. "Tell that to your foot soldiers."

Madoc realized he'd reduced the heel of bread to a heap of crumbs. "The Welsh have their ways, and the Normans theirs," he said as he brushed the crumbs off the table and the ever-hungry hounds licked them up. "Time will tell which is effective, so perhaps we should discuss something other than warfare."

"You're right," Uncle Lloyd magnanimously agreed. "Three to one John's overthrown before he has an heir."

"I don't think politics is a fitting subject, either," Madoc said quickly, and trying not to show his exasperation in front of the Normans. He loved his uncle like a second father, but there were times Lloyd could test the patience of a saint—and he was no saint.

"Speaking of heirs, I had hoped to meet your son this evening," the lady remarked.

God help him, it would have been better to talk about John—or anything else. But he was trapped now. "Owain is fostered elsewhere, my lady," he truthfully and succinctly replied.

Mercifully, the servants arrived to remove the

last of the fruit and the linens and take down the table before he had to say more. Nevertheless, he took steps to avoid having to talk about Owain, or the boy's mother. "Nobody knows or tells the history of Wales better than my uncle, my lady. Perhaps you'd care to hear some of his tales?"

Uncle Lloyd smiled proudly as he made way for the servants taking down the trestle table. "Aye, my lady, there are plenty of exciting tales. Battles galore and clever tricks and love—oh, sweet Jesu, the lords of Llanpowell have always been known for love."

"Is that so?" Lady Roslynn replied, sliding Madoc a vaguely quizzical look. "I should like to hear all about Lord Madoc's family."

Did she really, or was she saying that only because it was expected? And why the devil was he *blushing?*

He saw no need to linger. After all, he'd heard these stories a thousand times before, so once the tables were taken apart and removed, benches set in a circle around the hearth and seats resumed, he left his guests to speak to Ivor. Meanwhile, Lloyd launched into the story of how Madoc's ancestors had fought off the Romans, and then any Northmen who dared to venture this far inland.

As he joined Ivor, who was nearly hidden behind a pillar, he noted that Lady Roslynn appeared genuinely interested and even Lord Alfred relaxed, although perhaps that was merely the effect of the *braggot*.

After exchanging a few words in greeting, Madoc drew Ivor farther back behind the pillar. "You checked the dowry?" he asked quietly.

"Aye, it's as much as you said," he replied. "Eight hundred marks' worth of goods and silver, including some of the finest jewels I've ever seen."

Ivor tilted his head to study his friend in the flickering light of the flambeaux. "You're not thinking of agreeing to this marriage, are you, Madoc?"

It was on the tip of Madoc's tongue to say no. He didn't want to marry a woman he'd never seen before, and especially one sent by John. But then he remembered the fire in Lady Roslynn's eyes, her shapely figure, those full red lips and her vibrant boldness as she confronted him and the Norman who'd brought her.

He also thought of the life Lady Roslynn must have endured in John's court. He'd heard enough of the king and his courtiers to guess that it hadn't been easy for a proud and beautiful woman like her.

So instead, he slowly and cautiously replied, "When all is said and done, I may not have much choice in this. John and his favorites like William de Braose are powerful men who can crush us if they choose."

"But she's a traitor's widow!"

"*She* wasn't the traitor," Madoc replied, "and you're always telling me we need money to get the castle repaired and buy feed for the winter, and there's that fellow in the south with those good bows, and we could use more armor, too. With a selfish weakling like John on the throne, war's more likely than not."

"Not to mention she's beautiful," Ivor said flatly, as if he were taking a tally of fleeces.

Madoc saw no need to acknowledge the obvious. "Did you find out anything more about her from Lord Alfred's soldiers?"

"Apparently she's a quiet, gracious lady, and was no trouble at all on the journey. But she helped to get her husband captured, Madoc. She arranged some kind of trap for him."

"From what we know of Wimarc de Werre," Madoc replied, "and what she herself told me about him, I can't blame her. The man was a beast, Ivor, as well as a traitor to his king."

"It sounds as if you're halfway to agreeing to marry her."

"It means I'm not ready to say no. There's the dowry, and the fate of the lady to consider, too."

Ivor's sparse brown brows drew together over his straight, slender nose. "Why should her future be our concern?"

"Because she's a woman and we're honorable men. If I don't accept her, she says she's not going back to the king. She'd rather go to a convent."

"Then let her go to a convent, if that's what she prefers."

"I don't think it is," Madoc replied, "or she would have done that instead of coming here with Lord Alfred."

"So if it's marriage she wants, let her marry—but why should it be you?"

"Because Lord Alfred says that's the only way I'll get the money I was promised," Madoc answered, trying to focus on what he could do with the dowry rather than envisioning Lady Roslynn in his bed and in his arms.

Ivor regarded his friend with sympathy and a bit of remorse, too. "Look you, Madoc, we all know you were heartbroken when Gwendolyn died, but there are plenty of honorable Welshwomen who'd be happy to marry you. And I know I've told you more than once we're not well off, but we can get by without this dowry."

Once again Ivor proved that, like everyone at Llanpowell, he believed Madoc's marriage to Gwendolyn had been one of love and happiness, in spite of how it had come about. Nobody knew what had happened between the bride and groom on their wedding night, and the other nights afterward. Nor was he about to tell him.

"Our lives would be easier and safer with the money, though," Madoc pointed out. "That's why I went to John's aid in the first place. You were right to warn me, Ivor. You said there'd be a catch somewhere. But it's too late now. It's marry the woman John has sent and get the dowry, or let her go and the money with her."

"Then no more alliance with John, either," Ivor said, and it was clear he considered this a good thing.

"Aye, but what will happen to Llanpowell?"

Ivor sighed and shook his head. "Glad I am it's not me making such decisions," he admitted. "When do you have to give Lord Alfred your answer?"

"He'll stay two days, then he's going back to court."

"Not much time, is it?"

"No. Rest assured, Ivor, I'll think carefully on the matter before I decide."

Madoc gave his friend a wry smile, although he was feeling anything but amused. "Now I had best go back before Uncle Lloyd drinks himself under the bench and Lord Alfred with him."

AFTER A RESTLESS NIGHT and a mass presided over by an elderly Welsh priest, Roslynn sat in the hall of Llanpowell, breaking the fast. Lord Madoc, who'd been as plainly dressed as before in a leather tunic, linen shirt, wool breeches and boots, with his swordbelt around his narrow waist, had already eaten and departed. He'd said very little as he consumed his bread, cheese and ale. She'd said even less and asked no questions, determined not to encourage him in the slightest. That also meant she had no idea where he'd gone, or why.

Lord Alfred had been seated at Lord Madoc's right. He hadn't touched a morsel and could barely hold up his head, having had too much of that Welsh mead, no doubt.

Sitting beside her, Lord Madoc's uncle seemed as merry and in favor of the marriage as he'd been the day before.

"I warned you about the *braggot,* didn't I?" he said as he clapped the slightly green-faced Lord Alfred on the shoulder. "Normans haven't the stomach for it. Got to be brought up to it, you see. Now me, I can drink a bucket and be—"

Lord Alfred bolted from the table, clutching his stomach as he ran.

"Blessed Saint Dafydd, no capacity for *braggot* at all," Lloyd sighed with a sorrowful shake of his head.

"Any man who drinks a bucket of anything might be sick in the morning," Roslynn observed, feeling duty-bound to stand up for her countryman, even if she didn't like him and he had treated this journey as an extremely onerous duty.

"That's true enough, my lady, true enough," Lloyd replied. "You look a little peaked yourself. I hope you're not coming down with something."

"I am rarely ill."

"Well, there's a mercy."

The older Welshman's heartfelt response made Roslynn wonder if Lord Madoc's first wife had been somewhat delicate. Or perhaps he simply didn't want his nephew to lose another spouse.

"Madoc's healthy as a young ram," Lloyd continued. "Strong, too. And virile. His son was born just over nine months after he married Gwendolyn. Such a pity she died so young and so soon after marriage."

Not sure what to say to that, if anything, Roslynn concentrated on finishing her bread and peas porridge, and wondering how she could avoid the lord of Llanpowell for the rest of the day. Perhaps she should remain in the hall, although the sun was shining and the sky was cloudless.

Maybe she should stay in the upper chamber. She could always do a little sewing, perhaps finish the piece of embroidered trim she was making for her blue—

A cry came from the battlements.

Had Lord Madoc returned already? Her heartbeat quickened, then raced even more as several of the soldiers not already on duty grabbed their weapons and rushed out of the hall.

CHAPTER FOUR

"WHAT IS IT?" Roslynn demanded of Lord Madoc's uncle as she started to stand. "Is the castle under attack?"

"No, no," Lloyd hastened to assure her, patting her arm. "Them over the mountain have been after the sheep on the north slope, that's all.

"There's no need for you to worry, my lady," he continued as she slowly resumed her seat. "They'll have gone back to their own land by now. Madoc and his men will make certain of it, though, and see how many sheep were taken, and ensure that the shepherd and the rest of the flock are safe. And come tomorrow, the thieves will find themselves lacking an equal number of sheep."

"Won't Lord Madoc try to catch them and get his own sheep back?" she asked incredulously.

"No."

"But why not? Especially if he knows who's taking his sheep."

"It's a sort of feud, my lady," Lloyd explained.

A *sort* of feud? "Is this a Welsh custom of some kind?"

He colored and ran a hand over his beard. "I'd better let Madoc tell you about it," he said, before resuming his usual jovial expression. "It's nothing to get upset about, my lady. Just accept that every now and then, a few sheep will go missing, and Madoc or his men will go to collect the same number from Trefor's flock."

"I should think a feud of any kind is a serious business," Roslynn replied. "Who is this Trefor?"

Lloyd looked as if he wished he were anywhere else. "It's Madoc's brother taking his sheep. Trefor has fewer men and the lesser estate, though, you see, so Madoc doesn't think it's fair to set the law on him."

In that, Lord Madoc was quite a contrast to the king. John would stop at nothing to get his brothers' lands and titles.

"But never mind about Trefor now," Lloyd said. "Come to the kitchen, my lady, and have a pastry. Hywel's a dab hand with them."

Since there was nothing else for her to do, Roslynn dutifully rose to go with him, although pastries were the last thing on her mind.

MADOC SILENTLY cursed as he galloped along the rutted road leading up the northern slope of the highest hill of his estate. Of course Trefor would choose this time to harass him. No doubt he wanted to embarrass his brother in front of his Norman guests. Perhaps Trefor had learned the purpose of their visit and considered that even more reason to trouble him.

Madoc spotted a man running along the ridge—Trefor himself, Madoc realized with a surge of anger.

He immediately turned his horse to follow, but once at the top of the hill, he discovered a mist covering the slope just beyond the ridge, like a white curtain.

Cursing aloud this time, Madoc slipped from his saddle. His black gelding snorted and stamped, as anxious to give chase as his master. Unfortunately, from here it would be too dangerous to ride at a gallop, or even a canter. There could be hidden holes and loose scree that could cause a horse to slip or fall.

"Steady, Cigfran, steady," he murmured, running a hand over the horse's strong neck as his men caught up to them.

"Should we go after him, Madoc?" Ioan asked when he and the others reached the top of the ridge and dismounted.

"No."

Trying to give chase on foot would be just as

risky as on horseback. Besides, although he and most of his men had lived all of their lives on these hills and could run like deer, Trefor was just as familiar with the land and as fleet of foot.

Madoc's curt answer brought at least one groan of frustration from his men. Ioan, no doubt, for he was young and anxious to fight because he was good at it. Or maybe Hugh the Beak, who had the biggest nose in Llanpowell and was an expert with both sword and bow.

"I said no," Madoc repeated. "He's gone to ground like a fox. We'll never catch him."

"Madoc!"

Taking hold of Cigfran's reins, Madoc followed the call of his name, his disgruntled men behind him. He soon found Emlyn, the oldest and best of his shepherds. The gray-bearded man held a lamb in his arms as if it were a child, and at his feet lay a larger white shape splashed with violent red.

A ewe dead and a lamb left to starve, or be the prey of fox, wolf, eagle or hawk.

It was a cruel thing to do, and something new for Trefor.

"A fox?" he asked the shepherd, although he already knew the answer. A fox would have killed the lamb, too.

"Men for certain," Emlyn replied.

"Only the one ewe dead?"

"No," Emlyn replied. "Five more—and the big black ram is missing."

Madoc called Trefor an earthy Welsh epithet as he looked across the brow of the rise to the higher land, where Pontyrmwr, Trefor's small estate, lay. He'd been counting on that ram to build his flock. Trefor would recognize the value of it, too. No wonder he'd taken it, the vindictive, disgraceful lout.

Maybe he'd gotten more vicious and aggressive because he'd heard of Lady Roslynn's dowry and assumed Madoc meant to have it, although that was still no excuse.

"Not a broken branch, not a hoof- or footprint," Emlyn noted. "Like magic it is, how they come and go, invisible as demons."

"Aye, like demons, but no magic," Madoc said. "Trefor knows these hills as well as we do."

Emlyn sighed as the lamb in his arms continued to pleat plaintively. "Aye, that he does. I never thought he'd use that knowledge against us, though."

"He's not the man he was," Madoc muttered. Indeed, once he'd thought his older brother the epitome of a noble warrior—handsome, brave, skilled with weapons, irresistible to women but too honorable to take advantage of it. He'd trotted after

Trefor like an admiring puppy and tried to imitate his brother in every way.

Until his brother's wedding day, when Trefor had disgraced not just himself, but his family, and nearly destroyed an alliance that had held for three generations.

Madoc turned to the man who'd met his patrol yesterday to tell him the Normans had come. "Dafydd, take ten men and get me six sheep in kind from Trefor's flock and try to find the black ram. No killing any of his animals, though. My quarrel is with my brother, not his livestock or his people who depend on him."

Dafydd nodded, then fingered the hilt of his sword. "What if them with the ram put up a fight?"

"No killing, not even for the ram."

Madoc saw his men's displeasure and ignored it, as he always did. His brother was still his brother, and he wouldn't be the cause of Trefor's death, for hanging was the punishment for theft. He wouldn't attack Pontyrmwr unless Trefor attacked Llanpowell. He wouldn't sacrifice other lives because of this feud with his bitter, resentful brother.

"You three," he said to the men standing nearest him, "help Emlyn with the carcasses. You'll see to the lamb, Emlyn?"

"Aye, Madoc. I've got a ewe lost one."

Madoc knew Emlyn would skin the dead lamb and put the pelt over the living one, then put it to suck at the ewe's teat. If all went well, the ewe would accept the living lamb as her own.

Content that he had done all that was necessary, Madoc gestured to the rest of the men to follow him back to their horses. There was no reason to linger here, and he had guests at home.

Not that he was in any particular hurry to meet with them again.

LLOYD WAS AT Madoc's heels the moment he dismounted in the courtyard. "Was it Trefor and his men?"

"Aye."

Uncle Lloyd's face turned red and his dark eyes glowered. "I'm so ashamed of that boy, I could spit!"

"We'll get our recompense," Madoc assured him, dismissing the stable boy and leading Cigfran to the stable. "He's taken the black ram, though."

Lloyd cursed as he followed Madoc inside the dimmer, hay-scented stable. "He always had a good eye for an animal."

So he had, Madoc reflected, whether for horses, hounds, sheep or women.

What would Trefor make of Lady Roslynn? Would

he take her to wife if she were offered to him, even by John? Or would he say no woman, not even a beautiful one with a large dowry, was worth that alliance?

As for her spirited nature, Trefor had always preferred more placid women, like Gwendolyn.

Uncle Lloyd upended a bucket and settled himself upon it. Madoc put his saddle and blanket on the stand outside the stall, then began to rub Cigfran down with a handful of straw.

The motions helped to calm him, and the familiar scent of horse and leather reminded him that if he had much to regret, he also had much to be thankful for. No matter what Trefor said or did, *he* had Llanpowell—and justly so. Whatever Trefor thought, he hadn't stolen it from his brother. Trefor had lost Llanpowell and his title by his own selfish, dishonorable behavior.

"I trust you've been entertaining our guests in my absence," Madoc said to his uncharacteristically silent uncle, who sat twisting a piece of straw around his thick fingers.

"Aye, I have." Lloyd cleared his throat and tossed aside the straw. "I had to tell Lady Roslynn a bit about your troubles with Trefor."

That was unfortunate. Although he should have expected that some explanation of that morning's alarm might be necessary, he would rather the Normans didn't know about his conflict with his brother. John liked to pit Welsh noble against Welsh noble, the better to keep their attention on each other and away from whatever he was up to. "What did you tell her?"

"Just that you've a quarrel with your brother and it's nothing for her to worry about."

"Aye, it's not." Especially if she was leaving. And thank God Lloyd hadn't said more. "Where are the Normans now? In the hall?"

"Last time I saw Lord Alfred, he was lying on his cot, moaning, poor man." Uncle Lloyd sighed with completely bogus sympathy. "Like all the Normans, the man can't handle even a bit of *braggot*."

Lloyd's false gravity gave way to a bright-eyed grin. "He's got to be feeling better by now, though. I'd be feeling better with a pretty woman to nurse me. Lady Roslynn's tended to him with great kindness, Madoc, although he's only got himself to blame for his state."

"You shouldn't have offered him the *braggot*," Madoc said as he filled the manger with fresh hay.

"Not his mother, am I? And I did warn him, the day they arrived, before you came charging into the hall like the wrath of God."

"If I looked like the wrath of God, it was because Dafydd told me an armed party of Normans had

come. I thought Llanpowell was being attacked."
Madoc straightened his tunic and adjusted his
swordbelt before giving his uncle his formal smile.
"Well? I look amiable enough now, don't I?"

Uncle Lloyd wrinkled his nose. "You *look* fine,
but you smell of the stables. It's a fine, sunny day
and the river's nearby. Why not go for a swim?"

A surreptitious sniff proved his uncle wasn't
exactly wrong, and while it was not shameful for a
man to smell like a horse, he didn't want Lord Alfred to go back to the king and his courtiers and tell
them the Welsh smelled bad.

"All right," he agreed, "if you'll bring me some
linen, I'll be down by the alders. Quickly, mind. I
can't loll about like a lad with nothing to do."

"Right you are, Madoc!" Lloyd cried, already
halfway to the stable doors. "You head off and I'll
be there quick as a fox."

SITTING ON A STOOL behind the wooden screen painted
with a hunting scene and beside the cot of the snoring
Lord Alfred, Roslynn heard a commotion in the yard
and guessed Lord Madoc and his men had returned.

If they had, she wasn't sure what she should do.
Stay here with Lord Alfred, or go to greet him?
Then what? Ask him about the feud? Try to find out
how it had started and why, as if she cared?

Or use it to her advantage?

She could question Lord Madoc's reluctance to go after the thief, implying he was a coward. A man as obviously proud as he would surely take offense at that. Or she could suggest the Welsh must be childish, indulging in such petty games.

As tempting as that was, she might rouse his temper too much. If she did follow such a course, she would have to ensure that she wasn't alone with him, which shouldn't be difficult.

Before she could decide what she would do, she heard the sound of brisk footsteps approaching.

Whoever it was, she would be calm and aloof. She would be polite but distant. She would—

It wasn't Lord Madoc who came to stand at the foot of the cot. To her disappointment—a response she should *not* feel, she told herself—it was his uncle.

"Poor man can't hold his drink, can he?" he whispered loudly, regarding Lord Alfred as he might a sick child.

"He should be fine by this evening," she quietly replied. "I don't think you should offer him any more *braggot*."

"I won't," he agreed. "Look you, my lady, Madoc's come back and he wants to see you. Since it's such a fine day, he'll wait for you down by the river, in a little grove of alders. Very pretty spot for a conversation, if you'll join him."

Roslynn wanted to get out of the stuffy confines of the hall and there was no real need for her to stay by Lord Alfred's side; nevertheless, she hesitated. It might not be considered a wise or honorable thing to leave the castle without Lord Alfred to escort her. On the other hand, her host might consider it an insult if she refused his invitation, especially since they would be with his uncle, and so not alone. "Very well."

"Excellent!" Lloyd cried.

As she rose to join him, he reached around to grab a square of linen on the table beside the bed. She'd been bathing Lord Alfred's face when he was awake and complaining of evil Welsh brews. This large square, however, was dry.

Lloyd used it to wipe his brow, then tucked it into his belt. "I was in a rush to find you, and I sweat like a horse."

Accepting his explanation, she took his arm and together they left the hall, passing the servants replacing the flambeaux in iron holders on the walls. Roslynn felt their watchful eyes and wondered if there would ever be a time when she would no longer be the subject of gossip and speculation.

Outside, the weather was still fine, with a breeze redolent of fresh grass and warm summer days to come. Despite their curiosity, the servants at their chores and soldiers on guard duty went about their duties efficiently, although without the haste of colder days.

The yard itself was tidy, with nothing out of place, and the buildings were all in good repair.

As they were nearing the gate, the steward came hurrying around the side of one of the smaller buildings, probably a storehouse, as fast as his limp would permit. "Well now!" he cried. "Where are you two off to? And without Lord Alfred?"

"Lord Alfred's sleeping and Madoc sent me to fetch Lady Roslynn," Lloyd answered. "Wants to have a little chat with her down by the river on this lovely day."

"Then I won't keep you," Ivor replied, giving them a smile that didn't impress Roslynn. It was too much like Wimarc's—more a barring of the teeth than an expression of pleasure. "One thing you'd better learn if you're to live in Llanpowell, my lady—if Madoc gives an order, he expects it to be obeyed, and quickly, too."

"Or what?" she asked.

"If you're a soldier, night duty and short rations," Ivor answered. "If you're his friend, his eyes alone can make you feel you've sinned. If you're his wife…"

His smile widened as he shrugged. "I don't know. Gwendolyn never disobeyed, did she, Lloyd?

A very sweet, quiet wife she was for Madoc—quite different from you, my lady."

Had Lord Madoc not said he *liked* spirited women? What, then, did the steward mean by this? Was he trying to insult her, or intimidate her or make her afraid of his master?

Whatever he was trying to do, she wouldn't let him see that he was affecting her in any way.

Instead, she gave him a smile as condescending as his own. "Poor man, to lose such a model of a wife. But surely you don't begrudge Lord Madoc another chance for happiness in marriage, especially since it means a powerful alliance and wealth, too?"

She caught a flash of annoyance in the steward's eyes, although it was quickly replaced with another patronizing smile. "Indeed, my lady, some would consider your arrival most fortunate."

But not this man.

Yet perhaps she shouldn't be surprised. He was Welsh, and she was not, and his animosity could be based on no more than that.

Deciding to give him the benefit of the doubt, she said with cool politeness, "Since I don't wish to upset your master in any way, we had best be on our way."

"WHATEVER IVOR SAYS, never you fear about going against Madoc, my lady," Lloyd assured her, trotting to keep up with her brisk pace as they went out the gate. "My nephew's a bit stubborn and gruff sometimes, but he'd never hurt a woman. Never hurts anybody, except in self-defense or a tournament and then, God grant you, he's something to see."

Lloyd's words might have assuaged her fears, was she not well aware that pain could also be inflicted with a look or a word or a gesture. It didn't have to be slaps or blows.

"No need to worry about how Madoc will treat you, my lady," Lloyd persisted. "A soft heart for the women, him. And don't be troubling yourself about Ivor. He's got a grudge against Normans, you see, not just you in particular."

So, it was as she'd suspected, and she was glad she hadn't sounded as offended as she'd felt.

"Ivor can be like an old mother hen, too, the way he fusses. But he wants Madoc to be happy, as do we all, so if Madoc wants you, Ivor'll come round in time and so will everyone else who thinks it's a mistake."

She wondered if she should give Lord Madoc's uncle an indication of the unlikely possibility of a marriage, at least enough to warn him that the union he seemed so keen to promote was by no means certain.

"Unless I'm losing my capabilities, I'm sure

Madoc *does* want you," Lloyd continued so enthusiastically, it suddenly seemed a shame to ruin his expectations. "Ever since Gwendolyn died, he's had women chasing him and men trying to marry him off to their daughters or sisters, but he's never had that gleam in his eyes he gets when he looks at you, my lady."

This was surely empty flattery. She hadn't noticed any special gleam in Lord Madoc's eyes when he looked at her.

Haven't you? a small, hopeful voice whispered. *Haven't you felt his desire calling to your own?*

No, she had not. She must not. To listen to the urges of her body was folly.

Lloyd led her along a path that skirted the village at the south end of the castle, sparing her the necessity of walking through the market square, where more people would no doubt stop and stare at her. Whether he had done so on purpose or not, she wasn't sure, but she was grateful nonetheless.

The narrow river ran between banks of mossy red stones. A small, crooked wharf had been built close to the village and low-drafted boats were tied there or pulled up on the bank close by. Across the river was a forest of willow, ash and oak, pine and alders, so close together it was as if the trees were competing to see which one could reach the river first.

Farther downstream she could hear the happy

shouts of children at play and the occasional sharp reprimand of a mother. The language was Welsh, the tone universal.

"Ah, like heaven itself, isn't it?" Lloyd said with a sigh as they walked around a curve of the bank, so they were out of sight of the village, if not the high outer walls of the castle.

He pointed at the grove of leafy alders ahead. "I told you it was a pretty spot."

"It is indeed," she agreed, admiring the rugged beauty of the trees, rocks and river, with the rise of the mountain behind.

Then they entered the grove, and Roslynn's jaw dropped. A man was rising from the river—a completely naked man. His back to them, he stretched his long, powerful arms over his head as if he was worshipping the sun. Water glistened on his muscular torso, while his black, waving hair spread over his broad, powerful shoulders as he shook himself, like a great bear.

The Bear of Brecon.

CHAPTER FIVE

BLUSHING WITH embarrassment, hot with indignation, Roslynn stumbled backward, almost tripping
on her skirts. She immediately gathered them in
her hands and walked swiftly away, the need to
maintain some dignity the only thing preventing
her from breaking into a run.

Did Madoc ap Gruffydd think that she would be
so overwhelmed by lust at the sight of his magnificent body that she would fall into his arms, begging
to be his bride? Or had seduction been his aim,
whether or not they wed? Had all his previous talk
of honor been a lie after all?

Had she been deceived again?

"My lady!"

She paid no heed to Lord Madoc's uncle, nor did
she slacken her pace. He must have been in on
this...this disgusting exhibition, and here she'd
been thinking him a kindly old man, who was

perhaps a little too keen on his nephew remarrying and overly fond of drink.

"My lady, please! Stop and let me explain!" Lloyd called, panting.

He sounded as if he could scarcely draw breath, and while she didn't think any explanation could ever excuse what had just happened, she would not have him fall ill, no matter what he'd done.

As she waited, arms crossed, foot tapping impatiently, Lloyd came to a stop, breathing hard, his hand on his chest. "No need to rush off so, my lady! An accident, is all."

So he said, but the laughter in his eyes betrayed him.

"Hear this," she said. "This is the second time you've played me for a fool, and it will be the last. And if you and your nephew think seeing him naked is going to make me more keen to marry him, you're wrong. Wimarc de Werre was as handsome as any maiden's dream and he was the most evil, cruel, corrupt man in England. I will never again be swayed by such considerations."

"Madoc had no hand in this, I promise you!" Lloyd protested, apparently aghast. "It was all my doing."

She imperiously raised a brow. "He didn't send you to bring me to the river so that I could see his exposed magnificence, such as it is?"

"No. It was all my own idea, my lady. He came home hot and sweaty and needed a wash, so I suggested the river and I thought you..." He paused and took a deep breath. "Look you, my lady, he's been alone too long. He needs a wife, my lady, and he likes you."

"No doubt my dowry won't come amiss, either."

"I'd be lying if I said it wouldn't be welcome, but money or not, I've never seen him look at a woman the way he looks at you. And a woman could do a lot worse than my nephew. You've got to admit, he's a fine figure of a man."

"He could be another Apollo and that would matter less to me than how he treats the lowliest servant in his castle."

Lloyd's eyes lit up like a torch. "Ah! Well, then, my lady—"

"Uncle!"

Madoc came striding toward them over the uneven ground. His wet hair dampened the shoulders of his leather tunic. The shirt beneath was open at the neck, and his swordbelt was slung low about his narrow hips, as if he'd dressed in a hurry. "What is Lady Roslynn doing here?"

Regardless of the ire in his eyes, she faced him squarely. "I was asked to come to the river by your uncle—to talk to you, he said. Apparently he was under the mistaken impression that I would be anxious to marry you if I saw you naked. Let me assure you, my lord, lest you harbor any similar notions, that how my prospective husband looks—dressed or otherwise—is among the least of my concerns."

"And I assure *you,* my lady," the lord of Llanpowell growled, his face reddening, "that had I known what my uncle intended, I would never have gone in the river."

Lord Madoc's glance darted to his uncle, who had started to sidle backward toward the castle. "Where are you going, Uncle?"

Lloyd stopped and spread his hands placatingly. "Why, back to the hall, of course, so you two can have a little time alone without that gloomy Norman watching over you like a crow in a treetop. You're an honorable man and she's an honorable lady, so why not use this opportunity to have a little chat? It's not as if you'll be slipping away for a romantic rendezvous, although—"

"Uncle," Lord Madoc warned.

"Until later, then," Lloyd said, and in spite of their anger, he gave them a grin and a shrug before he hurried away with absolutely no hint that he was short of breath.

The sly trickster! Roslynn thought. He'd only

pretended to be winded so that she would stop and listen to him.

Fortunately, Lord Madoc seemed as annoyed by her arrival as she was at discovering him naked, so perhaps it *had* been Lloyd's idea alone to bring her to the riverbank.

As she reached that conclusion, her anger began to diminish. It lessened even more when Lord Madoc gravely said, "He's my uncle and I love him, but he can be aggravation in the flesh when he gets an idea. He likes you, my lady, and wants us to wed and no doubt thought this a good way to encourage us. But believe me, that was his idea alone, not mine. If I'd had any inkling, I wouldn't have been…"

He flushed. "I wouldn't have been in the river," he finished almost defiantly, as if daring her to contradict him. "I'm no peacock to be preening as God made me, my lady."

He was so annoyed and flustered, her heart went out to him. She could well imagine how she would feel if the situations had been reversed and Lord Madoc had come upon her bathing in the river, naked, water streaming down her…

"I believe you, my lord," she said after inwardly giving her head a shake. "I can tell you're no jack-a-dandy."

Certainly he dressed nothing like the vain men of the king's court, or her late, conceited husband.

Lord Madoc's broad shoulders relaxed. "Then I'll forgive him."

She suspected Lord Madoc had forgiven his uncle many things and many times. That would be a promising sign for a happy marriage—if she were staying.

Then he smiled, a warm, open smile that heated her even more than the sight of his naked body— although the memory of his body was more than enough to warm her, too.

"Shall we return to the hall?" he inquired, holding out his arm and nodding toward the castle walls.

"Yes," she agreed, lightly laying her fingertips on his strong forearm.

She could feel his muscle and realized the Bear of Brecon was a robust man, indeed.

"Unfortunately, my uncle's taken a notion into his head that I'm never going to be happy again until I take another wife," Lord Madoc said, his voice both apologetic and frustrated as they walked side by side. "Yet I think you, of all women, can appreciate that I would rather live as I do now than be miserably wed."

"I agree that it is better to be alone than to be bound to a person you can neither like nor respect."

"Aye. That's a whole different kind of loneliness."

He spoke as if he had intimate knowledge of that state, and she began to suspect his first marriage hadn't been a happy one.

If so, how much easier it would be for her to win his affections…if she were staying. If she could even consider marrying again, and a man like him.

They continued in silence until they neared the village. Sliding Lord Madoc a glance, she wondered what the villagers would think when they saw them thus, then decided it didn't matter. They were simply walking together. What worse scandal could come of that than that which she had already endured?

"My uncle said he told you a bit about my trouble with my brother."

"A little," she replied.

"Trefor thinks I did him a great wrong and so seeks to punish me in return."

Even if she wasn't staying, she wanted to know what had brought brothers to such a pass. "Did you?"

Madoc stopped beside a low stone fence bordering a farmyard. Within its confines lay a small cottage, with a lazy trail of smoke rising from an opening in the slate roof. Close to an outbuilding, chickens scratched in the dirt. A dog tied to the door rose, growling, then seemed to think better of it and returned to its slumber.

Meanwhile, Lord Madoc rested his hips against

the enclosure and looked off into the distance. "My elder brother was in the wrong, without doubt, but he doesn't see it that way. All Trefor sees is that I wed the woman he was to marry, and became the heir of Llanpowell instead of him."

He had married a bride intended for another? Willingly? Or for some other reason that would have made for an unhappy union?

And how did he become the heir, if his older brother still lived?

However it happened, those were causes for enmity indeed.

"It was his fault," Lord Madoc said. "Trefor came to his wedding so drunk he could hardly stand. That would have been bad enough, but he started bragging about what else he'd been up to the night before, with a harlot. I tried to get him out of the hall, but I wasn't quick enough. They all heard him—the bride, her parents, my parents, our families, the guests, the servants.

"Gwendolyn's parents were all for calling off the wedding, ending an alliance that had lasted for three generations, and she swore she'd hate Trefor till the day she died. To save the alliance, to prevent Gwendolyn's humiliation, and my parents', too, I offered to marry Gwendolyn instead."

So, in a way, he *had* been forced, much as John

had forced her to come here, because the alternative seemed so much worse.

Lord Madoc looked at Roslynn, his expression as open and honest as Wimarc's had never been. "I won't lie and say that was a hardship. I'd been in love with Gwendolyn for years, but thinking she was Trefor's and so out of reach."

Again, she fought unnecessary disappointment. What did it matter to her if he'd been happily or unhappily wed? She wasn't going to try to take another woman's place in his heart.

As for how he'd come to understand loneliness so well, it could be that he'd learned of those feelings through a friend's experience. She need have no compassion for him.

"We wed that same day," he went on. "I thought that was the end of our troubles, bad as it was, until my father decreed that Trefor was no longer his heir and must never come back to Llanpowell. He could have Pontyrmwr, a small estate on the northern border of Llanpowell. *I* was now my father's heir.

"That wasn't my doing, yet Trefor thinks I stole his birthright, as well as his bride. He won't acknowledge that he disgraced the family with his conduct and could have broken an important alliance—that he alone is to blame for his misfortune."

"However the breach between you came about, it's most unfortunate," Roslynn said quietly. "Your family should be your best, strongest ally, not your enemy."

"I'm not his enemy, but we can be neither friends nor allies as long as he keeps stealing my sheep."

"Perhaps he'll stop soon," she replied. "Maybe one day he'll realize that he was in the wrong and cease to resent you. I shall pray for it."

"If prayers could help…" Madoc muttered, shaking his head.

He didn't finish that thought, but he had told her something nonetheless: even if he felt himself in the right and his brother wrong, he wanted an end to the feud.

With a sigh, he pushed himself off the fence and held out his arm to escort her to the castle once again. She was reluctant to ask more about his brother or his first wife, although she was full of questions, especially about Gwendolyn and how she had felt about their marriage.

"Lloyd tells me you were taking good care of Lord Alfred," Madoc observed as they drew near the village green.

Not wanting to appear cowardly or upset by the gossip of strangers, Roslynn didn't suggest going around it. Instead, she steeled herself for stares and whispers, and prepared to ignore them. "It was an easy task. It was only that Welsh mead. He should be feeling better when he wakes up."

"It's the sweetness of it," Madoc explained. "Makes for a mighty ache in the head the next day if you have too much of it, even if you're used to it."

"It doesn't seem to affect your uncle."

Madoc laughed, a low rumble of delight that could have been how Zeus sounded when amused by mortal antics. "Don't ever tell him, but Bron waters his down."

Roslynn stared at him with amused shock. "My lord, I believe you may be as devious as he is!"

The merriment in his eyes diminished. "He drinks more than he should and I don't want to lose him. He had a bad fall two years ago, stumbling down some steps when he was in his cups. I've had his wine and *braggot* diluted ever since."

It was a deception, and she hated deceit, yet she had to admit this solution allowed Lloyd to keep his pride, unlike forbidding him to drink at all or taking the cup from his hand as if he were a child.

They reached the main market street, which mercifully wasn't as crowded as it would have been in the morning. Most of the village women would have already made their purchases for the day; only the poorest were still haggling over the remainders. A

few children ran among the stone or wooden buildings and a couple of dogs fought over a muddy
bone. She could hear the ring of the smith's hammer
in the forge across the green.

"I suppose Lord Alfred will leave tomorrow as
he vowed, with or without you?" Madoc asked.

"Yes," she confirmed, "and since he's returning
to court, he'll leave without me."

"Then it's to the nearest convent for you? That
would be Llanllyr, of the Cistercians. Or have you
another one in mind?"

"I do. Haverholme, of the Gilbertines, is in Lincolnshire, not far from my parents' estate."

So she had planned, yet as she walked beside this
tall, handsome man who loved his frustrating uncle
and who had tried to save his family's honor only
to be at war with his brother, the prospect of life as
a nun held even less appeal than it had before. But
if it was the church or return to the king's court,
what other choice did she have?

After they had passed the green, Madoc stopped
in the shadow of the baker's, a two-storied half-
timbered edifice with a stall for selling fresh bread
and pastries on the lower level and ovens in the
yard. The scent of his goods wafted around them,
homey and wholesome.

"If you'd rather not go to a convent," Lord Madoc

said, "I'll provide you with an escort to anywhere else, so you may travel in safety."

His offer was very tempting, or so it should have been. "If I leave here, the safest, best place for me, my family and my friends would be Haverholme. Otherwise John might blame them for my disobedience, as well as try to marry me off again."

As he stood before her, Madoc's dark, searching eyes locked on to hers. "You would sacrifice your future for them?"

She felt compelled to answer honestly. "I wish I *did* have other choices, my lord, for I'd rather not be a nun. I want to be married, to have a family and children."

"So do I. I want a wife, Roslynn, and children at my knee. I want a woman who isn't afraid to tell me what she thinks, who is bold, as well as beautiful. I want a woman like you, Roslynn."

"Are you…" She took a deep breath and tried to calm her tumultuous emotions, to quiet her inquisitive mind, for there was only one question of importance to ask. "Do you want to marry me, my lord?"

"Yes."

A single, simple word, yet in his deep brown eyes she saw all the emotions that were rushing through her, too—doubt and hope, dread and excitement. And desire.

Oh, yes, she could see the desire there, felt it between them like a current, even as she struggled against it like a shipwrecked sailor caught in a raging sea.

For lust must not color her decision. She had let it guide her before and it had led to disaster.

What did she really know of the lord of Llanpowell? That he was handsome, hot-tempered and stirred her blood. That he seemed kind and sympathetic and generous. That he was good to his uncle and that his people respected him. That his brother stole from him and yet he reacted not with malice and spite, but forbearance.

Was that enough? Could she possibly trust her judgment that had been so flawed when it came to another handsome man?

And what of his fiery temper? He claimed he never hit women, but what proof did she have? What certainty that he wouldn't turn into another Wimarc once the vows were spoken?

Yet in spite of all her fears and doubts and the terrible experience of her first marriage, her heart urged her to accept him, while her body fairly shouted that she become his wife and share his bed.

She must not be swayed by her fallible emotions, not even when he stood before her close enough to kiss, and even though she desperately wanted to feel those strong arms about her and taste his lips with her own.

But even as she fought against her inclination and desire, she pictured a group of healthy, happy children clustered about her, the boys with dark, waving hair and brown eyes that glowed with happiness, and little girls with hair like hers, blue eyes and smiling faces.

In the end, it was this image that was too appealing to disregard, and too hard to dismiss.

"I would consider it," she allowed, her voice surprisingly steady.

And then she thought of something else. She mustn't capitulate without conditions. She must tell him what she required from a husband. If he objected, she must refuse, even if that meant never being in his arms and angering the king. "If we marry, you must give me your word that you'll treat me with respect, and that you will never strike me or berate me before the household."

He nodded. "Understandable requests and easily granted. As it happens, I have a condition, too."

He drew her farther into the shadows of the buildings and inched closer, as if she were a nervous horse he was trying to saddle. "As you don't want a brutish husband, I don't want a reluctant wife. If you cannot come to my bed eagerly, if the thought of being in my arms is repulsive to you, we will speak no more of marriage."

He was in earnest. This handsome, incredibly attractive man was actually willing to admit that a woman might be reluctant to make love with him.

Now he was no arrogant warlord. He was as modest, as humble and uncertain, as a boy seeking his first kiss.

How she wished she could assure him she would gladly fulfill her wifely duties. Unfortunately, she could not be certain. Wimarc had hurt, frightened and humiliated her so often, she wasn't sure she wouldn't balk when Madoc started to make love to her, even if her body seemed anxious to find out.

"I can only promise to try," she answered truthfully. "But I think—I hope—that if you're patient and gentle with me, if you accept that I may not be as eager as you might wish at first, I am willing to share your bed and do all a wife should."

"I can be gentle," he whispered, gently taking hold of her shoulders and drawing her closer. "Patient, too. You have my word on that."

He lightly slid his hands down her slender arms and took hold of her hands, even though his eyes smoldered with yearning. "You see? Gentle."

Encouraged by his self-control, she didn't pull away. She could believe Madoc of Llanpowell would not hurt her as Wimarc had, that he would treat her with kindness and respect.

Yet despite her fervent hope and passionate longing, when Madoc's lips brushed over hers, the old fear rose up within her. She stiffened, fighting the panic, assuring herself she was safe, commanding her body to relax, her mind to forget. But it was not to be.

Madoc moved back, his brow furrowed with query, his eyes full of disappointment and dismay.

Not rage.

He was not Wimarc, a ravening wolf in the guise of a man. He was not John, the lecherous king who used his power to force women to do his bidding. He was not a courtier who thought the widow of a traitor should welcome his lascivious attention.

Madoc ap Gruffydd wasn't sly and calculating; his thoughts and feelings were plain to read in his face and voice. He spoke to her not as a thing to be captured and used, but as a person and his equal in some ways, if not all.

Marriage to him could be her last, best chance for happiness and contentment, and she would be a fool to lose it because of what had happened in her past.

So she took his face between her palms, raised herself on her toes and kissed him.

CHAPTER SIX

WILLINGLY, DESPERATELY, Roslynn captured his mouth with hers, needing to show him that she would truly accept this marriage, and him.

His strong arms enveloped her, making her feel warm and safe, as well as desired. A low moan of acquiescence broke from her throat when he parted her lips with his tongue and gently pushed his own inside the moist warmth of her mouth.

Still kissing her, he moved her back against the wooden wall of the bakery. Her breath caught as his hand slid up her ribs to her breast and lightly kneaded it, the sensation astonishingly pleasurable.

This was no rough grabbing, as if she were made of wood or stone. He caressed her gently, tenderly, as if she were precious.

In that moment, she realized she wanted Madoc as she had never wanted Wimarc, not even when she'd believed herself head over heels in love with him.

"Tell me to stop and I will," Madoc promised as his mouth glided along the curve of her cheek.

"Don't stop," she whispered, while her hands began an urgent journey of their own…until he broke the kiss and put his hand over hers.

"Do you really *want* to marry me, Roslynn?" he asked in an urgent whisper.

Could he not hear the thudding of her heart, feel the need of her body, sense her yearning and see the hope in her eyes?

Maybe he simply needed to hear her say it aloud.

"Yes, Madoc ap Gruffydd, lord of Llanpowell, I want to marry you."

His smile made her feel she had made the best decision of her life, and she tugged him close and pressed her lips to his again.

But this embrace did not last long.

"No more, my lady," he softly chided as he stepped back. "We had best get back to the hall. I won't have you wondering if I seduced you into marriage."

He spoke as if he could do just that, if he only tried.

The delightful warmth within her cooled. "Very well, my lord," she said, starting forward.

He grabbed her hand and drew her back, his black brows knit over his straight nose. "What's wrong?"

Since he asked, she told him. "I've already been tricked into marriage once by honeyed words and seductive kisses. I wouldn't like to believe I'm so stupid that I could be deceived again."

"I spoke without thinking, Roslynn," Madoc replied, looking sincerely penitent. "Forgive my hasty words. Or are you sorry you agreed to the marriage?"

How many men of his stature would apologize, let alone be remorseful? How many would seek to confirm her assent already given? Was this not another sign of the difference between Madoc and her first husband? "I'm still willing to marry you, my lord."

"Good," he replied.

His brown eyes sparkled and his lips curved up with a mischievous grin that made him look years younger as he took her hand and led her from the shadows of the bakery toward the castle. "Uncle Lloyd will be so pleased."

"And Lord Alfred so relieved," she added, desperately hoping that she was right to trust the lord of Llanpowell and that she hadn't made another disastrous mistake.

MADOC FELT as if he'd won a tournament single-handedly until they entered the courtyard of Llanpowell and found Uncle Lloyd, his arms spread wide, dancing in front of the Norman nobleman's horse as if his feet were on fire.

Lord Alfred turned his glaring face toward the returning couple. "So, my lady, you have come back at last. We were about to ride out in search of you."

Letting go of Roslynn's hand, Madoc strode past his uncle and came to a halt in front of the Norman's horse.

"Lady Roslynn is my guest," he said as his anger kindled. "No harm will come to her here, from me or any man. As I am an honorable knight, it's an insult to me to imply otherwise."

Lord Alfred sniffed with disdain. "Whatever *you* claim, this lady is my responsibility and—"

"If you're wise, you'll say no more," Madoc warned, although the man was John's emissary and no doubt powerful at court.

"Then perhaps, my lady, *you'll* explain where you've been with this man," Lord Alfred snapped as he ran his gaze over her.

"Certainly," she replied with a coolness that reminded Madoc of his brother. Trefor had always been calm in a catastrophe, until the night before his wedding. "We've been walking through the village discussing our upcoming marriage."

Lord Alfred was so startled, he nearly fell off his horse, while Uncle Lloyd let out a delighted yelp and rushed to embrace Roslynn. "By all the saints of Wales, I knew it!"

Although she'd made the announcement with a

lack of enthusiasm, at least she hadn't been reluctant to make it, Madoc thought as he surreptitiously surveyed the servants and soldiers who were in the yard.

As he'd expected, many were surprised. A few clearly weren't pleased, and many more were wary. Hopefully once Lord Alfred and his men were gone, they'd come around. After all, his own mother had been a Norman, and she'd been well regarded by the people of Llanpowell.

He didn't see Ivor anywhere; he was likely elsewhere on estate business. As for how his steward would react when he heard the news... Ivor wouldn't be pleased, but surely he would see the merit of Madoc's decision. Eventually.

"Is this true?" Lord Alfred demanded.

"Aye, we're to be married," Madoc said as his uncle left the lady and slapped him heartily on the back. "Tomorrow, if she agrees."

Before she changes her mind.

Lady Roslynn gasped, while Lord Alfred looked as stunned as if he'd been asked to perform the ceremony.

He shouldn't have been so impetuous, so influenced by his own desire...but it was too late now. He had spoken loudly and clearly, and couldn't pull the words back into his mouth even if he wanted to.

"That leaves little time to invite and prepare for guests or a feast," she replied.

"Of course. Forgive my haste, my lady. I should have realized you would wish to summon family or friends to the celebration."

"And no time to plan the feast," Uncle Lloyd added under his breath. "Thank God we've got plenty of wine and *braggot* in the buttery."

Madoc ignored him and continued to address Lady Roslynn. "Naturally the ceremony can be delayed, if you would prefer."

Lord Alfred made a strangled noise in his throat. No doubt he wanted the wedding over and done with before he returned to court. However, his wishes were nothing compared to those of Lady Roslynn, who was regarding him with that cool, slightly demure manner so at odds with her passionate kiss.

He commanded himself to subdue his lust and act like a civilized nobleman. He was no barbarian, after all, and he'd meant what he said about not forcing her before she was ready. He could control himself. He had before, he could do so again, however difficult it might be.

Her thoughtful frown replaced by calm acceptance, Lady Roslynn shook her head. "No, there is no one I wish to invite, so therefore no reason to delay," she said.

It was hardly an enthused response, but certainly better than a refusal or prevarication. Indeed, he should be relieved his sudden announcement hadn't sent her fleeing.

"Then Lord Alfred can return to court as he so ardently wishes," she continued.

"I do," Lord Alfred declared as he dismounted, smiling, although it made the man look more like a gargoyle than anything else. "The king will be pleased."

Madoc didn't give a hang whether John would be pleased or not. *He* was pleased, the lady was willing, and now they would have money to help make Llanpowell even more safe and secure.

"Come on inside, all of you," Uncle Lloyd commanded, once again forgetting Madoc was a grown man, and the lord of Llanpowell. "Let's have a drink to celebrate the happy news."

"You go ahead, Uncle," Madoc said. "I should find Ivor. As you said, I've not allowed much time for preparations."

And it might help Ivor accept his decision if he told him personally, Madoc reasoned. It might also help him get his raging desire back under control.

"Oh, aye. He's in the armory, I think."

Uncle Lloyd chuckled as he commandeered Lady Roslynn by slipping his arm through hers. "He'll be fit to be tied that he's only got a day. Good thing the buttery's full since the alewife made her delivery.

"Now come along, my lady," he said, giving her a wink. "Such a wise decision and no more anger about the river, is there?"

"No, I'm not angry about that, but you still should not have done it," she said, smiling at Lloyd in a way that made Madoc's heart skip a beat, and tomorrow seemed years away.

INSIDE THE ARMORY Madoc paused to let his eyes adjust to the gloom. Because it contained the castle's weapons, the armory had no windows or other natural light; oil lamps, candles and flambeaux provided illumination, depending on who was inside and what they were doing. At present there was only one lamp lit, at the far end of the square room beneath the barracks and beside the stables.

"Ivor?" Madoc called.

"Here!" came the answer, from near that single source of light.

Walking past spears and pikes leaning against the stone walls, racks of swords and shelves of bows and pieces of armor, quivers hanging on pegs and worktables covered with bits of wood, feathers and leather, Madoc found Ivor near a shelf of bent or broken swords, a quill in his ink-stained fingers. A small table with a pot of ink and parchment scrolls, as well as the oil lamp that reeked of sheep tallow, stood nearby.

"We'll soon be able to replace all those," Madoc said, nodding at the ancient and battered weapons that, even if repaired, would never be as good as the new ones Roslynn's dowry could provide.

Ivor frowned as he put down the quill. "How are you going to pay…" His expression slowly changed, to one of undisguised displeasure. "You're going to marry the Norman."

Madoc leaned a shoulder against the shelves and crossed his arms. He hadn't expected Ivor to be delighted. Even so, he wasn't pleased by his friend's blatant disapproval.

However, and whether Ivor agreed or not, his decision had been made. "Aye, I am."

To Madoc's silent relief, Ivor made no arguments as he picked up one of the parchments and began to roll it up. "When?"

"Tomorrow."

Ivor's brows shot up. "So soon?"

"I don't see any reason to wait. The sooner I marry, the sooner we can put the dowry to use."

And the sooner he would find Lady Roslynn in his bed.

Whatever her previous experience, her kiss had been...encouraging.

"Oh, aye, of course, and we might need the weapons," Ivor said glumly. "Trefor won't take this news well. He'll probably think you're planning to use the money and this alliance with the king to take what's left of his land."

Madoc hadn't considered Trefor's reaction, although he should have. However, he wouldn't let his brother's possible actions dissuade him now. "I don't want his land. I never have and I never will."

"You've got most of it just the same," Ivor noted. "And here's a rich bride, and through her, stronger ties to King John. He'll be angry, Madoc—maybe angry enough to do something serious."

Madoc fingered the hilt of a rusty sword on the wooden shelf beside him. "God, I hope not. I hope he'll show some sense for once."

"Sense was never his strong point," Ivor replied, standing with his weight on his good leg. "What will you do if he raises a force against you?"

"Defend myself and what's mine. I'm doing nothing wrong marrying Lady Roslynn."

"Well, let's pray we're wrong and he's content with Pontyrmwr and his latest mischief for a while," Ivor said as he started to gather up the rest of the scrolls and put them on a smaller shelf near the table. "I'd better get to the kitchen stores and see what we've got for the feast. You might have given me a few more days, Madoc."

Despite his apparent vexation, Ivor finally smiled. "Well, she's so lovely, I can't say I blame you—but Hywel will have an epic fit of temper, I don't doubt, so if he comes at me with a cleaver, it'll be all your fault," he finished as he started for the door. "Are you coming?"

"In a moment. I'll just have a look at these blades. And if Hywel comes at you with a cleaver, send him to me," Madoc replied, staying where he was.

WITH IVOR GONE, Madoc didn't examine any of the swords or other weapons. He sat on the edge of the table, arms crossed, head bowed in silent contemplation.

It was quiet here and, in spite of the presence of so many weapons, peaceful. The only sound was the spluttering of the wick soaked in tallow, the only light that of the flickering flame.

Had he truly made the right decision? Was he doing what was best for his people and himself? Or had his judgment been swayed by the lady's beauty and spirit, his loneliness and the passion she aroused within him?

Should he have told her more, about his marriage to Gwendolyn and all that had come after? Would it have made a difference to her? Was that what had kept him from speaking of Gwendolyn, little Owain and the birth that had taken his mother's life?

Whatever the reason, he had not, and the die was cast, Madoc thought as he rose and picked up the lamp and walked toward the door. His choice had been made, this path taken. Lady Roslynn had accepted him and his word had been given, so there could be no going back now.

Except with disgrace and dishonor.

THE NEXT MORNING, Madoc stood in the hall, waiting for his bride. The castle's chapel was too small to hold the servants, soldiers and villagers who'd arrived to witness the ceremony, as well as take part in the feast, so the ceremony had to take place in the hall. Madoc hoped it wasn't a bad omen that it was raining fit to drown a duck.

He shifted from foot to foot, fighting the urge to tug on his finest, and most uncomfortable, tunic. He hadn't worn that garment since his last wedding, and it had never fit properly then, either.

Lord Alfred had gone to bring Lady Roslynn from her chamber, while Uncle Lloyd was beaming as if he'd arranged the marriage himself.

Despite Ivor's disapproval, which had been obvious throughout the evening meal last night, his steward was in attendance, too.

Just as Madoc was beginning to seriously contemplate sending someone up to the tower chamber to see what was causing the delay, Lady Roslynn appeared at the bottom of the stairwell, her hand on Lord Alfred's arm.

A veritable bolt of exhilaration combined with desire struck Madoc. Roslynn's dark red gown of expensive samite was simple, but well fitted, accentuating her breasts and narrow waist before flaring at the hips. The band of gold embroidery around the square neck drew attention to the valley of her cleavage. A white silken veil brushed her soft cheeks and hid most of her thick, dark hair. She wore only a plain gold crucifix, but her intelligent blue eyes sparkled brighter than any jewels, and her full lips reminded him of her kiss.

Gwendolyn had been pretty, demure and sweet, and once he had believed he loved her, yet she had never stirred his heart or his desire as Lady Roslynn did.

While Lady Roslynn and Lord Alfred approached the dais and a ripple of excitement ran through the assembly, Father Elwy moved to stand in front of Madoc and his bride. Then Madoc took hold of the bride's cool hand and the priest began to address all those gathered there.

"Does any man here know of any impediments to the marriage between Madoc ap Gruffydd ap Iolo, lord of Llanpowell, and Lady Roslynn de Werre, widow, daughter of Lord James de Briston? If so, you must declare it."

Madoc held his breath, fearing someone would protest his marriage to a Norman and the widow of a traitor, or Trefor somehow interrupt, trying to ruin any chance for his brother's happiness and prosperity.

It seemed Lady Roslynn also shared his dread, for her grip tightened as if she feared she might be snatched away.

Or because she was tempted to flee?

No, surely not, for if she'd had second thoughts or come to regret her decision, a woman like her wouldn't hesitate to say so, or provide some excuse to delay the wedding.

Father Elwy looked pointedly at Madoc, who realized with a start that he'd been silent too long. To compensate and prove that he had no regrets about his decision, he spoke loudly and clearly, enunciating every word, first in Welsh, then in Norman French for Lord Alfred and the lady. "Once we are wed, my wife will be entitled to a third of my estate upon my death, as the law decrees. She will also have any household goods she has brought as her dower, as well as an equivalent sum in silver to that which she has brought with her."

Another animated murmur ran through the crowd. This could be considered generous, although Madoc thought it only just. Nevertheless, he could see he had surprised and pleased the lady, too, and was glad.

"The ring, my lord," Father Elwy prompted.

Madoc took his mother's ring from his belt and handed it to Father Elwy, who blessed it with the sign of the cross, then returned it to him.

"I take Lady Roslynn de Werre for my wife," he vowed, his voice loud and steady as he took hold of her hand and placed the ring on the fourth finger of her left hand.

"I will honor and respect her, protect her and be faithful to her, for the rest of my life. This I swear in the name of the Father," he said as he pushed the ring past the first knuckle. "And the Son," he continued as he moved it past the second. "And the Holy Ghost," he finished as it reached its resting place.

The priest nodded and again made the sign of the cross, blessing their union.

"Praise God and all the saints, they're married!" Uncle Lloyd cried, smacking Lord Alfred on his arm. "Soon, babies to come and the laughter of children. Now let's eat and drink to their health and happiness!"

"Not yet, Uncle," Madoc said. He raised his voice and spoke again, with equally firm resolve. "Whatever King John wants, Lady Roslynn is *my* choice. She will be my wife, bear my children and be the chatelaine of this household. You will give her the same respect you give to me, or you can leave Llanpowell."

"As I have freely chosen Lord Madoc ap Gruffydd of Llanpowell to be my husband," Lady Roslynn unexpectedly added, "I promise to do my utmost to be a worthy wife."

Then she raised herself on her toes and kissed him full on the lips, in front of all the people—and it wasn't just a chaste kiss for show. She kissed him with passion and fervent intent as if to prove to them all that he was indeed her choice.

He forgot where they were, or why, and responded as if they were alone, the bed close to hand. He had never wanted any woman as he wanted Roslynn now—and not just to make love. He wanted this woman to be his chatelaine, as well as his lover, to be the mother of his children and the heart of his home, as he would be its guardian and protector.

So he returned her kiss with passion and desire, hope and longing, until somebody coughed and reminded him they were not, in fact, alone.

Madoc drew back and smiled at his bride, who

blushed and looked away like the most bashful of maidens. Yet he was sure she was not, and that thought excited him even more.

Unfortunately, their pleasure would have to wait until after the wedding feast.

"Out of the way, Madoc!" Uncle Lloyd cried as he pushed past his nephew to envelope the slender Roslynn in a hug, then heartily buss her on both cheeks. "No keeping the bride to yourself—at least not yet!"

CHAPTER SEVEN

AT THE WEDDING FEAST that followed, Lord Alfred sat to Madoc's left at the high table on the dais. He was clearly pleased and, Roslynn had no doubt, secretly relieved that he could return to the king and report that John's orders had been carried out.

Madoc's uncle was on her right, and when he wasn't eating or drinking, he was telling her what a fine fellow his nephew was.

Unfortunately, although the food was very good and well prepared, Roslynn's appetite seemed to have deserted her—no doubt because she was still taken aback and not a little overwhelmed to be sitting in the hall of Llanpowell, the bride of a man she barely knew and within a short time of meeting him. Although she'd agreed to the marriage, she'd been shocked by his decision to have the ceremony so soon, yet when he'd allowed her more time, she'd realized there was no reason to wait. Her word had been given, and there was no one she wanted to invite to the wilds of Wales to see her married, even supposing they would come.

Madoc's near silence didn't help to ease her discomfort, although it did provide a welcome contrast to her first husband's behavior on that other wedding day. Wimarc had moved among their guests with voluble good cheer, dispensing greetings and compliments as if he were a magnanimous monarch.

Their clothing was just as dissimilar. Wimarc had been as brightly attired as a peacock in silk and samite, while Madoc wore a tunic of plain black wool that was too tight across his broad shoulders and powerful chest, equally plain breeches and boots that looked out of place on a groom, even if they were polished.

Yet it wasn't Lord Madoc's taciturn presence or his simple clothing that was so unnerving. It was what she saw if she happened to look him directly in the eye. Something heated and primitive smoldered in those dark depths, something that made her want to reach for the sensation-dulling wine. And if they accidentally touched…

But she mustn't consume too much wine. She wanted to have her wits about her when she and her husband…when they…

She swallowed the bit of roasted beef in her mouth and tried to keep her attention on the minstrel who was playing a jaunty tune. Unfortunately, he sang in Welsh, so she began to survey the rest of the people in the hall—the villagers thrilled to be at such an event, the richer among them acting as if they had expected nothing less than an invitation to the lord's marriage; the soldiers, getting quietly drunk and loudly competitive, comparing their prowess with weapons, women, and apparently just about anything men could compare; the servants, moving swiftly and surely among them, exchanging pleasantries with the villagers, and a few of the younger maidservants flirting with the soldiers.

Not the shy Bron, though. She kept to herself and went about her duties quickly and quietly, albeit with a genial smile on her pretty face while she deftly avoided any attempt to caress her.

Roslynn knew exactly how Bron felt. She had spent many a meal at the king's court avoiding unwanted attention, although it seemed Bron wasn't upset by the men's actions. It was as if she simply didn't care enough about any of them to respond, whether with pleasure or a slap.

Roslynn spotted Ivor, the steward, as watchful as a dog on the scent from his place nearest the high table. She had caught a glimpse of the steward's expression at the conclusion of the wedding ceremony and knew he still didn't accept her, or want her for the lady of Llanpowell.

She didn't have to like him, and he didn't have to like her. She was the lady, he the steward; they merely had to cooperate.

It wasn't his dislike of her that troubled her the most; it was his hypocrisy.

Wimarc had been a master of such deceit. Even at their wedding, when he'd behaved like a loving, happy groom, he'd been planning and scheming rebellion with most of the guests.

Madoc reached out and covered her hand with his. Startled, she recoiled as if she'd been pinched and he quickly withdrew it.

"I was wondering what brought that frown to my bride's face," he said, sounding faintly apologetic.

She regretted reacting so strongly; nevertheless, she answered honestly. "I fear your steward objects to our marriage."

"Ivor the Purse Strings is suspicious by nature and he doesn't trust foreigners, and he especially doesn't trust John," Madoc admitted with unexpected candor. "He has another reason for disliking Normans, though, peculiar to himself. He blames them for his lameness. When his mother was big with child, she was accosted by a group of Norman soldiers and fell. It brought on her labor and Ivor was born with a crippled leg. Whether it was the fault of the fall or early labor, no one could say, but he blames the Normans nonetheless. Still, he liked my mother well enough and she was a Norman."

He frowned when he saw her surprise. "Nobody told you that, eh?"

She reached for her goblet, then pulled back her hand without touching it. "I was told very little about you, my lord, and even less about Llanpowell. It's comforting to hear I won't be the first Norman chatelaine here. I hope all your people will come to accept me, too."

"If I didn't think that possible, I wouldn't have married you. As for Ivor, *I* rule here, not him, so this was my decision to make, not his. He's as stubborn as me, though, especially when he thinks he's right, so you may have to give him time. But I have no doubt he'll come round eventually, just like those who opposed my father's marriage."

He inclined his head toward his uncle, who was still listening with rapt attention to the minstrel.

"Your uncle?" she whispered incredulously.

"He was the worst of them all, so they say," Madoc quietly replied with a little smile that made her heart race. "He was proved wrong, and now he seems to think Norman women are the next things to angels on earth."

"What's that about women?" Lloyd asked as the minstrel concluded a very long ballad.

"I was telling her that you liked my mother very much."

"So did everyone. A fine woman she was, but oh, the temper! Could flay the skin off your back with a look." He sighed and shook his head. "How I miss her!" Then he grinned merrily. "But no sad faces now. Pleased she'd be tonight, I'm sure. Aye, this reminds me of your parents' wedding, Madoc. What a time that was! I was drunk for a week, when I wasn't chasing after the girls and catching a few of them, too! Not a one of them as pretty as you, my lady, Welsh beauties though they were."

Although his eyes shone with laughter, Lloyd heaved another heavy and mournful sigh. "Ah, I was younger and faster then. I'd never catch a one of them now."

"Unless they wanted you to," Roslynn suggested, trying to join in the merriment. "I'm sure I'm not the only woman who finds you handsome still."

"Go on with you! I know flattery when I hear it!" Lloyd cried, although he grinned with delight and beamed at Madoc. "There now, it's a kindhearted girl you've married, nephew, making me feel as young as you!"

"Perhaps I ought to tell the maidservants to hide," Madoc suggested.

"Go ahead," Lloyd challenged. "If your lady wife is right, there'll be one or two won't take any heed."

"Then we might be having another wedding soon, I suppose."

"Perish the notion!" Lloyd cried. "I'm not like you! Why, I couldn't stay faithful to one woman, nor the memory of one, either. Fine thing to do a woman, swear to be faithful when you know it's impossible."

Roslynn took a sip of wine. She was relieved to think Madoc wasn't the sort of husband to take lovers, but dismayed by what Lloyd had said, too. If Madoc had loved his first wife so much he'd never had a lover since her death, how could *she* possibly take that woman's place in his heart or in his life? Perhaps she shouldn't even try....

Clapping began near the door to the hall and Roslynn looked up to see a gray-haired man in a forest-green tunic carrying a harp coming toward the dais.

"Ah, here's Ianto!" Lloyd cried. "The best bard in Wales. I thought he'd never get here."

Lloyd jumped to his feet. "Make way there for Ianto!"

When he reached the dais, the bard bowed to Madoc and then to her, smiling, while the servants hurried forward to clear away the last of the fruit tart and roasted chestnuts from the high table and bring the bard a stool.

Ianto didn't begin to play once he was seated. Instead, he looked at Roslynn in a most disconcerting fashion and ran his fingers lightly over the strings as if they were his pet.

Curious about the delay, unsettled by the bard's scrutiny, Roslynn leaned toward Madoc and whispered, "What's he waiting for?"

"He's considering which song best suits the bride."

Roslynn didn't find that a comforting thought, especially when it seemed such a time-consuming task.

At last the middle-aged man struck a chord and began to sing in Welsh. Most of the people in the hall started to smile and several put their hands over their mouths to smother laughter.

Madoc, however, sat as still as a stone, while the steward looked just as grim. Made even more uneasy by their reactions, Roslynn glanced at Lloyd— to see his lips twitching as if he, too, was trying not to laugh out loud.

Exactly what sort of song had the bard chosen?

"Might one inquire what that fellow is singing about?" Lord Alfred asked Madoc, obviously likewise puzzled and suspicious.

"It's about a mermaid and the mortal man who loves her," Madoc replied.

"She's a slippery thing, you see," Lloyd supplied, his eyes twinkling, "and he has a hard time keeping hold of her when——"

Madoc abruptly shoved back his chair. "Now the groom will sing to his bride," he declared. "In her own language, so she'll understand."

Roslynn flushed and said nothing, but she was pleased he had risen to defend her dignity. A bawdy song about mermaids and their human lovers was hardly appropriate at the wedding of two nobles.

The bard handed Madoc his harp and her husband settled himself on the dais, then began to play. His song was sweeter, slower, about a lad who dreams of the perfect love but fears he'll never find it. Every verse ended with the young man trying to hope, yet afraid it was pointless, until the song ended with a haunting wistfulness.

Afraid she was going to start to cry, which would be mortifying, Roslynn rose abruptly. "If you'll excuse me, my lord, I wish to retire."

Madoc returned the harp to the bard. "It's early yet. Are you unwell?"

It was not his fault she was upset. He couldn't have known the effect that song would have on her—indeed, she wouldn't have guessed it herself. Yet now more than ever she wished she'd never met Wimarc. Never fallen under his spell, never begged to marry him. How much she would give to be an innocent bride with no past mistakes and foolish choices to stain this night!

Not sure what to say, what explanation she could offer that wouldn't reduce her to tears, she said, "I merely wish to retire. Have I your permission?"

Several people began to snicker.

Frowning, Madoc slid a sternly rebuking glance at them before inclining his head. "Of course."

Determined to be dignified, Roslynn held her head high as she started toward the stairs. Yet that only seemed to make the people more amused, and the farther she got from the dais, the louder their laughter grew.

Until a roar of approval rang through the hall.

Wondering what had caused that outburst, she glanced back, to see Madoc coming after her with purposeful strides and a most determined gleam in his dark eyes as if he planned to pick her up and carry her off and throw her down...

Not again! Never again!

On the verge of panic, not caring if any of the men saw her ankles or even her calves, Roslynn gathered up her skirts and ran as fast as she could for the stairs, narrowly avoiding a collision with a servant carrying away a tray of empty goblets.

"Out of the way!" Madoc called out close behind her, his warning followed by a tremendous crash.

Gaining the stairs, Roslynn didn't look back. She clutched the handrail carved into the curving wall and dashed up the steps, seeking the sanctuary of the upper chamber.

Not again! Never again!

The words rang in her mind, her heart, her soul, as she ran into the room, dimly lit by a single beeswax candle on the dressing table, slammed the door closed and slid the bolt home. But the bolt was old, the latch, too—no real deterrent to a strong, determined man.

Her heart thundering in her chest, she backed away from the door and waited breathlessly for the kick, the crash, the curses, the slaps. Getting shoved onto the bed, her skirts pushed up—

Instead, there was a light rap of knuckles on the door, and Madoc's voice, low and courteous. "My lady, may I come in?"

With shaking fingers she wiped the tears from her damp cheeks with the edge of her veil and reminded herself that he was not Wimarc. He was Madoc ap Gruffydd of Llanpowell, and her husband by her own choice.

He was not Wimarc. He had promised to be gentle.

Her hands still trembling, she drew back the bolt,

then moved away as Madoc entered and closed the door behind him.

"I didn't mean to frighten you," he said with every appearance of remorse. "Everybody assumed you were anxious to be alone with me when you started to run. So did I. But that's not why you ran, is it?"

There was no point denying that she'd been afraid, and still was, now that she was his and they were alone. "I shouldn't have behaved like a terrified child, but after being married to Wimarc—"

"You thought I was coming after you to take my selfish pleasure," he said, sparing her the necessity of putting her fear into words.

"Yes, I'm sorry. It was foolish of me."

The candle spluttered, the dim light flickering over his angular features as he shook his head. "No need to apologize to me, my lady. I know the feeling, you see. When I was a boy, my horse reared and threw me into a bog. I thought I was going to be sucked under the mud and drown. By the time they got me out, I had mud in my mouth and up my nose. Ever since then, the very smell of wet leaves and mud can make my stomach knot with dread."

He regarded her steadily. "You should never be afraid of me, Roslynn. I swear on my honor as lord of Llanpowell that even if I'm in a rage, I'll never hurt you."

She saw the truth of his words in his eyes and heard his sincerity.

"I believe you," she whispered, meaning it.

He gave her a wry little smile that removed the last of her lingering fear. "I'll admit it was flattering to think my bride wanted to be with me so much, she'd leave the feast early and run to the bedchamber. The bard's probably already making up a song about the lovesick lord of Llanpowell and how he chased after his bride."

Lovesick?

He came a little closer. "I hope you won't feel the need to run from the hall every night. Otherwise my people might think you don't like me."

Roslynn wrapped her arms around herself as if she could cage her tumultuous emotions. "I won't."

His glance flicked to the curtained bed.

Feeling like both a fool and a coward, she hurried to the dressing table, sat and, with fumbling fingers, began to remove her veil.

He came up behind her without saying a word. She felt his hands brush the back of her neck and realized he was undoing the laces of her gown. Very slowly. Painstakingly slowly.

Unsure what to do, she bit her lip and clasped her hands in her lap as he continued, until he parted the back of her gown and ran his fingertips along her spine. She sat bolt upright then, for although she wore her shift of lawn, it was as if she were naked, and his touch sent little lightning bolts racing across her skin.

"Don't be afraid, Roslynn," he whispered, his voice husky, his Welsh accent stronger. "I told you I could be patient and gentle. See, very patient, me."

He began to pull out the combs that held her hair in place, until it fell unbound about her shoulders, almost to her waist.

"Your hair is as beautiful as the rest of you," he murmured, "and as soft as your lips. I'm a fortunate man to have such a bride."

"I hope you always think so, my lord...my husband."

He reached down and pulled her to her feet, then drew her into his embrace. He kissed her gently at first, and tenderly, as she had always dreamed a lover would kiss, and she responded in kind, with grateful wonderment. Then with increasing ardor.

But Madoc was no hasty, selfish partner, no domineering male to take without regard for her feelings. He didn't treat her as something to be used simply to sate his own needs. He kissed as if they had a month, a year, a lifetime, to make love.

Her every sense was aware of him—his flesh beneath her fingers, the scent of his woolen tunic and leather boots, the delicate stroke of his powerful hands that she yearned to feel upon her naked skin.

He caressed her back, her arms, before lightly cupping her breast, and when he brushed the pad of his thumb across her taut nipple, she nearly swooned with the pleasure of it. Her need increasing, she pressed her body more fervently against him, silently urging him to take her to his bed.

He angled closer to her and, although she felt his arousal, he made no effort to hold her any tighter, his excitement kept in check by his undoubtedly powerful will. Nevertheless, she could sense his desire lurking like an animal only temporarily tamed.

As her fears kept her passion caged.

Until now. Until she had married this man who could set her free and release her from the chains of her past.

Holding him tight, she relaxed against him, her passion burning hotter as she parted her lips and pushed her tongue into Madoc's warm, wet mouth.

CHAPTER EIGHT

ONLY THE CERTAINTY that he must take care and not frighten his bride prevented Madoc from yanking the back of Roslynn's gown open so that he could feel her warm, soft, naked flesh.

Instead, he tried to content himself—for now—with ardent kisses and caresses, with words of endearment and encouragement, so that she would welcome his embrace.

"And here I was afraid you'd be reluctant," he murmured as he broke their kiss to move his mouth along her skin and run his hands through the thick cascade of her hair.

Roslynn smiled, as seductive as Salome, before she suddenly pushed him away. For one horrible moment, he feared even the little they'd done so far had been too much for her—until she tugged down her sleeves and began to wiggle out of her gown.

He fought the urge to tear off his own clothes.

She must take the lead, at least for tonight, so she could be sure he wouldn't force her.

So rather than do what his lust demanded, he stayed still and watched as she stepped out of her gown and stood before him clad only in that thin, almost transparent shift, her skin golden in the candlelight. She looked like an angel—although her expression was more lustful and seductive than any angel's could ever be.

When she reached for his belt and wordlessly began to unbuckle it, he nearly lost his rapidly fading self-control. His throat went dry and he couldn't speak, not even to mumble.

She drew off his belt with excruciating leisure, setting it on the table beside her veil. Then she stepped forward and slowly raised his tunic up and over his head and laid it on the stool. She took her time undoing the laces at the neck of his linen shirt, but at last it, too, was off, so that he wore only his breeches and boots.

She looked away as if suddenly shy—and perhaps she was. Whatever desire was moving her now, perhaps she'd already been as bold as past experience would allow. Maybe now they should even stop, if going further would distress her, for no matter how aroused he was or how much he yearned to feel her body beneath his, he wouldn't make love with her if she would be afraid.

But when she looked back at him, it wasn't fear or even reluctance he saw.

It was…admiration. "You have the most magnificent body I've ever seen."

He was so relieved, he burst out laughing, even as he blushed. "God save you, my lady, you'll be turning my head with such compliments," he said, while his appreciation for her compliment turned swiftly to passionate desire. "You're as beautiful as a goddess, and I'm the luckiest man in Wales."

She licked her full lips. "I believe I'm the luckiest woman."

He needed no other encouragement. He swept her into his arms and carried her, as light as goose down, to the bed.

As she scrambled under the coverlet of blanchet, he tugged off his boots. Her back to him, he blew out the candle, removed his breeches, climbed in and lay beside her.

She made no move to turn toward him on the feather bed.

"Roslynn?" he softly inquired, laying a hand on her shoulder.

She rolled toward him, her expression almost impossible to see in the darkness. "I am willing."

He heard the fear beneath the words and silently cursed Wimarc de Werre to the depths of hell for all eternity. That brute hadn't just taken away her innocence, he'd robbed her of the pleasure of anticipation, too, and replaced it with fear and dread. Whatever the cause, however, her fear was real and he must act accordingly. "If you'd rather not, I'll sleep on the floor."

He'd done it often enough before.

"I do want you, Madoc," she whispered, her voice small in the darkness, tears lurking on the edge, "but I can't rid my mind of the memories and the fear they bring. They come unbidden, and I can't prevent it."

"Perhaps those memories can be replaced by what *I* do," he said, hoping it could be so if he took his time, if he was tender and gentle and patient.

He gently moved her onto her back so that he could kiss her properly. He brushed her hair away from her cheeks and lightly slid his lips across her soft, pliant mouth, while his hand slid lightly down her naked arm, then up again.

It was no hardship, after all, to love her slowly, if that was what it took to make it enjoyable for her. He would gladly make love as if they had all the time in the world, and then some.

When she didn't protest, his mouth moved to her neck and the throbbing, swift pulse there.

He could feel her relax and he slid her shift from

her shoulder before nuzzling it lower, until her perfect breast was exposed to his lips and tongue.

As MADOC KISSED and caressed her, the terrible memories began to recede and the worst of Roslynn's fears melted away. Madoc wasn't Wimarc. He was a gentle, considerate lover, of the sort she had dreamed of in her youth. He was what a husband *should* be like, a man who considered her needs, as well as his own.

And, oh, how glorious his passion was, as he kissed and caressed her and whispered soft Welsh words. She didn't know what they meant, but she understood that they were compliments and encouragement, and she responded like a rosebud unfurling in the sun.

Yet despite her growing need and his zealous excitement, Madoc still didn't hurry. He took time to lick and stroke, caress and fondle, to arouse her to such heights of anticipation, she thought she would go mad with frustration if he didn't enter her. Even when she parted her legs and wrapped them around his slender waist, so that he was right where he ought to be, he paused to lave her breasts and tease her taut nipples.

"Oh, please, Madoc!" she pleaded, arching and writhing as the tension built and built. "Don't make me wait any longer!"

"As you wish," he murmured as, with an ease she

would have thought impossible before, he slid inside her at last.

She clenched her teeth, waiting for that other pain...which did not come. "It doesn't hurt," she whispered, amazed and relieved.

"Because I made sure you were ready for me," he said softly, his voice warm in the dark. "A difference it makes, you see."

It certainly did.

"Nor *should* it hurt, or will it again."

Believing him, she raised her hips and clenched her muscles, savoring the sensation of Madoc ap Gruffydd inside her.

That was the end of his patience—and hers.

As she gripped him and spoke encouraging words of her own, his thrusts quickened. His breathing grew ragged and hoarse, while her whole body tightened like fleece being twisted from a spindle into yarn.

Now she was tense not with the need to keep from crying out in pain lest it lead to blows and curses, but from an unfamiliar, increasing anticipation.

Until with a great groan, Madoc bucked and thrust deep and the tension within her snapped like a rope being cut. Panting, she clutched him tightly as wave after wave of release throbbed through her.

Never had she experienced anything so good. Never.

It was as if she were a virgin again, making love for the very first time.

She *had* made love for the very first time. Before, it had been...rutting. Or rather, her husband had rutted and she had been forced to endure it.

As her body relaxed, she uncoupled her legs and Madoc laid his head on her breasts. "By all the saints, that was...incredible," he murmured.

"Incredible," she agreed, wrapping her arms around him, happy he was still inside her.

She felt his lips turning up into a grin. "I thought it might be."

"Is that why you agreed to marry me?"

"I confess it was one of the reasons." He moved to lie beside her. "Did that never enter your mind when you were trying to decide?"

"Yes," she admitted, "but I only hoped it wouldn't be too painful. I had no idea making love could be so wonderful."

"It isn't always. You have to be with the right person for you."

"Am I the right person for you?"

"Indeed you are." He raised himself on his elbow, his face barely visible in the darkness, but she could tell his expression was serious. "I didn't just want you in my bed, Roslynn, although you are the most desirable woman I've ever met. Nor did I marry you only for your dowry, or because John sent you and I am his ally. I didn't choose you because it was time I took a wife, or because I think you'll be an excellent chatelaine."

He put his hand on her leg and moved it upward toward that other place still throbbing with excitement. "I married you because you are the most vibrant, spirited woman I've ever met. Because you stood in front of me as bold as Boedicea when you gave me your conditions. Because you *had* conditions, and I respect that. Because you're intelligent and diplomatic, as well as beautiful. That is why I want you, Roslynn, in this bed, in my hall and in my life."

Thrilled beyond measure by his softly spoken declaration, she didn't know what to say.

Instead, she showed him. With enthusiastic delight, she began to arouse him with her lips and her fingers, her hands and her body, moving over him as sinuous as a wave, until she was atop him. His breathing ragged, his body responded as if they hadn't just made love. She raised herself and, as he lay panting, eased him inside her. He groaned as she rocked and moved and shifted like a tree undulating in the breeze, doing all that she could to bring him to ecstasy. She leaned forward so that he could lick and suck her nipples, and run his tongue over her breasts, followed by his hands. Soon, he gripped her shoulders and arched, groaning loudly as he filled her once more with his seed, while she, too, felt that incredible rush of release.

Sweat-slicked and delighted, happy and content as she had never been, Roslynn bent down to kiss him lightly before she moved away.

He laughed with pleasure, the sound like the low rumble of thunder in the distance, before he caught her hand and held it. "Wonderful you are, *fy rhosyn*—my rose."

His rose. "And you're a fine man, Madoc ap Gruffydd."

"Well now, that's good to hear. I'd make love with you again for that, but I think you've completely worn me out."

"Then we should sleep."

"Aye. Come close to me, *fy rhosyn,* and let me keep you warm."

Roslynn needed no other urging, and with Madoc's warm, strong arms about her, she drifted off into a deep and dreamless sleep of the sort she hadn't known in months.

ROSLYNN WOKE when the dawn's first light shone into their chamber. She turned away, hiding her face from it against the warm, naked body of her husband.

Her kind, gentle husband who had loved her with such amazing passion and tenderness.

"Who is this brownie who wakes me?" he muttered, his voice low and husky as he opened his eyes and smiled at her. "A very shapely sprite she is, unless I'm much mistaken."

"Who is this young god beside me?" she replied, brushing a lock of his dark hair from his eyes. "Apollo? Mars? Zeus himself, perhaps?"

"No god, me, but a mortal man, although you, my beauty, would surely put Venus herself to shame."

"I think your uncle isn't the only flatterer in the family."

"Who do you think taught me the art?" Madoc asked with a mischievous grin. "Although I can't say I've ever had such inspiration before."

She laughed as if she were a girl again. "You are going to make me vain, my lord."

He frowned. "What is this 'my lord'? Too formal for bed, Roslynn-fy-rhosyn."

Roslynn-my-rose. Wimarc had only called her terrible things—but he was dead and gone and could never hurt or insult her again.

"I shall have to call you something special, too," she said, kissing him lightly. "Not the Bear of Brecon. That's far too fierce."

"It's only the Normans call me that. The Welsh

call me…" He frowned. "No, I won't tell you. It's beneath my dignity."

Now extremely curious, she said, "Your uncle is sure to tell me sooner or later."

"Aye, you're right." He sighed. "Mumble-mouth."

Were the Welsh deaf or that desperate for a nickname? "You haven't mumbled at all since I've been here. You speak very clearly."

Indeed, his voice was one of the most attractive she had ever heard, too.

Madoc ruefully shook his head. "It was different when I was a boy. A shy fellow I was, you see. I barely spoke in company—not that there was much chance to get a word in anyway, between Lloyd and my father and Trefor." His fingertips lightly brushed her arm. "I've grown bolder since."

"Indeed, you have. You're very bold," she chided, her voice serious, but her eyes revealing her enjoyment of his touch.

He began to stroke her arms and legs, her thighs and the warm, moist place between.

"How can I think of a nickname for you when you do that?" she asked, her voice low with growing desire.

"A problem, is it?"

"You know it is. Perhaps you don't want me to call you anything but Madoc."

"Just don't call me Mumble-mouth and I'll be happy."

"I like your mouth. Especially your lips."

"I'm glad," he said, shifting lower so that his face was next to her thighs.

"What are you doing?"

"Showing you what else I can do with my mouth."

CHAPTER NINE

WIMARC HAD NEVER done anything like *that* with her.

All thoughts of nicknames—and anything else—fled as Roslynn learned what else Madoc ap Gruffydd could do with his lips and tongue.

"I didn't…" she panted, shocked and delighted and amazed after she cried out in ecstasy just as she had the night before, her body thrumming with the same release. "I had no…"

"You liked it, though?" he asked, raising his head to look at her questioningly.

"Oh, yes."

Wanting to pleasure Madoc as he had her, she thought of one thing Wimarc had never made her do, for reasons known only to himself, so it bore no taint of past humiliation.

She slid lower on the bed and took Madoc into her mouth.

Judging by his groans and the way the sinews of his neck tightened, he found this very enjoyable. She moved as she thought would most excite him, until she was too aroused herself to continue. She swiftly rolled over and guided him into her yearning body.

He didn't hesitate or seem dismayed at the change of position. He made love to her with the same powerful thrusts, and soon she—scarcely believing it could be possible—once more felt that exhilarating tightening and release. As did he.

Afterward, he fell back beside her. "Sweet merciful heavens, you're a wonder, you are."

"I wanted to give you pleasure."

"Oh, that you did, Roslynn-fy-rhosyn. That you did."

She snuggled against him and traced the hairs on his chest with her fingertip. To think she had found such happiness here, in the wilds of Wales, and because the king had—

A cry of alarm sounded outside.

Naked, Madoc leaped from the bed and went to the window, where he called out to the guards running along the wall walk toward the gates. As she sat up, clutching the sheet to her naked breasts, she saw that rain fell in a steady stream, making all look gray.

After receiving an answer in Welsh, Madoc muttered something under his breath and hurried to tug on his breeches and boots before he grabbed his swordbelt.

"What is it?" Roslynn demanded. "What's happening? Is it an attack?"

"Trefor's too much of a coward for that," Madoc grimly replied as he strode from the room.

HIS FEET PLANTED, arms akimbo, ignoring the fact that he wore only his breeches and boots despite the rain, Madoc glared at the short, stocky man in the yard standing before him with a bundle at his feet. Rhodri had been a foot soldier in Llanpowell until he'd chosen to leave with Trefor. Now he was second-in-command at Pontyrmwr.

Several of the men of Llanpowell, some still obviously the worse for wine, ale or *braggot*, waited warily nearby, their hands on the hilts of their swords. A few servants, likewise recovering from the celebrations, hovered near the entrances to the hall, the kitchen and the stables. Neither Ivor nor Uncle Lloyd nor—thank God—the Norman nobleman, were there.

If Trefor had attacked Llanpowell in force this morning, it could have gone very ill indeed. Instead, he'd apparently sent only Rhodri alone, with a white flag of truce tucked into his belt.

Grinning scornfully, his black hair and beard as tightly curled as fleece, Rhodri held out a rolled parchment sealed with wax.

"Trefor sent this with his wedding gift," he said, nudging the bundle at his feet. "Good wishes for the bride and groom, no doubt."

"*I* doubt," Madoc muttered as he grabbed the scroll.

"Since my job's done, I'll be leaving," Rhodri said. "I'm not wanting to linger in case I come down with whatever it is your men have, for a sorry, sickly lot they are."

Madoc's men grumbled among themselves, while Ioan and Hugh started forward until a swift warning glance from Madoc made them halt.

Rhodri smirked even more and it was all Madoc could do not to strike him.

"I wish you joy of your new wife, Madoc," Rhodri sneered. "I hope she lives longer than Gwendolyn."

White cloth or not, Madoc would have drawn his sword and struck him down for that insolent remark, except that Rhodri's mouth fell open and he stared at something over Madoc's shoulder as if beholding an unearthly vision.

Madoc turned to see what had captured Rhodri's attention and wiped the smirk off his face.

It was Roslynn, wearing a gown of light green wool, looking as fresh as spring, with a cloak thrown over her slender shoulders against the slackening rain. The hood only partly hid her torrent of thick brown hair, still tousled as if she'd just risen from the marriage bed, which she had.

Madoc's ire disappeared, replaced by pride and pleasure. Let Trefor do or say what he would in his childish spite; *he* had Roslynn.

She had also brought him his cloak, which she put around his shoulders with a motion like a caress before she ran a quizzical gaze over Rhodri.

"Welcome to Llanpowell," she said, as gracious as a queen. "Unfortunately, I fear you come too late to celebrate. The wedding feast is over."

Her words seemed to shake Rhodri from his stupor, yet before he could speak, Madoc did. "This is Rhodri ap Meirion, Trefor's second-in-command. He's brought us a wedding gift from my brother."

"Oh? How kind of them both," Roslynn replied, her voice as melodious as a nightingale's song.

Yet beneath the words there was a tang of disdain that made Rhodri flush.

"Like I said, I'll be leaving," Rhodri snapped in Welsh as he turned on his well-worn heel and marched toward the gate.

Let him go back to Trefor and tell him of his brother's marvelous, beautiful bride, Madoc thought, feeling like he could crow with delight from the battlements.

"What do you suppose your brother's sent us?"

Roslynn asked warily, reminding Madoc of the parchment in his hand and the bundle still on the ground at his feet.

"I doubt it's anything good," he replied. "Probably rotten meat."

The parchment would also likely contain the sort of message he wouldn't want everyone in Llanpowell to hear, and if the gift was as disgusting as he feared, he'd rather keep that quiet, too, at least as much as possible.

"We should open my brother's message and gift in private," he said. He handed Roslynn the parchment before bending down to pick up the bundle, noting with relief that it didn't drip blood.

When they entered the hall, Uncle Lloyd was still asleep on a bench, snoring lightly. The wooden screen was in place near the dais, so Lord Alfred must be abed, too, which was a mercy. Madoc didn't want the Norman, and through him, the king, to know too much about his dispute with his brother.

Once in their chamber, Madoc set the bundle on the stool and removed his wet cloak before untying the leather strips that held it closed.

A sheep's skin with black fleece spilled onto the flagstone floor.

Madoc knew at once what it was. Trefor had killed his black ram.

"The spiteful, malicious *cnaf*," he growled as he held out his hand. "Give me the parchment. Let's hear what my despicable brother has to say."

Roslynn wordlessly put the message in his outstretched hand, then took off her cloak and laid it at the foot of the bed.

"'For you, dear brother,'" Madoc read aloud after he tore off the wax seal, "'and your Norman widow bride, a bit of repayment for the woman you stole from me. I wish you such joy of the lady as you deserve.'"

Madoc threw the parchment across the room. "You see what a malicious lout he is?"

Her expression composed, Roslynn began to gather up the fleece. "I see that he knows how to upset you."

"What do you mean?" Madoc demanded, annoyed that she could be so calm in the face of Trefor's insults.

"He plays upon you like a bard on a harp, or a nettle in your boot," she said, her visage still serene as she faced him with her arms full of fleece. "Are you so sure this is your ram?"

"There aren't many sheep in Wales that size and color," he snapped. "He's done this for vengeance, so of course it's my ram."

"So now will you have him arrested for theft and brought before the king's eyre for judgment?"

God save him, she was a cool one. "That may be

the Norman way, but it isn't mine. He's still my brother, and I will have my justice in my own way."

"As you will. I'll see that this fleece is spun into wool, perhaps to make a fine new tunic for you."

She turned as if she meant to see to it at once.

He had been too harsh. After all, this was not her doing, and she had just given him the best night— and morning—of his life.

"I'm sorry to be so churlish," he said, rolling his shoulders to ease the tension. "You're right. He does know how to goad me. He always has. I still won't attack Pontyrmwr or arrest him and bring him before the king's court for theft. I won't have his death on my conscience."

Too.

"But I *will* make it more difficult for him to do such things," he added, "starting today."

He got a shirt and pulled it on, then his tunic and his swordbelt before he started for the door. "First, I'll lead a patrol around the border of my estate to make sure he hasn't done anything else, or worse."

DESPITE WHAT had happened, Roslynn dutifully attended mass presided over by Father Elwy. Many of the servants were there, but few of the soldiers. Most of the garrison who weren't on sentry duty had ridden out with Madoc.

She tried to maintain a decorous demeanor and behave with the appropriate dignity, even if her mind kept wandering. She especially tried not to recall her wedding night and being in Madoc's arms, for it must surely be sinful to relive such moments in a chapel.

It was less pleasant, but also less wicked—she hoped—to consider Madoc's relationship with his brother, and what Trefor had done. Although Madoc had held his temper in check, he'd been furiously angry.

So why, if he was continually enraged by Trefor's trespass and other illegal acts, did Madoc allow this situation to continue? Why did he not put an end to it, either by force or legal means?

Why had she stayed with Wimarc? her own conscience chided. *Why didn't she flee the day after they were married, when she had learned the sort of man he truly was?*

Because she'd believed she had no choice. She had nowhere else to go. She had been too stubborn, too foolishly certain she knew what she was doing and that Wimarc loved her, for her family to welcome her back.

Perhaps Madoc thought he had no alternative, either. Perhaps, in spite of everything, he still loved his brother.

After the mass ended, Roslynn and the rest of the

household went to the hall to break the fast. The commotion of their arrival awakened Uncle Lloyd, who was sleeping on the same bench he'd occupied during the feasting the night before.

"Sweet Saint Dafydd and Bridget, too," he muttered as he put a hand to his head and slowly sat up. "An invasion, is it?"

"It's time to break the fast," Roslynn said with a smile as she sat beside him. She wanted Lloyd, and everyone here, to know that she was happy and pleased with her husband.

"Ah!" Lloyd looked around, clearly a little baffled. "Mass is over?"

"Just now," she said as several servants hurried to set up the tables and others to put away the pallets and blankets they'd slept on.

Lloyd cringed at the noise some of the men made as they put together a table near him. "Can't you be quiet about it?" he complained, before addressing Roslynn again. "You look well, my lady."

"I feel very well."

The older man's face lit up with delight. "Do you now?" He looked around the hall and his brows drew together in a frown. "Where's Madoc?" Then he grinned. "Or is the poor man so worn out, he's still abed?"

"He's ridden out on patrol."

Before Lloyd could ask any questions, or make any more observations, she quickly told him about Trefor's gift.

"Damn the lad," Lloyd muttered, shaking his head. "What's he got to do such things for? He was always the bright light in his parents' eyes, so why begrudge Madoc some happiness? It's not as if that will bring Gwendolyn back, either."

Roslynn saw an opportunity to learn more about Madoc's past. "Madoc's parents favored his brother?"

"Aye, although they were proud of Madoc, too. He was just such a shy boy, nobody could make out what he was thinking half the time."

Surely one had only to look in Madoc's eyes to know what he was thinking—unless one didn't take the trouble. Or perhaps he had grown more open over the years, after his favored brother was gone.

Lord Alfred came around the wooden screen. He looked a bit tired, yet well. He was also dressed in his mail and armor and cloak, as if he was about to depart. Confirming her observation, his squire followed, carrying his baggage.

Roslynn rose and went to meet them, trailed by Uncle Lloyd. "You'll eat before you leave, my lord?" she asked.

"Yes, thank you," he replied, casting his gaze around the hall. "Where is Lord Madoc?"

"He had estate business to attend to."

"What business?"

Roslynn regarded him coolly, secure in the knowledge that he had no more power over her. "Important business, of course, since it prevents him from taking his leave of you."

She slipped her arm through Lord Alfred's as easily as a fish glides through water, and steered him toward the dais. "Come and eat heartily, my lord, for you have a long journey ahead of you. And when you get to court, you must be sure to tell the king how pleased I am with the husband he so wisely chose for me. Indeed, I believe I'll be grateful to him for the rest of my life."

Lord Alfred checked his steps and studied her face, trying to gauge if she was sincere or not.

"I mean that, my lord," she assured him.

Lloyd's delighted smile stretched from ear to ear. "There now, my lady!" he crowed. "Did I not tell you my nephew is a marvel?"

"Indeed he is," she agreed.

A SHORT WHILE LATER, after Lord Alfred and his men had eaten and departed, Roslynn went to the kitchen to see the steward. As chatelaine, it was part of her duties to oversee the accounts the steward kept, and she saw no reason to wait to begin.

Lloyd had told her that Ivor had a workroom near the kitchen where he conducted the business of the estate and kept the lists of expenditures and household goods. She hadn't been in that part of the castle before and had assumed it housed only the kitchen, storerooms and the buttery.

She easily spotted Hywel, the cook, a large man with a shining pate who was adding rosemary to an iron pot over the fire in the hearth, and asked him where Ivor's workroom was.

Hywel pointed to a half-open door just beyond the kitchen. "He's in there now, my lady," he said, his voice loud enough to be heard over the talking, chopping, kneading and banging pots as the other kitchen servants went about their tasks.

With a grateful nod, she headed for the door and pushed it open. It moved without a sound on well-oiled hinges.

Ivor was indeed inside, seated at a scarred trestle table that looked as if it had been retired from the hall. Sunlight came in through a single high narrow window to illuminate the room. An open purse was at the steward's elbow and five small piles of silver coins rested in front of him on the table, as well as a small piece of parchment that looked like some kind of list.

The room itself was a good size, but between the table, Ivor's chair and the shelves that contained other scrolls, and a chest with a large iron lock, there wasn't much room for anyone or anything else.

"Good day, Ivor," she said.

He looked up with surprise. "My lady!" he cried as he rose from his chair. "To what do I owe this honor, and the morning after your wedding, too?"

"I thought I should become familiar with the household accounts as soon as possible," she replied, giving him a smile.

Ivor frowned and began to roll up the scroll. "Madoc didn't tell you then? There's no need for you to involve yourself in such things. I supervise all the purchasing and give the accounts directly to Madoc."

"That may have been the procedure while Lord Madoc had no wife. However, now that he has, it's my responsibility to manage the household expenditures. Naturally I leave it to Madoc to discuss the accounts for arms and other things related to the garrison."

"Your devotion to your responsibilities is to be commended, my lady," Ivor replied with a smile as condescending as Wimarc's had ever been as he put the rolled scroll on the table. "But I'm sure there's plenty enough for you to do without bothering with the accounts. Besides, you're new here, my lady, while I have known most of the merchants we do business with for years, so they know better than to try to cheat me."

"I'm sure that's quite true," she replied, "but any merchants who try to cheat *me* will quickly find themselves with no more business at Llanpowell."

She was not incompetent, after all.

She *was* the lady of Llanpowell and it was not for the steward to tell her what she could, or could not, do.

Nevertheless, and in spite of her growing indignation, she reminded herself that this man was Madoc's friend. She was also a stranger here and her arrival and the marriage had happened suddenly and without warning. Most important of all, she wanted to fit into the life of Llanpowell and avoid conflict, so Roslynn fought to remain composed, overlook Ivor's manner and instead do all she could to convince him she was capable.

"I can read and write and calculate," she assured him. "My mother made sure of it. I quite enjoy that part of a chatelaine's duties, much more than embroidery or other women's work."

She would even find common ground with him, if she could. "Is there not something satisfying about tallying up the accounts? Don't you feel a sense of triumph when you come upon a mistake and then discover where it occurred and correct it?"

"I've never heard a woman say such things," Ivor

replied with undisguised astonishment, and not a little doubt.

"It's quite true," she said, tucking her hands into her long cuffs. "My father's steward said I would have made an excellent clerk, had I been born a man."

"I cannot imagine you anything but a beautiful woman," Ivor said. His lips jerked up, and she realized that was supposed to be a smile.

"I learn quickly, too," she went on, "and you can teach me about the local merchants and their prices as we go through the accounts together. I'll certainly expect you to assist me when it comes to negotiating purchases at first, because the merchants might be inclined to try to inflate the prices unless someone they know is with me."

Ivor clasped his hands behind his back. "Madoc has agreed to all this?"

"I'm sure he will. As chatelaine—"

"Then you haven't actually asked him?"

As much as she wanted to avoid conflict, there were limits to what she would countenance from the steward. Nevertheless, she fought to keep her voice level. "There was no need. I am well versed in a chatelaine's obligations and responsibilities and I intend to fulfill them, unless and until Madoc tells me otherwise."

Ivor seemed to shrink a little. "Forgive me, my

lady, for my reluctance. I would hate to think Madoc doesn't trust me anymore."

Is that why he'd been so resistant? "I'm quite certain he has every confidence and faith in you. It is simply that he now has a wife who's capable and willing to do all that a chatelaine should."

Ivor gave her a more genuine smile. "As long as he doesn't doubt my honesty."

"I'm sure he doesn't." She picked up the scroll that he'd put on the table, unrolled it and studied the list of items on it. "You have a remarkably neat hand, Ivor. I shall not have to squint at all."

Ivor came to stand beside her. "Thank you, my lady. As you can see, the trout at the wedding feast was a bargain…"

As THE MORNING progressed, Ivor became more genial and forthcoming, answering Roslynn's many other questions about goods and money paid while going through lists and tallies.

"I think that's enough for today," she said as the noise from the kitchen increased, telling her it must be getting near the hour for the noon meal.

She rose and arched her back. "You do have an eye for a bargain, Ivor. Madoc's lucky to have you for a steward."

"He's lucky to have you for a wife, my lady," Ivor

replied with an admiring smile, more accepting of her now that he knew she was capable of discussing and comprehending such matters. Like most men, he had believed otherwise until she gave him proof.

"I'll just put these scrolls away and come along shortly," he added.

Feeling she had won him over, or at least was well on the way to doing so, Roslynn nodded her head and left the room.

Had she turned back, however, she wouldn't have seen admiration or respect on the steward's face.

Only bitter, burning resentment.

CHAPTER TEN

IT WAS APPROACHING dusk when Madoc and his men returned to Llanpowell that day. He'd done everything he could think of to protect his land, his sheep and his people from his brother's selfish villainy.

Not only had he checked the border of his estate for any signs of trespass, he had gone to every shepherd and farmer and warned them to take special care and alert the castle if they noticed anything amiss. He'd also made sure that the signal fires were sheltered from the wet and ready to be lit at a moment's notice. He'd ordered extra patrols and put more men on watch at the castle.

Yet despite his brother's action and the need for increased vigilance, Madoc felt happier than he had since the day he married Gwendolyn, because he was going home to Roslynn. Beautiful, passionate, clever Roslynn…

"This marriage must agree with you, Madoc,"

Ioan noted as he rode beside him at the head of the patrol. "You're humming."

"Am I?"

"Aye. The song about the mermaid, too. A good sign, that. Must have been quite the wedding night."

Madoc was in too good a humor to be annoyed by Ioan's impertinence. "It was."

Ioan let out a low whistle. "My, my, who'd have thought it? I wish I'd been more polite to Lord Alfred when they arrived."

Madoc had forgotten that the often-insolent Ioan had been on sentry duty then. "What did you say to him?"

"Nothing so very rude," Ioan assured him, although his reddening cheeks suggested otherwise.

"Tell me," Madoc ordered.

When the lord of Llanpowell used that tone of voice, a man had best obey, so Ioan told him, albeit reluctantly, finishing with, "You see, Madoc? Not so bad."

Madoc envisioned the scene, especially Ioan's impudent manner as he addressed the haughty Norman from the wall. He would have been upset if Ioan had been rude to Lady Roslynn directly. Since it had been Lord Alfred, though, he was inclined to be magnanimous. "Next time, be more polite. You represent me, after all, and we don't want the Normans thinking we're insolent louts."

Ioan grinned with relief. "Aye, I'll be politeness itself the next time a Norman comes to the gates."

Madoc didn't believe that for a moment, but decided to let the matter rest.

"Since you seem so keen to be entertaining, how about a song?" he asked, for Ioan was the best singer in Llanpowell, with a rich tenor that could make the hall rafters vibrate.

"Gladly!" he replied, before launching into a song about a shepherd and his lass on their wedding day.

A particularly bawdy ballad it was, one that got progressively more bawdy, and funnier, with every verse. But it was a favorite with the men and soon even Madoc joined in until the song ended with a rousing chorus that left them all laughing.

"It's good to hear you laugh like that again, Madoc," Ioan said, wiping his eyes.

"It *feels* good," he replied.

"She must be some woman," Hugh the Beak noted behind them.

"She's a beauty," Ioan observed.

"A little skinny, though," somebody called out.

"Madoc likes them thin!" another cried.

"With huge chests!"

That comment was too insolent. Madoc twisted

in his saddle and glared at the youth who'd said it—young Gwillym, as skinny and pale as a plucked chicken, riding at the back of the group.

"Not meaning any harm, me, my lord," the young man stammered, blanching, which made his freckles look like spots of red dye. "I meant of gold, my lord. Chests of gold."

Although he believed the lad, Madoc wanted his men to appreciate that there were some things he wouldn't countenance, even in jest. "She's a lady and my wife, so there'll be no more talk like that about her body or her face. Is that clear?"

The men nodded their understanding and he knew they would obey.

To show them he wasn't angry, only resolved that his wife be respected, Madoc gave them a grin and said, "Since I'm used to you louts, you can make all the sport you like of me."

"And we will!" Ioan replied, to the amusement of the company.

Hugh started up another song about a battle between the Britons and the Romans, and they sang until they rode through the inner gate of the castle.

Where Lloyd was waiting for them. Madoc had hoped Roslynn would be there, too, but she was probably seeing that all was ready for the evening meal. She seemed a very conscientious woman, in every way.

Even so, the first thing he said to his uncle when he dismounted was, "Where's my wife?"

The last time he'd said those words, he realized, he'd been speaking of Gwendolyn and cringing inside.

"In your chamber waiting for you, I expect," Lloyd said. He drew him away from the hall, closer to the stables. "I heard what your brother did. Any more trouble from him?"

"Not yet."

"Good," Lloyd said with relief, before he shoved Madoc toward the hall. "Don't stand here talking to me. Go see your lovely wife."

As if he needed prompting, Madoc thought as he hurried to the hall.

As he'd expected, the hall was indeed prepared for the evening meal. Some of the returning soldiers, or those just ending their watch, as well as servants waiting to serve the food, were already gathered there. Father Elwy was in place to bless the meal. Not unexpectedly, Ivor wasn't, but he was no doubt still calculating how many weapons and stores they could buy with the dowry.

Madoc took the stairs to their bedchamber two at a time, then waited a moment to calm his racing blood before he entered. He must be patient and not impetuous. He must treat his wife gently until she felt completely safe with him.

He slowly eased open the door.

Clad only in her shift hiked up around her thighs, bent at the waist, Roslynn had one foot in a basin on the floor as she ran a soaking, soapy cloth up her bare leg from her ankle to her thigh.

His breath caught and his desire blazed at the sight.

But he mustn't let his desire overwhelm him. He mustn't frighten her with the intensity of his passion. So he took another moment to subdue the need raging through him like a brush fire before he cleared his throat.

She straightened at once. "Madoc!" she cried as she stepped quickly out of the basin, nearly knocking it over. "You're back."

He tried not to notice how sheer her thin lawn shift was, or to remember the feel of it beneath his fingers last night, even if soapy water from the cloth dripped onto it, making it nearly transparent. He could see the shadow between her legs, the ruddy tips of her taut nipples, the rounded swell of her breasts.

Swallowing hard, he struggled to control the need building inside him, for this was even more arousing than if she'd been naked.

With equal desire kindling in her eyes, Roslynn whispered his name.

He reached her in one long stride and snatched the damp cloth from her hand, tossing it into the basin and ignoring the splash of water on the floor. He put his arms around her and captured her mouth with all the intensity he felt.

Panting, she broke the kiss and stepped back. "We haven't time. The evening meal—"

"Can wait," he muttered, reaching for her, because it wasn't food he was hungry for. "A man has needs."

Then he saw the look on her face.

"Which this man can control," he said firmly, moving away from her. He had told her he would never force her, and he never would, no matter how much he wanted her.

She said nothing as she went to the chest containing her clothes and, with trembling hands, raised the lid.

God help him, he was a fool! A selfish, impetuous, unthinking fool! "Roslynn, I'm sorry. I was too hasty."

She pulled out a gown of rich brown, like damp earth, and held it in front of her. "I'm sorry, too, Madoc, that I cannot stop the panic that comes over me." She turned away. "I truly wish I could."

"It'll take time, that's all, until you're used to me and know me better," he said, smiling, even though in his heart, he dreaded it might always be like this. "Let me help you dress, or they'll be wondering what's keeping us."

She put the dress over her head, lifting her arms in a way that seemed designed to draw his attention to her breasts. In spite of the desire that aroused, he kept a rein on his passion and came to stand behind her to tie the laces in the back.

Even when she pulled her hair to one side, exposing the naked nape of her neck, he controlled himself, although it seemed every particle of his body urged him to kiss her there.

Instead, he focused on the leather laces, pulling them closed and tying a firm knot. He would not notice the rise and fall of her breasts, or remember the sight of her back, pale and naked in the moonlight, or the feel of her flesh beneath his seeking palms.

She abruptly turned toward him and, just as unexpectedly, took his face between her hands and kissed him full on the mouth. More, she leaned into him as if she wanted him to make love with her then and there.

"Take me," she commanded, her voice husky with longing and determination, too. "Take me as you will, Madoc. I want you and I'm willing. Please, Madoc, I'm sure you won't hurt me and I am not made of glass."

Drawing back, his anxious gaze searched her face, seeking confirmation.

Before he could be sure it was confirmation he saw and not mere compliance, her lips were on his and her tongue was pushing into his mouth and her hands were on his body—seemingly all over his body, as if she would feel every inch of him, clothed or bare.

Surely that was confirmation, especially when she attacked his breeches, freeing and stroking him until he thought he would burst.

Driven by need and excitement, he tore at the laces he had so recently tied, ripping the holes through which they were threaded in his haste to touch her skin, her breasts, to lick and kiss and suck her rosy nipples. She pulled off his tunic and shirt in one motion, exposing his naked torso to the cooler air and her touch.

His breathing hoarse, his need almost beyond his control, he angled her back against the dressing table, then lifted her so that she was sitting on the edge.

Her mouth, lips, tongue and fingertips explored his naked chest, gliding over the flesh like the soft graze of feathers. She sucked his nipple into her mouth and teased it with her tongue, making him groan as he pushed up her skirts to enter her.

But despite the impassioned urge driving him,

he kept a slim grasp on his willpower. He must still ensure that she was ready. That she would feel no pain.

His hand found the nakedness between her legs, warm and wet, and then his finger made the first foray. With a low moan, she shoved her body against the heel of his hand, the motion and the sound of her passionate yearning nearly making him spill his seed then and there.

Certain she was prepared, too aroused to take more time, he positioned himself between her legs and lifted them around his hips, her shift and skirt gathering about her thighs and waist.

"Yes, oh, yes," she gasped, grabbing his shoulders as he pushed inside her.

With a few strong thrusts, he was over the edge, his body bucking. She, too, cried out, as ecstasy overwhelmed her. Marveling, delighted, relieved and happy, Madoc held her close until their breathing slowed and his heartbeat returned to normal.

He helped her down, then swiftly retied his breeches.

"I've torn your gown," he said with remorse as she began to remove it and he picked up his discarded clothing.

"No matter. I have others and it can be repaired," she said lightly, giving him a satisfied look that told him better than words that she had enjoyed what they had done as much as he.

"I'll help you into another," he offered.

She chose the plain blue one and as he once more tied her laces, he brushed his lips across the nape of her neck. "Thank you for that, Roslynn-fy-rhosyn. Otherwise I might always have been afraid to lose myself in the desire you rouse in me."

"It was necessary for me, too, and it was very exciting, although I believe I prefer to make love in our bed," she replied, turning to face him and share another passionate, powerful kiss.

"We should go," she panted several moments later. "The evening meal will be ready."

"Lloyd won't wait for us, I'm sure. Let them begin without us."

"Won't they wonder…"

"They shouldn't be surprised. We're newly wedded, after all."

LATER THAT NIGHT, moving as furtively as a thief, Madoc returned to his bedchamber. He eased the door open, cursing the leather hinges that creaked so much, and slipped inside the chamber lit by a quarter moon that seemed to bob and weave among fast-moving clouds.

Making his way cautiously into the room, he bit

back a curse when he stubbed his toe on the stool that seemed to have been waiting to trap him.

"Madoc?" Roslynn queried sleepily from behind the bed curtains. "Where have you been?"

CHAPTER ELEVEN

"GOT TO KEEP UP my strength with a wife like you," Madoc replied, holding up the basket he was carrying for her to see. "Since we missed the evening meal entirely, I went to the kitchen to get whatever I could find."

Covering herself with the sheet, Roslyn raised herself on her elbow. She had no idea what o'clock it was, only that it must be well past midnight.

They never had gotten down to the hall after making love. They'd stayed to kiss and caress, talk and laugh, and share stories of their childhood. Madoc had apparently been an imp of a boy, albeit shy while she was no stranger to mischief, either, and it had been delightful to compare tales of childish exploits.

Not quite so delightful as making love, however, so they'd done that again, too, although they'd gone to the bed that time.

Yet she truly had enjoyed it when he'd taken her

at the dressing table, although for a different reason. She'd felt fear and panic at first, yet she'd overcome them. She'd been able to let Madoc love her with urgency, as if she had no past experience to taint her response to his desire.

As if she'd only ever had him for her husband.

Dressed in his shirt, unlaced and loose, breeches and barefoot despite the chilly floor, Madoc set the basket on the bed.

"I'm starving," she said as she peered inside and he sat beside her.

He had brought a loaf of barley bread, the remains of a wheel of thick cheese, some broken pieces of meat wrapped in a napkin and a wineskin half-full.

"It's no feast, I grant you," Madoc said as he ripped apart the small loaf and handed a half to her, "but I didn't want to wake anybody."

"Nobody saw you then?" she asked, wondering what they'd have made of the sight of their overlord sneaking into his own kitchen.

"No," he replied as he removed his boots. "Some of the dogs woke and sniffed and made a few noises until I told them—quietly—to settle. Not that it would make any difference if anyone had seen me, of course. I have every right to go through my own castle whatever the time of day."

He reached out to caress her cheek, then leaned

back against the pillows to eat his bread. "Are *you* embarrassed because they know what we've been up to? We're husband and wife, after all."

"We certainly are," she said, nestling against him as she chewed the delicious bread, enjoying this impromptu meal more than any feast, happier than she'd been since she'd met Wimarc. "I wish my parents could know how happy I am."

"We can send word to them if you'd like."

Shaking her head, she shifted away from him. "No. They won't want to hear from me. I disgraced and humiliated them, even worse than your brother disgraced and humiliated you."

"Wasn't it you who said families should protect each other?" he asked.

"I insisted on marrying a man of whom they didn't approve, and he turned out to be a traitor planning a rebellion. They surely want nothing to do with me, and why should they, when all I have given them is grief?"

"Except that now they have a fine new son-in-law and an alliance with the Welsh," Madoc pointed out. "Or do you think that will add to their shame?"

"No!" she quickly assured him. "Even if they don't know how fortunate I am in my husband, they've nothing against the Welsh that I know of."

"Perhaps this marriage will please them," he suggested.

She couldn't agree, even though she wanted to. "What if it doesn't? I've already brought them too much trouble."

"Very well then, no letter."

"No letter," she replied, although she began to wonder if she was wrong not to contact her parents. They would have heard of her journey to Wales and its purpose from friends at court. Maybe they could forgive her now that she was married to another, better man.

Or perhaps they'd never forgive her for what she'd done. She'd been so stubborn, so determined not to heed their words of caution.

When the food and the contents of the wineskin were gone, Madoc set the basket on the floor and rested against the pillows with a satisfied sigh.

"Are you happy?" she asked as she laid her head on his chest.

He ran his fingers up her bare arm, an expression on his face she was beginning to know well. "More than I ever thought I could be."

"I suppose we should sleep," she said with a sigh, even as her body tingled at his touch and she began to envision activities far removed from slumber.

"We can always sleep tomorrow night," he suggested with a smile that made her feel as if she were melting.

"I begin to think I've married an insatiable man."

"If I'm insatiable, it's only because you're my bride," he said, brushing his lips across hers.

Although she didn't pull away, she didn't respond with the passion his kiss usually aroused.

"What's wrong?" he asked with a frown.

Her first impulse was to deny that anything was the matter, to tell him a comfortable lie. But she had had enough of deception and so would be honest with him. "You're such a vital, passionate man, how can one woman ever satisfy you?"

His frown deepened. "You think I'll commit adultery? That I'm so lust-filled, I'll sate my needs with other women?"

"You asked me what was wrong, and I answered honestly."

He got out of bed and walked to the window, leaning one hand on the frame and looking out as if consulting the moon.

She, too, rose and, wrapping the sheet about her, went to stand beside him. "I could have lied to you, Madoc, as Wimarc so often lied to me. I could have flattered you or told you I was only wondering how I could please you more. Instead, I told you the truth, that I fear a man like you will have other women.

"I'm no innocent, naive bride to believe that all men treat their vows as sacred. I have seen things at court that make a mockery of marriage. I hope you aren't like that, but I've only just met you. How can I be sure? And you're so handsome, so vigorous, many women must want you. How can I compete against them all?"

He turned toward her and she knew she had upset him. "You're right. I can have my share of women if I choose, and I've not been chaste since Gwendolyn died. There have been women in towns and castles that I visited.

"But this isn't the court, and I'm not like those men. When I give my word, I keep it. I am your husband by vows of honor, our union blessed by a priest. Did I not keep my vow to be gentle and patient, even though my blood has never been so heated as when I was with you?"

His indignation lessened, replaced with a tenderness that thrilled her as much as his passion. "I'm grateful, too, that I have a truthful wife who tells me what she thinks."

"I'm sorry if I offended you, Madoc." She took his hand in hers and pressed a kiss upon the palm, for she could believe that he would indeed be faithful to her, as she would be to him. How many women could say that of their husbands and be certain? "I'm grateful that I have a man of honor for my husband."

As he bent his head to kiss her, a cock crowed somewhere in the yard below. Looking past him out the window, Roslynn realized that the sky was lightening with the sunrise.

"Morning," Madoc said, following her gaze. "And hardly a wink of sleep," he added.

The most delightful, welcome twinkle came to his usually serious eyes. "Now that we understand each other so well, I'd like nothing better than to go back to bed and sleep. Unfortunately, I've got to meet with the shepherds today. We have to pick a day for the gathering of the sheep for the shearing."

"And I still have much to learn about your household," she said, unwrapping the sheet and picking up her shift from the foot of the bed. It had been discarded during the night, tossed aside when she grew too hot.

He went to the washstand and poured some water from the ewer into the basin to wash his face. "You should talk to Ivor about the feast when the shearing's finished."

A feast—her first as chatelaine.

A different sort of dread and excitement grew within her, knowing she would be judged on her abilities to plan and host such an event, and on the meal itself, too. "I'll do so right away."

Madoc put on his tunic, then sat on the edge of the bed to pull on his boots. "Aye, and we'll need extra food the days of the washing and shearing, as well as the feast to follow the day after all of that is done. We'll have men from all the estates nearby to help us, as our men will go to help them when their time comes."

Not all his neighbors, she thought. Surely his brother wouldn't come to help him, nor would he send any of his men to help Trefor.

"Perhaps we could make it a marriage celebration, too," she suggested, "since we didn't invite your noble neighbors when we wed."

"If you'd like that, Roslynn-fy-rhosyn."

"I would," she said, thinking it would be the proper thing to do, and help maintain other necessary alliances.

"All right then. Do whatever you think best, and since it's your dowry paying for it, have whatever food you like. But I should warn you, Ivor can be tight with the purse strings."

She wasn't surprised to hear that. Something about his thin lips and narrow eyes had made her suspect he was at least a bit of a miser. However, she couldn't fault him for being careful with her husband's money.

As she went to her chest for a gown, she realized that Madoc was watching her in the dim light of dawn.

"I could forget my own name when I look at you," he said softly.

She flushed with delight. "I could forget that I have duties, too," she said, picking up the blue gown. "I shouldn't, though, not with so much to do."

She thought of something else. "Will your son come to the feast? I'd like to meet him."

When she saw the expression that came to Madoc's face, she was sorry she'd mentioned his son, until he shrugged and smiled.

"Why not? You should meet Owain. He should meet you, too, now that you're his stepmother."

Stepmother. She hadn't really thought of herself as that before, and now it seemed even more important for her to meet Owain.

Madoc came behind her and tugged her laces tight. "You're too tempting by half, *fy rhosyn,*" he said, his voice low. "We'd better leave while I still have the strength to resist you."

"And I, you," she agreed, even as her thoughts turned to the feast and all it would entail.

"HYWEL, HAVE YOU SEEN Ivor this morning?" Roslynn asked the cook a few days later after once again finding the steward's workroom locked and Ivor absent.

As usual, the kitchen was abustle with the efforts of the cook and his helpers to feed the household. Several women chopped and mixed and added various vegetables, herbs and spices to the iron pots hanging from the pot-cranes. Others made and presided over flat bake irons lying directly in the fire. A spit boy, wiping his sweaty young brow with his sleeve, turned several chickens, so close to them he was almost inside the hearth. Seated on a low wooden stool, an elderly, gray-haired male servant tended the built-in boiler cauldron, adding wood to the fire hole as necessary.

Standing at the table where he'd been spicing what appeared to be an entire ox, the cook wiped his large, bloody hands on his apron. "He was here before breaking the fast, my lady. I didn't see him leave."

"I heard him say something about going to the mill," Rhonwen, one of the maidservants, supplied as she cut onions for soup.

Another older servant, named Lowri, shook her head and stopped stirring the peas porridge. "I thought he said Milltonbury. That's the town about five miles from here," she added for Roslynn's benefit.

"What the devil would he be doing there?" Rhonwen demanded. "He's surely got no business there."

"Who are you to say where the steward's got business or not?" Lowri retorted, giving Rhonwen a sour look. "He can go where he likes, I should think!"

"But if the lady's looking for him, your foolish answer—"

"I heard him say Milltonbury," Lowri persisted. "Didn't you hear that, Hywel?"

"I didn't hear him say anything," the cook replied with an apologetic shrug. "Sorry, my lady. But if you find him, will you tell him I need to know what fish he's buying for the shearing feast? I hear the fishmonger's in a way to getting some good salmon."

"I was hoping to discuss such matters with him myself this morning," Roslynn replied, hiding her aggravation as she left them.

Unfortunately, every time she'd gone to see Ivor to go over the accounts together and discuss upcoming purchases for the feast, he hadn't been in his workroom, or anywhere else in the castle, apparently. Later, when she encountered him in the hall during meals, he was full of apologies and apparently sincere remorse for having been otherwise engaged.

The gathering of the sheep and the shearing feast to follow were a mere eight days away. It was Ivor's duty to help her with the selection and purchasing of the food and they shouldn't delay any longer, or they might not be able to find, let alone purchase, all the foodstuffs required.

She had two choices, Roslynn reasoned: wait for

Ivor to return, or go in search of him. The first would add to her frustration, the second was a blow to her pride. The steward should be coming to the chatelaine, not the other way around.

There was a third alternative, although it was one she would prefer not to consider: she could go to Madoc and have him order Ivor to meet with her.

That was the choice of last resort, for she really didn't want to complain to her husband, who had enough to think about without household concerns.

So instead, she swallowed her pride and went to find the steward, starting with the armory. The fletcher was there, making new arrows, and another man repairing some quivers. They had no idea where Ivor was.

He wasn't in the stables, or the loft above them. None of the grooms or stable boys had spoken to him that day.

He wasn't at the dovecote, or the dairy, or the barracks, or in the servants' quarters. Every storehouse was locked, so he couldn't be in one of them. She even looked in the chapel, where Father Elwy was at prayer.

He must have gone to the mill or Milltonbury, as Lowri had suggested. Unfortunately, by the time he returned, it would be too late to discuss the feast, or anything else, before the evening meal.

Frustrated and dismayed, Roslynn crossed the yard toward the gate, deciding she could *not* let this situation continue any longer. The shearing feast was simply too important to her and she must make sure the steward appreciated that fact.

CHAPTER TWELVE

ROSLYNN HEARD MADOC shouting commands before she saw him. He'd taken those men not on patrol or guard duty to the outer ward for practice with sword and shield, although mercifully there'd been no more trouble, and no sign of Trefor or his men since the day after their wedding. Although they hoped the lord of Pontyrmwr was content with his latest malicious act and not planning another raid, Madoc was taking no chances.

Once she saw the group of men, there was no mistaking her husband's superb body as he led them through their drills. Every lithe action of Madoc's powerful arms looked like a dance—except that he held a sword and shield and every move of that sword, every slash, could kill anyone who got too close.

He stopped when he saw her and lowered his shield, barely winded despite his efforts. He sheathed his sword before addressing his men as they, too, stopped what they were doing.

"That's enough for today, men. Hugh, I want your sword cleaned before you eat. It's a disgrace. If I see it like that again, you'll be cleaning the stables for a fortnight. Now get out of here, the lot of you, and go eat something. Some of you look like scarecrows."

As the men sheathed their swords and took their shields from their left arms, talking and laughing among themselves, Madoc hurried toward Roslynn, a smile on his face that sent the blood throbbing through her. "Had to see what I was up to, eh, my lady? Well, what do you think of my garrison?"

"I don't think any of them look like scarecrows, unless Welsh scarecrows are particularly large and brawny," she replied. "There was no need to stop the drill. I was merely passing by on my way to the mill."

His dark brows rose. "By yourself?"

"It's not far."

"Far enough that I don't want you to go alone," Madoc replied. He put up his hand to silence her before she could protest that unnecessary measure. "No need to get that stubborn look in your eye, *fy rhosyn*. I wouldn't put anything past that brother of mine, so I won't take any chances with my wife's safety. Go anywhere you like, but you've got to have guards to protect you."

She could tell by the expression on his face that he was adamant. "Very well."

"As it happens, since I've already dismissed the men, I can be your escort. What do you need to go to the mill for?"

"I want to speak to Ivor."

Perhaps meeting Madoc like this was a sign that she ought to speak to *him* now, not Ivor. Besides, it was getting late and there was no guarantee Ivor would even be at the mill when she got there.

"I have to speak to him about the feast," she said, "and other things, too. I've only had one discussion with him, and that was days ago, before I even knew about the feast. Ever since, he's never been in his workroom when I've gone there and it's been locked, so I can't check the lists of stores to know what we might already have for the feast, and what we need to purchase."

"He's a busy man, is Ivor," Madoc said with a shrug, "and he's right to keep his workroom locked when he's not present. There's a lot of money in there."

"I'm sure that's true, but even when I've set aside a time to meet with him, he never comes."

Madoc's brows lowered at that. "He's given you explanations, hasn't he?"

"Yes, but how can I plan the shearing feast if I never have a chance to speak with him?" she asked, some of her frustration seeping into her voice.

"That won't be for days yet," Madoc replied, taking her hand. "Plenty of time. And nobody expects anything fancy. All they want is plenty of good plain food and drink. Now, speaking of food, the evening meal must be almost ready and I'm hungry."

"I'm sure that would content most of the men, but if we're inviting the neighboring nobles, there will be women, too. They'll be meeting me for the first time and I want everything to be perfect, so the feast must be well planned, with nothing left to chance if I can avoid it."

Madoc laughed softly and put his arm around her. "Wanting to show you're up to the task, are you?"

"Yes."

"Nothing's ever perfect," he noted as he drew her into the shadow of the wall. "I'm sure I'll be the envy of every man there, and the women will be even more impressed by your beauty and your competence." His eyes sparkled with good humor. "If you really want to impress everybody, wear that red gown you wore when we married." He ran a tantalizing finger around the neck of her bodice. "The women will want to have the pattern of it and the men will be amazed at the fit. It fits you to perfection, that gown."

Comforted by his words, aroused by his touch, her mood shifted and longing spread like a warm mist through her body—until she recalled that this was hardly the time or place to fall under his seductive spell. "Madoc, don't. The guards will see us, and I'm serious about the feast."

"I don't care if anybody sees us. I'm serious about kissing you right now," he replied, pulling her into his arms.

"I'm not just worried about the feast," she said, even as she couldn't help leaning into him, so that their lips were nearly touching. "This is about respect—or the lack of it. By ignoring my concerns, Ivor is being disrespectful."

Madoc lightly brushed his mouth over hers. "Another man might mean that for a sign of disrespect, but not Ivor," he assured her. "Of course he respects you. You're my wife. And I'm sure if he doesn't meet with you at the appointed time, it's because something more urgent has occurred."

"I'd like to believe that, Madoc, but *every* time?"

Frowning, Madoc drew back. Part of her regretted that, yet Ivor's disrespect and disregard for her wishes was a serious problem.

"Do you want me to *order* him to talk to you?" Madoc asked.

"I truly don't wish to make trouble between you," she replied, "but this feast is important to me, Madoc. I don't want anyone believing you've been saddled with a wife who can't manage a feast. The women will then conclude I can't be a good wife and you shouldn't have married me."

"Ah, a matter of pride, is it?"

"Yes. I want people to think you made a good decision when you took me for your bride."

He caressed her cheek with his strong, callused hand. "As I want everyone to know I chose wisely and well, too."

His arms loose about her waist, his hands clasped behind her back, he leaned against the wall. "Well then, wife, I'll see that Ivor understands that this feast is very important and he should give it precedence. I appreciate you wanted to deal with this yourself and spare me the trouble, but I think it would be the better if I speak to him alone."

Madoc's lips curved up in a wry smile. "Granted, I'm not famous for my tact, but I think he'll be more likely to listen if I speak to him privately. And I don't want you two to be enemies. I need you both."

He pulled her close for a long, lingering, seductive kiss that made her wish they were in their bedchamber. "Albeit in very different ways."

She needed him, too. And wanted him. And his children.

She was already counting the days, every one

giving her more hope that her prayers would be answered.

Madoc drew back and sighed sorrowfully. "Alas, my lady, we had best part, or I fear we might find ourselves making love right here after all."

He was right, of course. They should each go about their daily business, and it would be an outrageous thing to make love here—yet she was tempted nonetheless.

However, her pride and the call of her responsibilities overpowered her desire. "Yes, we wouldn't want to upset the sentries."

He nodded, and grew serious. "And the sooner I speak with Ivor, the better it will be."

"MADOC!" Ivor cried when he realized who was walking down the road toward him a short while later. "Nothing the matter, I hope?"

"Nothing serious," Madoc replied as he fell into step beside him. "We need to have a little chat about the shearing, that's all."

"Everyone can come on the day, can't they? Or is it the weather you're worried about? Emlyn's sure it'll be fine. Or is it Trefor you're thinking of?"

"Killing my ram should be enough to content Trefor for a while. Roslynn says she hasn't had a chance to speak to you about the feast."

"There've been too many other things to deal with," Ivor replied, "and since the shearing's not for a while, there's plenty of time to arrange that."

"Roslynn doesn't think so, and it seems every time she tries to meet with you about it, you've been too busy."

"Aye, there's been a lot—" Ivor suddenly halted and frowned. "She's complained to you? Does she think I'm lying when I tell her where I've been and what I've been doing instead?"

Madoc was sorry to see Ivor upset, and over a feast at that. "I understand that you've got other calls upon your time, but she's anxious about the feast, you see, wanting to make a good impression on the neighbors. She wants everybody to know she's a capable chatelaine."

"I'm sure everyone will be duly impressed with your wife, Madoc. All they have to do is look at her."

Madoc laughed amiably as they started toward the castle again. "Well, aye, she's a beauty, but she's a bold, clever woman, too, and I want her to be happy. So you'll talk to her tomorrow about the arrangements, won't you, Ivor?"

"Of course, Madoc," Ivor replied, his tone not one of friend to friend, but as servant to master. "I don't want to be the cause of any trouble between you and your wife."

Madoc bit back a curse. "Look you, Ivor, I know you're a busy fellow and it's for the good of the estate, so I'm not blaming you a bit. It didn't occur to me that she would care so much, either."

Madoc was relieved to see Ivor's expression become more natural and good-humored. "It was a surprise to me, too," he replied, "but no harm done."

"Did she mention what sort of things she wants? Special dishes or wine?"

"No. I leave that all up to you and her. I told her she could have whatever she liked. That might have been a bit of a mistake, but I don't think she's likely to be extravagant and I know I can count on you to keep the costs reasonable."

"Aye, Madoc," Ivor said gravely, "you can count on me."

WHEN MADOC RODE into the courtyard after hunting the next morning, Roslynn met him by the stables, her face aglow with delight, her eyes bright with happiness.

"Your meeting with Ivor went well, I'm guessing," Madoc said as he handed the brace of quail to a stable boy while a groom took charge of the prancing Cigfran.

"It did, and we decided on everything for the feast and how much ale and wine we'll need.

Thank you for talking to him, Madoc. I feel so much better now."

"Thought you might," he said with a pleased smile, his hand finding hers so that, as they crossed the yard, they looked more like courting sweethearts than a lord and his lady.

HER EYES CLOSED and her body languid with sleepiness, Roslynn reached across the bed. The bedding was still warm where Madoc had lain, although his place was empty.

She cracked open her eyelids, to see her husband moving about in the dim chamber, only the merest hint of dawn brightening the sky beyond. He had warned her he would be up and out very early to help gather the sheep for the washing, which had to be done before the sheep were sheared. Otherwise, too much grease would affect the weight of the fleece when it was sold.

She had not asked him why he, the lord of Llanpowell, would help with such menial tasks. She had already learned he was the sort of overlord who valued camaraderie with his people. It was also, she had seen, as much a part of his leadership as his martial skills.

"Go back to sleep, *fy rhosyn*," he said softly. "No need for you to get up so early."

"I enjoy watching you dress," she replied. "After all, you're a very comely fellow."

"And you're a beautiful woman—but don't try to tempt me to stay, Delilah that you are. We hope to get the whole flock gathered and washed today."

She sat up and wrapped her hands around her knees, the sheet barely covering her breasts, and her dark hair loose about her shoulders. "I'm not trying to tempt you to stay. I just enjoy watching you get dressed."

He raised a brow as he buckled his belt. "Aye, with those big eyes of yours and naked under the sheets. What will you be doing today while I'm out earning my bread?"

"Earning mine, too. We need more candles and I found another chest of linen to be washed. I may find still more in the back of the main storeroom. And I want to see how much yarn Bethyn was able to spin from the ram's fleece. I should meet with Ivor again, as well. I'm worried we won't have enough salmon. And no doubt your uncle will follow me and offer much advice.

"Not that I'm complaining," she hastened to assure him. "I need his help, since I don't speak Welsh yet."

"Yet, is it? Delighted I am you're willing to learn. But you'll have to do without Uncle Lloyd today. We need him at the pens. We always find some sheep with earmarks we don't know, and Lloyd is the expert. He remembers every earmark for fifty miles."

Madoc paused as he sat on the stool to pull on his boots. "Why don't you come to the pens for a little while? Lloyd can demonstrate his expertise."

"I'd like that," she replied, although she probably shouldn't take the time.

Like the shearing itself, gathering was a major undertaking, requiring all the shepherds, tenants and soldiers who could be spared, and they would all have to be fed. She wouldn't be doing the cooking herself, of course, but it meant more tasks to supervise in addition to those preparations for the major feast when the shearing was finished.

Madoc gave her a pleased smile as he stamped his booted feet on the floor before standing. "I'll look forward to that when I'm hot and sweating."

"I will, too. I like you hot and sweaty."

His eyes widened even as he shook his head. "What did I tell you? Delilah for sure!" he exclaimed as he went to the door. "Fortunately, my will is strong, so I can tear myself away—if only just." He paused with his hand on the latch. "Why don't you go back to sleep for a little bit. It's awhile before mass, and we won't need Lloyd till the noon."

"I might just do that," she said, yawning as he smiled a farewell and went out.

Enjoying the warmth of the thick coverlet and soft feather bed, she snuggled back down, resting her hands on her stomach, hoping she was indeed already with child. Her courses were late and she'd been more tired than usual the past few days.

However, it was early yet and she'd had no other signs, so she wouldn't tell Madoc what she hoped, not when he was so busy with the gathering and shearing. She would wait until she was certain, then she would share the wonderful news.

CHAPTER THIRTEEN

AFTER MASS WAS OVER, Roslynn hurried to Uncle Lloyd and took his arm to walk back to the hall to break the fast. "I'd like to see the flock when it's been brought to the pens. Will you take me with you when you go? Madoc says you can identify all the earmarks within fifty miles."

"Aye, my lady, with pleasure," Lloyd replied, beaming, before doubt clouded his genial face. "It'll be noisy and, frankly, my lady, so many sheep together will stink. Are you sure you want to come?"

"Quite sure," she said, suppressing the urge to tell him that since he'd tricked her into seeing Madoc naked, he shouldn't be surprised if she wanted to see her husband bare-chested and sweat-slicked.

Something about Lloyd's subsequent expression, however, suggested he might not be quite so incapable of guessing her motives as she'd thought. "Well, then, who am I to deny you? It will be my pleasure."

"Thank you," she said happily. "I'd better go to

the kitchen and tell Ivor of my plans before I break the fast. Otherwise, he'll likely be gone before I'm finished."

She hurried away to the kitchen. Because they'd be feeding all the men who'd helped gather the sheep, they need to have much more than the usual amount of food prepared. The meals would be simple, though—stew, roasted mutton and pork and beef, pottages of peas and leeks, thick slices of bread and cheese, and tarts to finish. Casks of ale were ready to be tapped. No wine after such work, Madoc had decreed. Ale was better.

The servants were so engaged in their work, few noticed her enter except the spit boy, who looked as if he was half-roasted himself as he turned an enormous joint over the fire. He opened his mouth to announce her entrance, until she said, "I've come to see Ivor."

She swiftly continued toward Ivor's workroom, to find the door ajar.

Even more surprising, Ivor wasn't there. Some parchments were still on the table, as well as a half-eaten piece of bread and a cup of mead. There were no bags of coins on the table, and the chest banded with iron was still locked. It appeared as if he'd been called away suddenly, although she'd heard nothing that would indicate such a necessity.

She was about to turn back to the kitchen to ask Hywel what had happened when she spotted a parchment on the floor, over by the wall, as if it had rolled off the table.

She picked it up, noting that it was relatively free of dust, so it must have fallen recently. She was about to put it on the table with the others when she saw the last line of writing on it.

The name belonged to the wine merchant who had delivered several barrels the day before. She'd seen him arrive from the doorway of the storehouse where the apples were stored on open racks, for the wine merchant was hard to miss. He was large and loud, but also amusing, so although she had much to do, she'd lingered a moment to listen to his jovial banter with Lloyd. She'd noted the number of barrels, wanting to be sure they had enough wine in store, and counted twenty-five of them.

But the number on the list was thirty and the sum beside it consistent with thirty barrels of wine at Davies's price, not twenty-five.

She was about to unroll the scroll farther when a shadow fell across the table and Ivor walked into the room, a quizzical expression on his face as his glance flicked to the parchment in her hand. "Is there something you need, my lady?"

"I came to tell you that I'll be going with Lloyd

to see the sheep brought down from the hills," she said, resisting the urge to shove the parchment up her sleeve. "You must have left in a great hurry, for I found this on the floor and you're the least careless man I've ever met."

"There was a dispute among the grooms that needed to be sorted out before they came to blows, which they very nearly did," Ivor replied as she put the parchment on the table. "Is there anything else, my lady?"

"No," she said, moving to the door. "I should be back well before the men are finished."

As she left the steward, Roslynn tried to convince herself that the discrepancy was merely a rare error. She should have simply drawn his attention to it so the entry could be corrected.

Unfortunately, she couldn't rid herself of a lingering suspicion. Ivor was a neat and meticulous sort of man, not the kind to make careless errors, or not find them if he did.

How could she be certain if this was a genuine mistake, or if there was something more sinister afoot? She had only found this difference by chance, for she'd always left it to Ivor to oversee the unloading of goods. She must be more vigilant in the future and, whenever possible and without raising any suspicion on Ivor's part, keep her own record of deliveries, so that later she could compare the numbers Ivor recorded against her own.

Hopefully she was wrong to worry, and this was merely an error, for even the most careful of men must surely make mistakes.

But if she was right, she must be very sure that a crime had been committed and have the evidence to prove it before she accused Madoc's trusted friend.

WHEN ROSLYNN AND LLOYD arrived at the sheep pens later that day, the first half of the flock had already been brought down from the mountain to the river, although it hadn't yet been fully separated into ewes and lambs.

The busy men answered Lloyd's greeting, then went back to work. They'd formed a line from the large pen holding all the sheep to a smaller one for the lambs. Madoc himself, half-naked and sweating as she'd expected, was in the pen with the sheep, and she watched with both amazement and admiration as he bent down, grabbed a skittish lamb by its fleece and deftly tossed it over the fence to the man just outside it. That man caught the lamb, then threw it to the next in line. The lamb proceeded in that manner all the way to the pen containing several frightened, bleating lambs, until the last man put it over the fence and inside with the others. Meanwhile, Madoc had already picked up another and sent it after the first.

"What if they drop a lamb?" Roslynn asked Lloyd in amazement. "Won't it be hurt? Or break a leg?"

"Lambs' bones are like butter," he assured her as he hoisted himself onto the top of the wooden fence of the larger, temporarily erected pen. "Just needs a splint and it should heal fine. Emlyn could do it in his sleep."

"Which man is—?"

"Ah, Lloyd, here you are and about time, too," one of the shepherds called out, pointing at a sheep's ear as he held the animal in place by its fleece. "Where's this one from?"

"Pencwmb," Lloyd replied without hesitation. "That's to the south, Sir Ector's land," he added for her benefit. "Come a long way, that sheep has. It's got to be ten miles or more."

She wondered what they would do if they found one of Trefor's sheep among those of Llanpowell, but thought it best not to ask. "With no fences, I'm surprised the sheep don't wander all over Wales."

"Bred to a place, they are," Lloyd explained. "Ewes graze where their mothers did, and their mothers before them. Sometimes they move, if they smell a fox or wolf, and some are wanderers, but that's not usual for a sheep."

"Roslynn!"

Wiping the beads of perspiration from his forehead with his forearm, Madoc waded toward them through the flock of sheep and lambs like it was a living river. When he reached the wooden barrier, he put his hands on the top and, with the agility of a mountain goat, vaulted over it to join them. "Here you are then," he said, his hands on his hips and a smile on his face.

"Here we are," she replied, speaking loudly to be heard over the animals.

"Lloyd-y-Brawd!" another man in the sheep pen shouted, pointing to another sheep.

"Cwm Myrmydden," Lloyd replied.

"God love you, it's been years since we've had one from there," he said to Roslynn, who was trying not to have too many lustful thoughts about her husband. Judging by the look in his eyes, he was having a few about her, too.

A commotion broke out in the line of men passing the lambs to the pen. A lamb with a black nose and crooked leg had managed to wiggle free of his handler. Despite its impediment, the little beast dashed toward the pen of ewes, heading straight for Roslynn. It had almost reached her when it was surrounded by some of the dogs. Confused and frightened, the poor little creature halted, bleating as if desperately calling for its mother.

Ignoring the dogs, Roslynn hurried to scoop the trembling, terrified lamb in her arms. Cradling it, she stroked its back to calm it.

"Poor thing's frightened nearly to death," she said as she turned back toward her husband.

Instead of looking sympathetic, Madoc grimly lifted it from her arms and deposited it in the pen with the other lambs. "I'd best get back to work," he muttered, jumping back over the fence and walking as quickly away from them as he could through the crowd of sheep.

"What did I do wrong?" a baffled Roslynn asked Lloyd over the sound of the bleating, milling animals. "Should I not have picked it up?"

"I think you caught him off guard, that's all."

"By picking up a lamb? I may be a lady, but—"

"Not that," Lloyd replied, shaking his head. "I don't know exactly what was going through my nephew's head, but to see you with that lamb in your arms…well, it looked like you were holding a babe. I thought so, and maybe so did he."

"Madoc said he wants more children."

"No doubt he does. It was probably just the surprise caught him off guard and made him think of

Gwendolyn, you see, and how she died. God save us, my lady, I've never seen him so upset. He's a strong man, is Madoc, but not that day."

"How did his first wife die?" Roslynn asked as quietly as she could and still be heard. "No one's ever told me."

"In childbirth. They couldn't stop the bleeding after Owain was born."

Roslynn moved her hands instinctively to her stomach, stopping before she rested them there, lest she betray her hopes. It was no secret women died in childbirth and it was already affecting the happiness she felt at the possibility of giving Madoc a child. Even so, to learn that he had lost one wife already in such a way... It made the dread that much more palpable, even if many women bore children safely and lived.

She realized this might also explain why Madoc's son was not at Llanpowell, where he would be a living reminder of the mother he'd lost, and how. Madoc wouldn't be the first father to find the sight of such a child difficult to bear.

"So I wouldn't put too much store in the change that came over Madoc just now," his uncle concluded. "Bad memories, I'm sure, and nothing more." His gaze grew significantly speculative. "A babe would help vanquish those bad memories."

She was still determined not to tell anyone she might be with child until she could be certain, and Madoc should know first. "Then let us hope I bear a child soon."

MADOC ROLLED his shoulders, then arched his back to ease the ache as the last of the washed sheep scrambled up the bank of the makeshift pool. It had been a long day, as such days always were, and he was glad to see the end of it.

Most of the men who'd helped with the gathering and washing had already gone to the castle to be fed, including Lloyd. He had remained to the end in part because he felt it was his duty, but also because he wanted to have a little peace and quiet as he made his way home, the better to think about what he'd say to Roslynn.

He'd seen her shock and dismay at his reaction to the sight of the lamb in her arms, and more especially the tender, motherly look on her face before that. He had immediately envisioned a babe, not a lamb, in her slender arms—a babe with dark hair and blue eyes likes hers. Or Owain.

Yet after the shock of that vision, after he had so brusquely spoken and left her, had come a longing so powerful, it had hit him like a boulder rolling down a mountain.

Then came guilt, and fear, the memory of Gwendolyn as she lay dying, and the promise he had not kept.

Ivor, who never helped with the gathering because of his leg, appeared, limping quickly toward him.

"What is it?" Madoc asked, hurrying forward, fearing some major domestic catastrophe had brought that grim expression to his steward's face.

"Has Lady Roslynn spoken to you about the cost of the meal today and the feast to come?"

"No, not yet," Madoc replied.

"It's a huge sum of money, Madoc—far more than we've ever spent before," Ivor said as he came to a halt in front of him.

That was a bit unsettling. "How much more?"

"Two hundred marks—and that might not be the end of it."

Madoc stared at him, aghast. "Why so much? Have prices risen?"

"It's not the prices, it's the food Lady Roslynn wants, as well as the quantity. Eels and salmon and other fish by the baskets. Enough flour—and the best kind—to last a month or more. And the wine… Madoc, the cost of the wine alone will stagger you."

He was already staggered. "Why didn't you tell me about this sooner?"

"Because you told me your wife was to have her way in this, and I didn't want to make trouble between you. But when I saw the final tally this morning, I thought I ought to make certain you knew. To be honest, Madoc, I doubted you did, or you would have set a limit."

Aye, so he would have. That was far too much for food and drink when there were weapons to buy and repair, and a fortress and garrison to maintain.

"You did right to tell me," Madoc said, starting toward the castle. Despite his agitation, he set a slower pace so that Ivor could keep up with him. "She was wrong to spend so much without consulting me. I'll see that she understands we aren't as wealthy as she seems to think."

"I'm sorry, Madoc," Ivor said as he walked beside him.

"Not as sorry as I am," the lord of Llanpowell muttered.

DETERMINED TO SPEAK to Roslynn about this extravagance at once, Madoc quickly ascertained from the shepherds, soldiers and servants gathered in the hall that she had gone to their bedchamber to wash and change before the last meal of the day.

He made his way through the tables and benches, nodding a greeting to Lloyd, who was already

seated with Emlyn and several of the older shepherds near the hearth.

"See how he hurries to be with her," he heard
Lloyd say, and the chuckles that followed.

He wished Uncle Lloyd would hold his tongue,
or at least show a little more respect. He was no boy
to be teased, but a grown man, and a nobleman, too.

He took the steps two at a time and shoved open
the bedchamber door—to find Roslynn seated in a
large wooden tub, her hair piled on top of her head,
and her naked breasts almost completely exposed
above the soapy water.

Everything he'd been about to say flew right out
of his head.

"Madoc!" she cried, covering her breasts with
her hands and blushing as if they weren't married.
"I wasn't expecting you so soon!" She glanced to
her left. "Bron, you may leave us."

Recovering quickly, remembering why he was
there, Madoc moved away from the door as the
blushing maidservant scurried past him.

Roslynn rose from the tub like a goddess from
the sea.

He cleared his throat and forced himself to con-
centrate. "Do you know how much you've spent on
the food for today and for the feast?"

Reaching for the large square of linen on the

stool beside it, Roslynn stepped out of the tub. "No. I haven't added it all up yet."

Droplets of water glistened on her smooth naked skin as she wrapped the towel about her. Damp tendrils of dark hair licked her cheek and the kissable nape of her neck. Her slender, shapely feet and ankles seemed a temptation all on their own.

Think, he commanded himself, even as his traitorous body heated with desire. "Ivor tells me it's at least two hundred marks. I didn't think you'd spend so much."

Roslynn's smooth cheeks turned pink as she rubbed herself dry. Did she have any idea how seductive that was? "He didn't tell *me* it was anywhere near that amount."

He imagined himself encased in a block of ice. "Did you ask him?"

"No."

She didn't sound very concerned, and that both cooled his ardor and annoyed him. "That's far too much for a feast."

"Surely it isn't extravagant for both a wedding *and* a shearing feast," she replied, letting the towel fall to the floor.

Was she purposefully trying to distract him?

Determined to keep his mind on the money, he turned away so that he couldn't see her. "That's more than I've spent on the last three shearing feasts and Christmases combined."

"I didn't get the most expensive things," she protested, "and I did try to keep the costs down, but when there are three hundred people expected…"

He spun around. "*How* many?" he demanded, glaring at her. Thank God she had put on her shift, thin linen though it was.

"Three hundred," she said, coloring as she reached for a green gown that laced at the sides. She'd worn it before and it fit her as well as the red gown she'd worn on their wedding day. "Your noble neighbors, the merchants from the town and Milltonbury, as well as the shepherds, garrison and servants."

"By the saints, woman, who *didn't* you invite?"

"Your brother."

Her calm answer momentarily deflated his anger, until he remembered how much the feast was costing him. "I didn't say you could spend like Croesus! It should only have been half that much at most."

"As you yourself said, my dowry is paying for it," she said quietly as she stepped into the dress and pulled it up over her shift.

"Nevertheless, your dowry belongs to me, not you," he reminded her. "I have uses for that money that don't include feeding everybody within fifty miles."

She went to the far side of the bed, so that it

stood between them. "I'm sorry if you feel I was too profligate. Unfortunately, it's too late. The guests have been invited and the provisions paid for." A little wrinkle appeared between her furrowed brows as she clasped her hands in front of her. "It was Ivor who complained to you, wasn't it?"

"As well he should, and if there's any fault to him, it's that he should have told me sooner."

"He should have told *me* sooner if I was spending more than you consider appropriate. I am no mind reader, after all."

He was about to point out that he was no Roman emperor with casks of coins to throw away, either, when there was a soft rap on the door.

"What?" Madoc called out.

The door eased open and Bron's head appeared. "I-if you please, my lord," she stammered, "there's visitors at the gate."

"What visitors?" he demanded.

"I—I don't know, my lord." Bron's gaze flicked uncertainly to Roslynn. "They're Normans, that's all I know."

"If they've come for the feast, they're early," Madoc snapped as he strode to the door.

CHAPTER FOURTEEN

MADOC FOUND UNCLE LLOYD already waiting on the hall steps.

"Ah, nephew, here you are then," he said, a hint of disappointment in his voice.

No doubt he'd been planning to greet the visitors in Madoc's absence, as he had greeted Lord Alfred's party before.

"Who are they?" Madoc demanded as two mounted soldiers, one carrying an unfamiliar banner, rode into the courtyard.

"Don't you know?"

"I don't recognize the banner. They must be nobles Roslynn invited for the feast."

Lloyd slid him a wary look. "She's invited a few, then?"

"Too many," he snapped. "She'll have run through her dowry in a month."

"Well now, that's a problem, I grant you, but she's a woman, after all, and they set great store on feasts and clothes and things. And no doubt she wants you to be proud of her."

Blessed Saint Dafydd, what had he done? "Aye," he muttered, his ire banished in an instant, replaced by regret—especially when he remembered how she'd retreated behind the bed, getting as far away from him as possible.

Because she still feared he would strike her in his temper?

His silent admonishment was interrupted when the man who was obviously the leader of the party appeared, seated on an embossed saddle on a very fine, snow-white palfrey adorned with costly accoutrements.

The man himself wore a chain-mail hauberk and coif, and a surcoat of scarlet covered by a very fine wool cloak the color of ripe blackberries and fastened with a gold brooch. His hair, cut in the Norman style, was gray, as was the beard below his hawklike nose. Behind him came more mounted soldiers, then a tall wooden wagon of the sort used by ladies and their maids, brightly painted, the windows covered by leather flaps. After the wagon came twenty more mounted soldiers, and then another smaller wagon covered with canvas.

"Norman, all right," Lloyd muttered, echoing Madoc's conclusion. He nodded at the wagon and raised a brow. "Do you suppose John's sent *me* a bride?"

His uncle's answer didn't lighten Madoc's mood. Instead, he resolved to act as a noble host should as he approached the Norman, so that Roslynn could be proud of *him,* even as the stranger ran a measuring gaze over Madoc that he didn't appreciate.

Before he could speak, however, the nobleman glanced toward the hall and seemed to turn to stone.

Madoc followed his gaze, to see Roslynn on the top step of the hall, dressed in that green gown that fit her like a well-made glove and illustrated the perfection of her slender figure. She hadn't put up her hair, only swiftly thrown a flowing white silk veil over her head.

Madoc looked back at the visitor who, being a man, was still staring at her.

It would be better, Madoc decided, if he went to Roslynn and asked who this man was before introductions were made and he made it clear Roslynn was his wife.

As he turned toward the hall, however, he realized she, too, was standing as still as if she'd seen Medusa, and her face was as white as her veil. Then, putting her hand to her head, she closed her eyes and began to sway.

Panic like nothing he'd ever felt before overwhelming him, he raced to the steps and caught her just as she crumpled like cheap mortar struck by a mason's hammer. "Help!" he shouted as he lifted his wife's limp body. "Help me!"

"Roslynn!" the Norman cried as he leaped from his horse and ran to the steps, despite his age and the weight of his armor.

"Send for a physician!" Madoc ordered Lloyd, ignoring the stranger.

"What have you done to her?" the Norman demanded, blocking Madoc's way as he moved to take her inside.

"Get out of my bloody way!"

"I'm her father!"

"I don't care if you're the archangel Gabriel. Get out of my way!"

"Yes, my dear, stand aside," a middle-aged lady in a blue mantle and white veil and wimple commanded as she made her way past Lloyd and the Norman. "Roslynn should be taken to bed."

Not caring who she was, either, Madoc shouldered the door open and carried his unconscious wife inside.

ROSLYNN SLOWLY OPENED her eyes, then blinked. Surely she was seeing things. "Mother?" she whispered incredulously.

"Daughter!" her mother whispered, squeezing Roslynn's hand. "How do you feel? Are you going to be ill?"

Removing the damp cloth on her forehead, Roslynn sat up. Although her veil had been removed, she was still dressed, and she was in her bedchamber at Llanpowell—with her mother, so long estranged, smiling at her with love in her eyes.

"Oh, Mother!" she cried as she threw her arms around Lady Eloise and held her close. "I feared I'd never see you again. That you were so angry and disgusted with me, you'd never want to come near me!"

Her mother held her just as tightly and stroked her hair. "We wanted to come to you the moment we heard about Wimarc's treason, but your father was ill. He had a cold that settled in his lungs and..." Her breath caught, telling Roslynn her father must have been very seriously ill. "I couldn't leave him. Then I fell ill, too. It's taken this long for us to be well enough to travel—but the moment the physician said we could do so, we went to court, only to find that you'd been sent to Wales to be married. We came here right away."

Lady Eloise drew back and anxiously studied her daughter's face. "I'm so sorry for everything that's happened. I never trusted Wimarc, but if I'd had any notion of what he was truly like, I would have locked you up in your chamber and risked your eternal hatred rather than let you marry him.

"We should have known something was terribly wrong when you didn't answer our letters, even if our messengers assured us that they had seen you and told us you were well."

"I never received your letters!" Roslynn cried, hating Wimarc even more, even if he was dead. "I thought you didn't want to have anything more to do with me because I'd been so selfish and childish."

As for the messengers themselves, there were often couriers coming and going at Castle de Werre. It would have been easy for Wimarc to ensure she never met them or received any letters they carried.

"We wrote to you at court, too," her mother said, "after we heard about his arrest."

"I never got those letters, either," she replied, the reason all too easy to guess. "The king, or one of his minions, must have ensured I didn't so I would think you didn't care what happened to me and would therefore make me more biddable. Oh, Mother, I've been such a fool!"

Her mother embraced her again. "You made a mistake, Roslynn, but so did we, not taking better care to learn more about Wimarc. When we heard what he'd done, I feared it would kill your father. Instead, he rallied, because he knew you couldn't be involved and he was as determined as I to go to the king and get you. We were just setting out when we heard from Lord Bernard—to our great relief and joy—that you weren't to be charged with treason. But, oh, if only we could have been with you at that terrible time!"

"If only I had listened to you," Roslynn replied, her heart burdened with her past mistakes, thinking of all the pain she could have spared them, and herself, if she had. "After Wimarc hurt me, I should have had faith in your love and the courage to go to you for help."

She shivered as she considered what else her mother had said. "And to think you were so ill and I didn't know!"

Her mother brushed a lock of hair back from Roslynn's flushed cheeks. "We met Alfred de Garleboine at an inn near Gloucester and he told us you were married and that you had done so willingly. Is this true, Roslynn? Did you really marry Madoc ap Gruffydd of your own free will?"

"Yes, Mother, I did."

"And this man, this Madoc, what sort of fellow is he?"

"He treats me well, Mother," she assured her.

So far, her fearful worry added as she recalled Madoc's rage before they'd been interrupted.

Her mother's relieved smile made her glad she'd said no more, and she started to get out of bed. "Where's Father?"

Dizzy, she sat back down. "I'm just a little light-headed," she said in answer to her mother's silent question. "I've been very busy with the preparations for the feast we're having after the sheep are sheared."

The feast that she had wanted to be perfect, and instead...

"I don't think it's that," her mother said as she rose and picked up the damp linen square that had been cooling Roslynn's brow. "I would say you're with child. I was often faint when I was carrying you, and there's a glow about your face, daughter, that I think only a babe brings."

Roslynn blushed, but didn't try to deny it. "It's too early to be certain, so I haven't told Madoc yet. I wanted to wait until I was sure."

"I think you should tell him now," her mother advised. "He seemed very worried about you, and might think you're seriously ill unless you do."

She was right, of course. And it might mollify Madoc's anger with her, she realized with a sickening and familiar sense of having to appease an irate man. "I will, but I'll also ask him to keep it a secret between us until I'm certain."

"So I should, too," her mother said. "Very well,

although I'd like to tell your father. He'll be very worried about you, too."

"All right, but no one else, please."

"Agreed," her mother replied. "Now, if you are feeling better, I think we should go below and relieve the anxieties of our husbands."

Roslynn nodded, wondering if she would ever again know a life without anxiety.

She had believed she had miraculously found such peace and security.

Until today.

MEANWHILE, BELOW IN THE HALL, the guilt-wracked lord of Llanpowell paced like a trained bear on a chain. On the dais, in Madoc's chair, sat Lord James de Briston, who was even more stiff of back and manner than Lord Alfred. Uncle Lloyd, the soldiers, shepherds, other laborers who'd come to help gather and the servants were talking quietly in small, wary groups, their manner subdued, as all waited to hear what had befallen the lady of Llanpowell—although none so much as her husband and her father.

His anxious gaze focused on the stairs, cursing himself for making such a fuss about the money for the feast, Madoc was too immersed in remorse and dread to pay attention to anyone or anything.

What did it matter how much Roslynn spent or

how many people she invited? It was important to her, and he had acted like a miser.

"You *are* Madoc ap Gruffydd, I presume?" Lord James suddenly demanded, his voice like a shout in the hushed hall.

"*Lord* Madoc ap Gruffydd," Madoc replied with the barest flicker of a glance at his father-in-law. Worried or not, he would brook no disrespect, and certainly not from a man who would give his daughter to the likes of Wimarc de Werre, no matter how much she'd insisted.

The Norman rose and came to stand in front of him, his gaze irate as he blocked Madoc's view of the stairs. "Then, *Lord* Madoc ap Gruffydd, hear this. Whether you're a friend of King John or not, if you've harmed my daughter in any way, I'll kill you."

Not the least bit intimidated, Madoc's lip curled with scorn. "*Now* you will protect her, when she doesn't require it? You would have done better to prevent her marriage to Wimarc de Werre."

His face reddening, Lord James coughed before he replied. "We had doubts about the man, but no proof of any wrongdoing. Do you think I would have allowed that marriage if I'd known de Werre's true nature?"

"As Roslynn's father, it was your *duty* to find out his true nature, as you call it," Madoc returned.

The man looked about to disagree, until he shook his head. "No, no excuses. We failed her—but I'll be damned before I fail her again, so if you hurt her, Welshman, you'll answer to me."

"A bit late with the threats, aren't you? Wimarc and John should have been threatened before me. And if you're as worried about her fate as you claim, why didn't you come to her assistance at court? She was in danger there as much as when she was married to Wimarc—more so, for as the widow of a traitor, she became the king's pawn to do with as he will, or risk death, unless her family prevented it."

"I was too ill to travel and so was my wife," Lord James retorted. "The moment we could, we did go to court, but it was too late. She'd already been sent to marry some Welshman we'd never heard of."

"So here she is, married to a man who will protect her better than you did."

"Father!"

Madoc whirled around to see Roslynn and her mother hurrying toward them. She looked a little pale, but otherwise well, and he heaved a sigh of heartfelt relief.

But it was not at him she looked; it was at the man beside him.

"My little sparrow!" Lord James cried as she fell into his embrace.

"Oh, Father!"

Madoc glanced at her mother, to see tears on her cheeks and joy in her eyes. Perhaps they *had* been too ill to come to their daughter's aid. Yet whatever their reason for not helping Roslynn, he was quite sure that if his child were in the same predicament that Roslynn had been, he would have done everything he could to protect her, even if he had to climb from his grave to do it.

Roslynn drew back and finally spoke to her husband. "You mustn't blame my parents for my marriage to Wimarc or what came after, Madoc. I gave them no choice, and Wimarc prevented their letters from reaching me, or I would have known they would help me."

She had obviously heard him condemning her father—another terrible blunder that could make her even more upset with him.

He hurried to try to undo the damage. "Forgive my hasty words, my lord. I hope you can understand I spoke to you as I did because I care about your daughter. I can well believe Wimarc capable of any evil."

And perhaps if she'd received those letters, she might not have done as the king commanded and come to Llanpowell, he suddenly realized.

Before he could say more to show his genuine

remorse, Uncle Lloyd came bustling up to the dais. "Well, now, here we are then," he said, gleefully rubbing his hands together. "Lowri, Bron! Let's get a table here, and food and drink. You must all be parched and starving and I'll not have it said the folk of Llanpowell are lacking in hospitality."

Determined to impress Lord James and his wife—as Roslynn hoped to impress his noble neighbors at the feast, he realized with another twinge of guilt—he assumed his most charming manner. "Allow me to introduce my uncle, Lloyd ap Iolo. A finer fellow you couldn't meet, although he did try to steal my bride from me the day she arrived."

"I never did!" Lloyd cried, blushing to the roots of his gray hair. "A misunderstanding it was, my lord and lady, that's all. I forgot to make the proper introductions, you see, so taken was I by her grace and beauty."

"As we all are in Llanpowell," Madoc graciously added, trusting Roslynn understood by his words and manner that he regretted their quarrel.

Just in case she didn't, he would make sure of it later, when they were alone.

CHAPTER FIFTEEN

AN ANXIOUS ROSLYNN wasn't sure what to make of her husband's behavior as the evening meal progressed. He was genial, polite and seemed to be taking great pains to impress her parents.

Before his angry outburst over the cost of the feast, she would have been delighted and pleased by this behavior, as well as proud. Now, though, she felt more dread than pleasure, fearful that he might be putting on a performance, as Wimarc had so often done, and that she had never really seen the true Madoc until today. Perhaps the whole time they had been together, he had been playing a part, assuming a mask, while the real Madoc had been hidden beneath.

Maybe she had been duped again, led astray once more by her lustful desires and her wish for a home and children at her knee.

And if she had been?

She would not stay at Llanpowell. This time, especially knowing that she still had her parents' love, she would flee.

Sick at heart, trying not to be swayed by Madoc's charm or his handsome face, she smiled when she deemed it necessary and spoke when he addressed her. She, too, could play a part, and she did so now—that of dutiful, even loving, wife.

Until she could take the strain no longer and said she wished to retire.

"Of course," Madoc replied, rising and putting out his hand to help her stand. "I'm exhausted myself, so if your parents will excuse me, I'll go with you."

Her mother voiced no objection and neither did her father, although what excuse could they give to force their host to stay?

It seemed a very long walk through the hall to the stairs tonight, and Roslynn's feet felt as heavy as rocks as they went up the steps. What would he say to her when they were alone? What would he do? Would the mask fall from his face and violent anger return, to be unleashed against her once they were alone?

She could scarcely breathe by the time Madoc opened the door. Breaking away from him, she hurried inside, fighting the tears that threatened to come.

Yet still, she whirled around to face him, determined to be brave and never again be humiliated by a man.

To find Madoc kneeling on the floor like the most humble penitent.

"Roslynn, forgive me," he said. "I shouldn't have gotten angry about the money for the feast, especially since I'd told you that you could have whatever you would. I was a fool to get so angry—but please know that even in my hottest temper, I will never hurt you. I'd sooner cut off my sword arm than strike you."

She could only stare in shocked disbelief as he got to his feet.

"I apologize for frightening you," he continued. "I'm sorry if I upset you and especially if I made you fear me."

She didn't know what to say, how to feel— whether relief, or joy or suspicion that this, too, was a trick.

"I mean it, Roslynn, with all my heart," he said softly, a longing in his eyes that seemed too sincere to be feigned. "I was a stupid fool, and I regret it deeply. Can you forgive me and forget I was such a lout?"

"You did frighten me," she admitted. "I was afraid you weren't the man I believed you to be." *And that I'd been duped again, led astray by my lust.*

"And now?" he asked warily, taking a single step toward her, apparently humbled.

How she longed to believe him sincerely penitent! How much she wished she could forgive and forget his anger and her fear.

"I was in the wrong, too, Madoc," she said instead, because it was true. "I should have ensured that Ivor kept me informed of the total amount we were spending and asked you if there was a limit. I promise you, I'll do so in the future, and be less extravagant."

"I don't care if you leave me a pauper, as long as you forgive me and believe I'll never hurt you," he said fervently, his gaze intense, as if he were trying to will her to forgive him by the power of his mind alone.

"I will, Madoc, I will," she said, telling herself she must try, or live in fear forever.

Had he not most humbly, sincerely apologized? Could she not see the genuine contrition in his dark eyes, so different from Wimarc's false expressions?

He leaned down as if to kiss her, then paused, a look of even graver concern creasing his brow. "Was it my selfish anger that made you ill?"

"No," she assured him, for that was true, too. "I think I'm with child, although it's early yet."

His eyes widened as he regarded her with delighted amazement. "A child! And so soon!"

Did he think... "The child is yours, Madoc, on

my honor," she said firmly, pulling away from him abruptly.

"I don't doubt that," he said at once, gently tugging her back into his arms and embracing her. "God save me, I'm making a mess of everything today! I'm happy, truly. It's just that childbirth is fraught with danger, Roslynn."

"I'm young and quite well, except for a little dizziness," she assured him, and herself. "I should be fine, and so should our child, although we should pray for health and a safe delivery."

"Aye," he whispered, holding her close. "Aye."

She clung to him tightly, ardently wishing she still didn't feel this skein of dread wrapped around her heart, slowly strangling the happiness she'd had with Madoc. She wished she wasn't afraid she might never again know that same untainted joy.

Surely she could. She must—or she would be imprisoned in fear and misery for the rest of her life.

"Please don't say anything to your uncle or anyone else just yet," she said softly. "It's still early and I would be completely certain first."

"I'll keep it to myself—as best I can," he added, smiling down at her. "I'm not known for my ability to keep secrets, but I'll try because you want it so. I want to do all in power to make you happy, *fy rhosyn*."

How could she not trust him when he looked at her thus? How could she not believe his contrition heartfelt and his words true?

"I want to make you happy, too," she whispered, reaching up to kiss him.

IT WAS NIGHT, and Madoc stood in a chamber like the one he shared with Roslynn...but it was different, too. The bed was gone, although it had always been there since Madoc was a boy. The walls were in shadow, so it was as if they didn't exist at all. There was no window, no door, the only light a single flickering candle...somewhere.

He heard a sob at his feet and looked down.

There, on a straw pallet, lay Gwendolyn, tears running down her sickly white face. Her hair was loose about her, damp with perspiration, and there was blood.

So much blood.

"Promise me, Madoc," she whispered weakly as a babe wailed nearby. "Promise me..."

"I promise," he murmured, kneeling beside her and taking her limp hand in his, feeling the life ebb out of her with the blood that could not be stopped.

A man appeared in the shadows across from him—Trefor, dressed for battle in mail and black surcoat, with a sneer upon his face. "You broke your promise, Madoc, even though it took the last of her life to ask it."

Trefor hadn't been there the day Owain was born and Gwendolyn had died.

His brother raised his sword and pointed it at Madoc. "You broke your promise to a dying woman. You don't deserve to live."

Madoc dropped Gwendolyn's lifeless hand and started to stand.

Uncle Lloyd, a goblet in his hand, walked out of the gloom and came to stand beside Trefor. "A fine nephew you are, breaking a promise," he jeered. "And here I thought you were better than that."

Madoc turned, ready to flee from their accusations—but where? And how? There was no door, no window, only darkness.

Then Roslynn appeared as if by magic, a bloody lamb in her arms and disgust in her eyes. "You broke your promise," she said, her voice hollow and lifeless, as if she were dying, too. "You broke the promise you made to a woman you claimed to love."

"You don't understand," he cried desperately. "I—"

"You broke your word," Roslynn intoned as she backed into the shadows and the babe's cries grew louder and louder. "You said you loved her and you broke your word. You said you loved her and you broke your—"

With a gasp, Madoc sat up. Panting, he looked around wildly. This was his chamber, the very room where Gwendolyn had died, and he had made his promise.

But he was in the bed and—thank God!—Roslynn slept peacefully beside him.

Leaning forward, he cradled his head in his hands and tried to calm his racing heart.

A dream. It had been a dream. One born of memory and dismay and guilt, but a dream just the same.

He took a few more deep breaths, then eased himself out of bed, stepping gingerly on the floor so he wouldn't wake Roslynn. He welcomed the chill of the cold air against his naked skin, for it confirmed he was awake, and that had been a nightmare.

He put his hand on the bedpost and took another gulp of air as he remembered the dream-Roslynn regarding him with disgust, holding that bloody lamb in her arms. An honorable woman, she would surely look at him with just that expression if she ever found out the truth, and about the promise made and broken.

"Madoc?"

He turned toward the bed. "I didn't mean to disturb you. It's early yet. Go back to sleep."

Instead of doing as he suggested, Roslynn raised

herself on her elbow and looked toward the window. "Can you tell if the day will be fair?"

Seeing no clouds hiding the stars, he was able to give her a smile. "No rain today, I think. A fine day for a feast."

"Good," she said, sinking back down into the feather bed. "Are you coming back to bed?"

"No," he replied. He'd never be able to fall asleep now. "I think I'll take a stroll on the wall walk and make sure the sentries are awake."

"Not like that, I hope," she replied, a hint of a smile on her face as she ran her gaze over his naked body. "You'll catch a chill."

"Might give the lads a turn, too," he noted with a laugh as he went to the chest and pulled out some dark, woolen breeches.

He hesitated. Since the shearing had been completed yesterday, he might as well dress for the feast later today. Guests could begin arriving at any time during the morning.

"Are you going to wear that?"

Madoc glanced down at the leather tunic he now held in his hands. It was his better one, not the one he wore most days. "What's wrong with it?"

"Your other black tunic would be better, the one you wore when we married."

"It doesn't fit properly."

"It's very fine wool."

"It's too uncomfortable."

"You look more like the nobleman you are in that tunic," she coaxed.

"No doubt I'd smell more like a nobleman if I dabbed myself with perfume like the king's courtiers," he muttered, disgruntled by her implication that he didn't look noble in his regular clothes.

Then he cursed himself for a fool. What did it matter what he wore? This was a day to make her proud, not cause more difficulties between them. "You're right. I'll change later."

"Thank you, Madoc."

She sounded so relieved, he didn't begrudge his acquiescence and went to kiss her soft cheek. "Now you rest, my lady. I'm sure everything's well prepared and the feast will be the best there's ever been in Llanpowell."

"I hope so, Madoc," she said, smiling up at him, her hair sleep tousled and spread upon the pillow, her blue eyes shining, her body naked beneath the coverlet.

Suddenly, checking to see if his sentries were awake at their posts didn't seem important at all....

THE SUN WAS WELL UP by the time Madoc strolled into the barracks, his nightmare all but forgotten in the pleasant aftermath of lovemaking.

Some of his men were sitting on their cots in the large room, others were lying on theirs, heads cushioned in their hands. A round hearth was in the middle of the room, unlit at this time of year. Pegs beside the cots held cloaks and swordbelts and bits of clothing, and basins and ewers rested upon a long table at the far end of the room, where more pegs held drying linen.

Every man sat up abruptly or leaped to attention as their overlord, tugging the damn black tunic down, closed the thick oaken door and turned to address them.

"Sit," he said, planting his feet, his hands clasped behind his back, "or stand as you prefer. I've just come to remind you to be on your best behavior today. My wife's put a lot of work into this feast, and I've spent a lot of money, so you better damn well behave like decent, God-fearing Welshmen. No drunkenness and no rowdy songs about mermaids or anything else, all right?"

"You *like* the mermaid song," Ioan protested, his voice grave but his blue-green eyes twinkling with merriment.

"How would it look to the Normans if my men are no better behaved than louts in a tavern?" Madoc replied. "Look you, I'm serious about this. I want today to go well, for my wife's sake, especially since she's—" He caught himself just in time. "Well, it's important to her, that's all."

Ioan's eyes widened and so did his grin. "I win the wager!" he cried, surveying his companions with triumph. "Pay up, and the next time I tell you a woman's with child because she's looking a little weary and a little plumper in the face, maybe you'll believe me. And now we've another reason to celebrate, eh, Madoc?"

Hugh the Beak, standing by the door, called out, "Here's hoping for another son for Llanpowell!"

"Aye, aye!" cried the men, fists pumping and grins all around.

Madoc cringed inwardly and cursed himself for a dolt. Yet despite his slip, he still should try to keep Roslynn's secret for as long as possible, as she'd asked.

"Did I say she was with child?" he demanded. "No, I did not, and you'd better not be making any more such wagers. It's insolent, and if it weren't the shearing feast today, I'd seriously consider having you all run from here to the top of the mountain and back again."

Most of the men flushed or looked sorry, but not Ioan. "Nothing wrong with a bit of wishful thinking, is there, my lord?"

Madoc hated feeling like he was lying to the men who would give their lives to protect him and his family. "I'm not saying she's not—but no more speculation and wagering, lads. I'll tell you the moment Lady Roslynn gives me leave. I don't want to be upsetting her now, or have her thinking I can't keep a confidence."

"While women can, eh?" Hugh the Beak asked skeptically.

"Well, that's how she wants it until she's sure," Madoc said.

"Then I'll just offer congratulations for some possible future eventuality," Ioan said as if he were a seer, peering into a magic glass.

"Ioan," Madoc warned, "one of these days, you're going to go too far and say too much. Now, all of you, mind you don't let it slip."

The way he had.

"We'll be careful, won't we, boys?" Ioan said. "It'll be sleeping in the barracks for Madoc if his wife finds out and how he snores!"

"I do not!"

"Well, and we don't want you to have any trouble with the wife. That's women for you—bane and blessing."

"Aye!" young Gwillym enthusiastically agreed. "You can never please them, can you?"

"Some of us *men* can," Hugh returned. "Remains to be seen if you ever will."

A shout came from the inner gate.

"Seems some of your guests are keen to get here," Ioan noted.

"Aye, so it seems," Madoc said, turning to leave and giving his tunic another tug. "Remember what I said, men—best behavior. Let's make the lady proud."

Hugh suddenly turned to look at Madoc with stunned horror on his face.

"What?" Madoc demanded, quickening his pace until he stood beside the Beak and could see for himself what had brought that expression to the man's features.

Trefor ap Gruffydd stood in the center of the courtyard of Llanpowell, as bold and arrogant as if he owned it.

CHAPTER SIXTEEN

WHAT THE DEVIL was *he* doing there?

The gall of his brother—for surely, as God made Adam, Roslynn would not have invited Trefor to the feast.

Or would she? Did she think this could be a way to make peace between them?

If so, he thought as he strode toward his brother, skirting the extra tables and benches already set out for the feast, one look at his brother's haughty, sneering face should tell her, or anyone, how impossible that was.

It had been nearly six years since Madoc had seen his brother up close, but Trefor hadn't changed, or at least, not much. Although he was a bit more unkempt and leaner in the face, he was still the same handsome fellow who could make every woman between here and the Hebrides swoon with desire with those bright blue eyes, the irises rimmed with black.

His looks wouldn't help him through the outer gates of Llanpowell, though, so how had he managed it? Madoc silently vowed to find out who was on duty, and when he did, they were going to regret...

There was a white flag of truce tucked in Trefor's belt. That would explain why he'd been allowed inside, for his men would respect that.

Trefor had not come alone. Rhodri and several other men—thieves and cutthroats by the look of them—were at the side yard near the stables, along with some mangy horses. Several men of Llanpowell, including the guards on the wall, were watching them, clearly ready to attack if Madoc gave the word.

"Greetings, Madoc," Trefor said with an insolent nod of the head when his brother reached him. "I see you're expecting plenty of company."

"Aye, but you weren't invited." *Or so he hoped.*

"Since when does a brother need an invitation to the home of his father and grandfather?" Trefor replied, telling Madoc he had *not* been invited or, being Trefor, he would have said so.

Trefor came toward him until they stood eye to eye. "What, a man can't visit his home—the home that should be his—on a feast day when every neighbor should be welcome?"

"The home you lost through your own dishonorable conduct," Madoc retorted.

"The estate you stole from me, along with Gwendolyn."

"You lost her when you came drunk and late to the wedding, and fresh from a brothel."

Trefor shifted his weight from side to side, like a man preparing to fight. "I never said that's where I'd been."

"No doubt you were too drunk to remember what you said, but you were sure enough that day," Madoc replied, rolling his shoulders to loosen the muscles, as he always did before he fought. "No doubt you don't remember the horror in our mother's eyes, or the look of shame in our father's."

"I know you had your excuse to take what was mine at last," his brother charged, his hand going to the hilt of his sword. "You'd waited for all your life for that chance, you selfish, scheming *mochyn!*"

"What are you but a thief and a scoundrel, to come onto my land and steal my sheep and kill my ram?" Madoc countered as he reached for his. "Or will you deny that, too?"

"I killed that ram, all right. Fine animal, that— as fine an animal as that woman John sent you, or so Rhodri tells me. If I'd known John would give his lackeys such rewards, Madoc, I might have sold myself to him, too. Rhodri says she's the prettiest Norman wench a man could ever hope to fu—"

Madoc's temper exploded and, with a roar of rage, he tackled his brother. They landed hard on the cobblestones and Madoc hit his brother everywhere and anywhere he could, until Ioan and Hugh pulled him away. Several of his men were around them, swords drawn, and more had surrounded Trefor's men.

"Flag of truce, Madoc," Hugh reminded him through clenched teeth. "You'll dishonor yourself if you kill him here and now."

"Aye, I hear you," Madoc muttered, although he was still enraged.

A table was overturned and a bench, but Madoc had no memory of how that had happened.

Rhodri helped Trefor, his nose bleeding, to his feet. "Aye, you would dishonor a flag of truce, wouldn't you," his brother sneered, his lip swelling and a bruise forming on his chin.

"Shut your stinking mouth and get out," Madoc commanded. "Take these rogues and leave Llanpowell and never come back, or so help me God, I *will* kill you."

Trefor smirked as he wiped the blood from his face with the back of his hand. "Temper, little brother, temper—although you never could rein it in, could you?"

"Get out of my castle before I throw you in my dungeon and leave you to the king's justice."

Trefor's eyes gleamed spitefully as he spread his arms wide. "What, you'd bring me before a Norman court? What would Uncle Lloyd say? Where is he, anyway?"

Madoc had no idea where Uncle Lloyd was, and didn't care.

"Who is this, Madoc?" Roslynn asked as she swept down the steps of the hall.

She was dressed in that beautiful red gown she'd worn on their wedding day. Her hair was uncovered and unbound and falling past her waist.

Pride and triumph surged through Madoc at the sight of her, and he sheathed his sword with a swiftly satisfied motion. "Come, brother, let me introduce you to my wife. Roslynn, this is my older brother, Trefor ap Gruffydd, lord of Pontyrmwr."

"Greetings and welcome," she said, her voice as sweet as honey, her manner as charming as a woman's could be. "You didn't tell me you look so much alike, Madoc, except that your brother's eyes are blue."

He had the delightful experience of seeing Trefor's blatant envy, until he hid it as he bowed.

"A delight to meet you at last, my lady," he said, and he had the effrontery to smile at her with the same smile that had endeared him to so many women. "Since I wasn't invited to the wedding, I thought I'd come along to the wedding feast, late though it is."

"Many people were not invited to the wedding ceremony," Roslynn coolly replied. "The king's escort was in some haste to return to court." She slid Madoc a smile that made him want to haul her close and kiss her with all the passion she aroused within him. "And my lord and I were in some haste, as well."

Trefor smirked again as he ran another measuring gaze over Roslynn. "No, you couldn't make John's lackey wait, or delay following his orders. Might upset the greedy fool, and we can't have that, can we?"

"My brother will be leaving now," Madoc announced.

"Unless the lady would like me to stay?" Trefor asked with that same outrageous impudence.

"I beg your pardon, but I think not," she replied. "It's unfortunate you chose this day to visit your brother, for although I'm sure there is much you could say to each other, we're expecting other company and your brother won't be able to give you the attention you deserve. Another time, perhaps?"

Another time?

"Never," Madoc growled. "My brother will *never* be welcome here."

"A delight it's been, if a short-lived one, my lady," Trefor said with another bow.

"Go!" Madoc ordered. "Before I order the archers to use you for target practice."

"If they could understand you, Mumble-mouth," Trefor retorted before going to one of the pathetic horses waiting near the stable.

He threw himself into the saddle and, followed by his men, rode out of the gates.

After they were gone, the guards turned back to watch beyond the walls, the soldiers returned to their duties and the servants, subdued and wary, began to go about the necessary business of preparing for the feast.

His shoulder aching, blood trickling down his neck from a scrape near his ear, Madoc turned to Roslynn. "You didn't invite him to the feast, did you?"

"Of course not," she replied. "But—"

"There are no buts with Trefor! He is never to be allowed in this castle again, *ever.* I don't even want to hear his name mentioned!"

She paled a little as she nodded her head. "As you wish, Madoc. Let me look at that cut."

"It's nothing," he growled, wiping the blood away with his hand.

"You've torn your tunic. You'll want to wash and change before you go to fetch Owain."

"I'm not going to get him."

That little wrinkle appeared between her eyes. "Surely there's time enough to—"

"I've changed my mind. It will be too much excitement for him and not the best circumstances for you two to meet," he snapped, before he turned on his heel and left her.

IN MANY WAYS, the shearing feast at Llanpowell was all that a celebratory feast should be. The food was excellent, plentiful and, for the nobles, exotic. Many of them had never before had eels cooked in ale, or mutton prepared in such a fashion, or leek soup with that particular combination of herbs and vegetables. There was roasted beef, boar and quail, expertly done, as well as savory stews and several kinds of bread, including some woven into intricate patterns. In addition to puddings and sweetmeats, baked fruit and pies added to the fare, and there was so much wine and ale, it was a wonder everyone in the hall wasn't drunk before the tables were cleared.

The entertainment was also varied, exciting and amusing, from the jugglers Roslynn had hired, to the bards and dancers, and especially the magician who astonished them all by pulling live birds from his beard.

Roslynn should have been happy, proud and satisfied, and pleased by the results.

Instead, she sat miserably beside Madoc, who was still simmering with rage, barely saying a word. Although she knew his encounter with his brother was responsible, she couldn't subdue the dread that he was going to find fault with something, or someone, and fly into a fit of temper again.

She was disappointed in other ways, too.

She had been anticipating meeting his son and hopefully establishing a friendship with him before her child was born, until Madoc had abruptly changed his mind.

And judging by the way several of the men of the garrison kept looking at her and smiling as if they shared a confidence, she could well believe Madoc had told them about her condition, regardless of his promise that he would keep that a secret between them.

So in spite of all her hopes and careful planning, all the time and trouble and worry, the feast was ruined for her before it had even started.

After the last of the food was finally cleared away, her grim and silent husband left the high table to join Ivor and some lesser Welsh nobles in another part of the hall.

She shifted restlessly in her chair, tempted to retire until Uncle Lloyd slid into Madoc's vacated chair. "A fine business this! I'm that ashamed of my nephew, I could spit!"

"It's unfortunate Madoc and his brother came to blows," Roslynn replied, "and that Madoc is still so angry about it."

"Madoc's done nothing wrong," his uncle retorted, clearly taken aback that she thought he'd referred to her husband. "He should have beaten Trefor to a pulp, the way he's been carrying on. No, it's Trefor I'm ashamed of. I wish I'd spanked the lad more often, that I do. Aye, and with a thick leather belt! Spoiled he is, and spoiled he was!"

"Family squabbles are a bad business," her father, who had been seated at a place of honor to the right of Madoc, agreed. "It often ends in misery for all concerned."

Whatever her misgivings, Roslynn didn't want her parents to worry about her, not after all she'd already put them through. "I'm sure Madoc and I will be quite all right."

"Trefor's never done anything worse than kill that ram before the wedding," Lloyd confirmed. "Still, coming here as bold as a king's whore— What the devil's the matter with him?" He shook his head again. "Madoc's going to have to kill him, I think, before there'll be peace."

"Surely not!" Lady Eloise cried, echoing her daughter's thoughts from her place beside her husband. "Whatever has happened between them, they are still brothers. For one to kill the other…it would be a terrible sin."

"Aye, but Trefor's giving poor Madoc little

choice. As for brother against brother, look you at John and his," Lloyd replied, reaching for Madoc's half-full goblet and draining it. "There's an example for you. Each one out for all they can get. But I never thought to see such conflict within my own family. A pity it is, and Trefor's to blame."

On the other side of the hall, and without even a glance in her direction, Madoc continued to converse with his friends.

Roslynn put her hand to her forehead. "If you'll excuse me, my head is aching. Too much excitement and fine food, no doubt."

Her mother was beside her in an instant.

"I'm quite all right," Roslynn said in answer to her mother's silent query. "It's been a long day, that's all. I'm sure I'll be fine in the morning. Please, stay and enjoy the rest of the entertainment."

Mercifully, or perhaps seeing that it was no use, her mother didn't protest or insist upon accompanying her.

As Roslynn left the hall, she paused to say goodnight to the most important guests from neighboring estates. She did not look to see if Madoc noticed she was retiring and she would be relieved if he didn't. She didn't want to be alone with him until he had calmed down.

Once inside their bedchamber, she closed the

door and leaned back against it for a moment before heaving a weary sigh and going to her dressing table. She sat heavily on the stool and drew off her expensive silk veil.

"Are you ill?"

She started at the sound of Madoc's voice. Shifting on the stool, she discovered him standing on the threshold, regarding her with worried eyes.

"Only tired," she said, wishing he would go, even if it seemed he was no longer enraged. She really was exhausted and wanted to sleep. Or at least not deal with her husband right now.

"Are you sure?" he persisted.

"I know how I feel, Madoc," she replied impatiently. "Please go back to the hall and celebrate with your friends. I'm sure they'll all want to congratulate you on our coming child."

Her breath caught when she realized what she'd said and how peevish she must have sounded. She shouldn't be chastising him after he'd been so angry earlier, lest he lose his temper again, and with her.

"Only a few know," Madoc muttered under his breath, although there was guilty confirmation in his eyes as he came into the room and closed the door. "I didn't come right out and say. Ioan guessed. Those that know have been ordered not to tell anyone else."

She rose and went to the window. "Nothing is ever your fault, is it, Madoc?" she demanded as she turned to face him. "You have an excuse for everything."

His eyes narrowed. "I have an *explanation*—or do you think Trefor is speaking the truth and I have only an *excuse* for holding Llanpowell?"

"I don't know what to think," she replied, trying to contain her frustration and failing. "You claim you're justified, yet when he steals from you, you act as if you feel guilty."

"You don't understand."

"No, you're right, I don't," she replied, her emotions spilling out in spite of her attempt to suppress them. "I don't understand what's happened between you and your brother. I don't understand why you play games with each other, stealing sheep and taking them back. I don't understand why you sent your son away, even if you loved his mother who died giving him life."

Regarding her, Madoc's visage was as still and stern as the effigy of a martyred saint. Only his eyes seemed alive, and they burned—but not with desire. With rage. "If you think I do these things because I *enjoy* them, or because I have a choice, you *don't* understand. And you don't know *me*."

Her heart racing, the panic returning, Roslynn backed away from him. She had never really known

Wimarc before he revealed his true nature after they were wed and she was tied to him for life. Obviously she hadn't known Madoc ap Gruffydd at all, either.

"By the saints, Roslynn, why do you look at me like that?" he demanded. "How many times must I tell you I won't hurt you?"

"How can I be sure?" she asked in a whisper, her hands clasped before her, wanting to trust him, but terrified that would be another disastrous mistake. "If, as you say, I don't know you, how can I ever be sure that you won't hurt me when you're angry?"

Suddenly it was as if his temper had been a candle, snuffed out in an instant. His eyes full of remorse, he held out his hands in supplication. "Because..." A different expression dawned on his face—both surprise and certainty. "Because I love you, *fy rhosyn.*"

She closed her eyes. To think she had yearned to hear him say those words.

But now she had seen the way he'd attacked his brother, the rage and the explosive violence he was capable of. She'd witnessed the sullen, brooding aftermath.

She could never again feel safe here.

"Wimarc claimed to love me, too," she said quietly. "And he beat me until I was black and blue."

"But *he* didn't mean those words," Madoc protested. "I've been as angry as I've ever gotten today, and I didn't strike you. I never will."

It was true that he hadn't laid a finger on her. He hadn't hit her, or thrown her down or done anything to physically harm her. He hadn't called her terrible names.

But the damage had been done. After what had transpired today, she could never be sure that he wouldn't lash out at her. That he wouldn't one day lose his temper and hurt her, either with his fists or his words.

It would be like walking along a perilous path, with unseen dangers lying in wait, every single day.

She had already lived that life as Wimarc's wife, and she had vowed not to do so ever again.

"Leave me, Madoc," she said. "I cannot be near you now."

He stared at her as if she'd struck him. "Roslynn—"

"Will you do as I ask, or not?"

Without another word, he left her.

AFTER HE WAS GONE, Roslynn sank down onto the cold stone floor and covered her face with her hands. She knew what she must do—what she had sworn to do.

Never again would she live always wondering if

today a man would take out his anger on her. If today he would lose his temper and strike her, claiming she had goaded him into it. She would not live always anxious, always fearful.

So she must leave, as she had not done before.

CHAPTER SEVENTEEN

"BY SAINT DAFYDD and Bridget and all the rest in Wales, what the devil's happened between you and your wife?" Lloyd demanded the next morning as he dragged his nephew from a straw pallet covered in rough blanchet in the hall. "She's leaving Llanpowell!"

Madoc kicked his foot to make his uncle let go of his ankle. "We had an argument," he muttered as he staggered to his feet. His mouth was dry as a cask six months empty, his head ached and his stomach—

Best not consider his stomach, or the amount of ale he'd consumed trying not to think about Roslynn, and Gwendolyn, or Trefor or Owain.

"She's leaving you, Madoc," Lloyd all but shouted, making the other men still sleeping around them snort and stir. "Going home with her parents, or so she's told Bron, who came to me in tears because she was too afraid to tell you herself, poor girl."

That couldn't be right. Roslynn wouldn't leave

him. He loved her. He'd told her so, and if she didn't love him yet, she certainly liked him. Besides, she was bearing his child... "She can't be going."

"Well, she says she is—*today,* you hot-tempered nit! *She's packing her things!*"

The look on Roslynn's face when she told him to go last night, and the tone of her voice, came back to him with the force of a blow.

His own aches and pains forgotten, desperately hoping Lloyd was wrong, he left his uncle and went at once to the bedchamber, taking the stairs two at a time just as he had on his second wedding night.

He opened the door and saw, to his dismay, that Uncle Lloyd was right. Roslynn was packing. "You're going away?"

"Yes. I'm going back to Briston with my parents," she replied, folding her hands before her, as calm as a nun as she regarded him with a resolve he despaired to see.

"Even if I apologize?"

"You've apologized before, Madoc. But how many more times will you lose your temper? How many more times will I be afraid that *this* time, you'll be angry enough to hit me?"

"I would never—"

"So you say, and so you no doubt believe. I'd like to believe it, too. But I've seen you attack your own brother as if you'd kill him with your bare hands, so how can I be certain? I can't, and I won't live with that uncertainty. Not ever again."

What fresh punishment was this? Madoc inwardly cried. Had he not suffered enough for his sins? Had he not given his word to her that she would be safe with him, shown her how much he cared for her?

Yet it still wasn't enough. "You'll *never* trust me, no matter what I do?"

She turned away and went back to her packing. "No."

She faced him once more, and the sorrow in her eyes, so much harder to bear than anger, smote him to the core. "This isn't easy for me, Madoc. I care for you very much, more than I ever would have thought possible. I wish with all my heart that things could be different. That I had met you before Wimarc. But I didn't.

"Perhaps if you were a docile man, it would be possible for us to have a happy life together, but then you wouldn't be Madoc ap Gruffydd. Nor am I foolish enough to believe that you could be otherwise, even if you tried. For good or ill, you are as you are, Madoc, and I am as I am."

He had his pride and he would not beg—but he wouldn't let her go easily, not Roslynn. He approached her slowly, cautiously, as he had the first time he had kissed her. "You claim you care for me, yet you'll leave me."

"I do care for you, but I must leave you."

He reached out to caress her smooth cheek, the feel of her skin warming him, as it always did. "If you truly care for me, how can you go?"

"Don't touch me, Madoc," she said, stepping back. "Not ever again. If you do, I might weaken. We might even make love and I might decide to stay. But soon, the dread and doubt would return and I would hate myself for weakening. I would always be watching and waiting, fearing that you're going to lose your temper and hurt me."

She held up her hand for silence before he could protest. "Yes, I know you've vowed not to and you meant it."

She went to him and, taking his hands, clasped them in hers as she looked up into his stricken face. "I've lived in fear before, and I will never live that way again, not even with you."

Just as he would never be able to stand in a bog, letting himself sink in the mire. "Then there is nothing I can say or do to make you stay?"

She shook her head. "No."

It would have been easier if she'd stabbed him. But even so, he would not give up. Not yet. "You carry my child, Roslynn."

She went to the bed, picked up her red gown and began to fold it. "You will be welcome to visit my parents' estate. My father will tell you how to get there."

How often would he be able to do that? Once a year? Twice? "According to the law, it will be *my* child, Roslynn, not yours."

She slowly turned toward him, the gown limp in her hands. "You would take my child from me?"

"If you think me a monster, what would stop me?" he asked, bitterness and sorrow and anguish welling up inside him.

"Nothing," she whispered. "But I thought…"

"What?"

"That you wouldn't care where your child was, as long as it lived and was well cared for."

"Why—" He fell silent as the answer struck him like a kick of a warhorse's hoof.

Owain.

She thought he wouldn't mind being away from his child because he had sent Owain from Llanpowell.

Because she didn't know the truth.

Because he couldn't bear to speak of it, to reveal the terrible thing he'd done, the promise he'd broken. Not even now.

God help him. God give him strength to endure. And not to beg, for as she had her resolve, he had his pride. "Go then," he muttered, reaching for the latch. "Send word when the babe is born."

"Madoc."

He hesitated, but didn't turn back.

"Have you any names for our child?"

He wanted to groan and cry to the heavens and tear out his hair. "Name the babe as you see fit, Roslynn," he said as he opened the door and walked out.

And live, he silently prayed as he walked slowly down the stairs.

FOR ROSLYNN, it seemed only a heartbeat—a painful heartbeat—from the time Madoc left her until she was in the yard watching her baggage being loaded onto a cart. This time, though, it wasn't Lord Alfred and his men who waited to escort her. It was her father and her mother, who was already in the large, heavy, brightly painted wagon that would take them back to Briston.

It wasn't raining anymore, but the sky was a dull gray and there were several large puddles to avoid, so she had to keep her eyes on the ground. That made it easier to avoid the people watching. She could hear some of them, though Hywel was in the doorway of the kitchen, with Lowri, Rhonwen and other kitchen servants, their distressed murmuring like the sound of far off waves. Lloyd stood at the entrance to the hall muttering to Bron, and several of the soldiers and other servants of Llanpowell were watching from the wall walk, the barracks, the stable and the various outbuildings, all whispering among themselves.

Just as she reached the wagon, she caught sight of Ivor by the armory out of the corner of her eye, with a satisfied smirk upon his face.

If Madoc had been there, she would have turned aside and, regardless of what had passed between them, told him at once of her suspicions and that Ivor was not to be trusted. That Madoc should take nothing his steward said at face value. That he should check the accounts carefully and confirm all recent deliveries with the merchants.

But Madoc was not there, and she had no idea where he was.

She thought of telling Lloyd and dismissed that idea. He would likely doubt her and she didn't want to try to justify her suspicions in the yard, nor did she have the time.

Nevertheless, she wouldn't let Ivor rob Madoc. She would write to Madoc after she arrived at Briston. She could make certain the letter was delivered into Madoc's hands alone. She owed him that much.

And if he chose not to believe her, at least she'd have tried.

Her father, who hadn't yet mounted his horse, opened the door of the wagon and helped her inside. It wasn't a particularly restful mode of travel, but her mother had made it as comfortable as possible, with plenty of cushions, after first insisting she not ride. Roslynn didn't care enough about how she was leaving to differ.

Nor had she given her parents an explanation for her request to go with them. They hadn't asked for any, either. Maybe, having seen Madoc's altered behavior at the feast, or because of his fierce confrontation with Trefor, they'd come to their own conclusions, or at least enough to make immediate questions unnecessary. Perhaps they sensed that she was too upset for questions and so would wait for an explanation.

Her father closed the door tight and gave her an encouraging smile. "Only a few days, and then you'll be safe at home," he said, before he went to his horse.

Home. Their home, once hers.

She surveyed the now-familiar walls and buildings of Llanpowell. In less than a month, this had come to be her home, because Madoc was there.

She turned away from the wagon's window as her father called the order to depart and the heavy, lumbering vehicle drawn by four huge draft horses began to move. Her mother put her arm around her, comforting without a word.

"Farewell, my lady!" Bron cried out, running closer, her arm waving frantically. "God bless you!"

"Oh, Mother," Roslynn whispered as she laid her head on Lady Eloise's shoulder.

ROSLYNN AWOKE with a start as the wagon jerked to a halt. She must have fallen asleep, although it was still day. "Mother, what—"

"Quiet!" Lady Eloise commanded, fear in her eyes, as well as her voice, her body tense, as she leaned forward and pulled back the leather flap over the window to peer cautiously outside. Roslynn immediately did the same on the other side.

Despite the constricted view, she could see a group of mounted men in the middle of the road, blocking their way.

Led by Trefor ap Gruffydd.

She swiftly drew back, lest he see her. Trefor had never seen her parents. Maybe he simply thought to rob some rich Normans. Nevertheless, whether it was robbery or some other motive, they could be in danger.

"Have you any weapon other than your eating knife?" she quietly asked her mother.

"No. Have you?"

Roslynn shook her head.

"Surely we'll be safe," her mother replied, her mouth a thin line of determination. "Your father and his men will protect us."

The moment she finished speaking, a gauntleted hand shoved back the leather flap over the wagon's window on Roslynn's side, and Trefor's face, so like Madoc's except for his piercing blue eyes, appeared in the opening. "Greetings, ladies."

His brows rose with recognition. "Especially you, Lady Roslynn," he said, his horse prancing nervously, although that didn't seem to bother Trefor of Pontyrmwr. "Since you've enjoyed my brother's hospitality, you must come and enjoy mine."

Her mother replied first, assuming her most dignified manner. "Thank you for the invitation. However, we would prefer to continue our journey."

Trefor's smile seemed a cruel version of Madoc's. "I'm sorry to disappoint you then, because you're staying with me regardless."

Roslynn and her mother answered at the same time and with the same words, although they referred to different people. "My husband—"

Trefor interrupted with a harsh caw of a laugh, nothing like Madoc's low rumble, "Husbands, is it? One's squatting on his estate like a toad in a hole and the other knows better than to try to fight when he and his men are outnumbered three to one."

His eyes widened with bogus surprise. "You look shocked, Lady Roslynn. Did you think I had only those few I brought to the feast? As if I would bring all my men to Llanpowell." His expression became grimly serious. "And since many more are with me now, you're coming to Pontyrmwr."

"Where you no doubt intend to ransom us, rogue that you are," Roslynn charged.

Trefor's brows rose again. "There's an idea. I hadn't thought of that."

Roslynn tried not to panic. "What *were* you going to do?" she demanded, even as one answer came to mind. She wouldn't be the first woman used to exact revenge against a husband.

"Why, have a little visit with my brother's bride," Trefor answered with a smile that was as cold as the North Sea. "And her charming parents, too. Now, we'd best be on our way. The roads can be treacherous in the dark."

He raised his hand, called something in Welsh and the wagon lurched into motion.

Roslynn reached for her mother's hand.

"Be brave, daughter," her mother said, although her face was pale and drawn.

Roslynn managed to give her mother an encouraging smile. "I will be. After all, I'm the daughter of Lady Eloise and Lord James de Briston, aren't I?"

ROSLYNN HAD ASSUMED Pontyrmwr would be like Llanpowell, only on a smaller scale and perhaps not so well maintained.

She was quite wrong. The castle, if it could even be called such, was not even half the size of Llanpowell. It had only one wall not nearly as tall, and while there was a wooden walk around the inner perimeter, no towers at all, not even by the narrow gate. Once inside the walls, it was easy to see that the only building made of stone was the round keep, and it appeared ancient.

Also in contrast to Llanpowell, the yard was unpaved and full of muddy holes. The few wooden buildings, including the stable, looked as if they might fall down at any moment.

Unfortunately, there were plenty of men both on the wall and in the yard, telling her that Trefor must spend most of whatever income his estate produced on soldiers. Judging by their looks and clothes, they were all mercenaries.

The door to the wagon opened and Trefor leaned inside. "This way, if you please," he said, holding his hand toward Roslynn, obviously expecting her to take it.

She'd rather touch a leech.

Ignoring him, she grasped the frame of the door to climb down. Her mother did likewise.

If their actions disturbed Trefor, he didn't show it as he led the way up the stone steps curving around the outside of the keep. Her father followed them while, under the watchful eye of Rhodri and the other men, their soldiers were escorted to another tumbledown building.

They would be safe, Roslynn told herself. Even if Trefor were willing to compel his brother to battle, surely he wouldn't want to risk the enmity of the Normans by killing a Norman nobleman and his family, as well as their escort.

The second level of the keep reached by the outer stair served for a hall. Cobwebs hung from the scarred, smoke-blackened beams that held up another floor above. The greasy rushes stank of spoiled food, the stench mingling with the scent of wet wool and damp dog. A rickety set of steps curved to the third and topmost level above.

More men were inside, lounging about as if they were Trefor's equals, regarding her with lustful eyes, until he glared at them and ordered them to go. Slowly, with scowls and shuffling feet, they obeyed, and Roslynn breathed a little easier—but only a little.

Trefor gestured for his prisoners to sit on a pair of benches beside a battered, nicked table at the far end of the room, then ordered a slovenly female of indeterminate age who stood gaping by the door to bring them some wine.

"Not as luxurious as Llanpowell, is it?" he said with a scowl. "Still, better than a hut in the woods— or a grave."

A chill ran down Roslynn's spine at his last words.

"You realize it would be an act of war if you killed us," her father declared. "King John would certainly take it as such."

Trefor laughed, the sound even more harsh in the cold stone building. "You think I'm afraid of John? A Welshman could never be afraid of a Norman and especially one like him. If he takes Pontyrmwr from me, I'll easily find sanctuary elsewhere." He nodded at the walls around him. "This isn't so much to lose when your birthright's been stolen."

The slovenly servant, her skirts ragged, her bodice stained, her brown scraggly hair loose, appeared with a tray bearing a plain copper carafe and some mugs. She sidled closer, her mouth hanging open as she regarded the three Normans.

Trefor grabbed the tray from her hands and spoke brusquely in Welsh. The woman bobbed a bow and scurried away.

"You have to forgive Myfanwy," he said as he set the tray on the end of the bench and poured wine into four mugs. "She's a bit simple in the head and she's never seen a Norman lord and lady up close before."

He handed out the wine, which Roslynn and her parents set on the bench without taking so much as a sip.

Trefor gave them a smirk of a smile. "Not good enough for you, eh? Well, well, maybe not—but it's the best I've got." He downed his in a gulp, then wiped his mouth with the back of his hand. "My lord and my lady, up you go to my chamber above. I want to speak to Madoc's wife alone."

CHAPTER EIGHTEEN

ROSLYNN'S FATHER rose to protest, but Trefor cut him short.

"My castle, my orders," he said bluntly. "Or if you don't want to go to my bedchamber—" his lips curved up in a smile that was very like Madoc's, except that it had nothing of her husband's honest good humor in it "—your daughter and I will. I was thinking you'd be worried if I took her where there was a bed, although there's no need. I'm a more honorable man than Madoc."

She didn't believe that, and they would still be alone here. "If you are as honorable as you say, why did you abduct us?"

"Honorable where women are concerned, then," he amended. "Unlike your husband."

"What do you mean?"

His glance slid to her parents. "I'll explain to you alone, my lady, or not at all."

Her mother rose with stately dignity. "We shall

do as you say. But if you harm our daughter, my husband's vengeance will be nothing compared to *mine,*" she said, before she started toward the stairs.

Her father followed, darting a threatening glare over his shoulder.

When they were gone, Trefor grabbed her father's cup and finished the wine before sitting across from her. "I can see where you get your manner. God, like a queen your mother is and you a princess. Maybe I should have helped John, too, like Madoc. Then John could pay me off with a fine wife."

"What do you want to say to me that you couldn't say in my parents' presence?"

Trefor rose abruptly. He walked a short distance away, then turned to face her. "I'm going to tell you the truth about your husband."

"You could have done that without sending them away."

"It's bad enough you looking at me with those big eyes of yours."

"If I disturb you so much, save your breath and let us go."

"God, you're a cool one! You must freeze the marrow of my brother's bones."

"If you prefer to think so," she replied, resting her hands on her stomach.

His gaze flicked to those protective, laced fingers. "Maybe not all the time."

She might have inadvertently revealed too much, as Madoc had done with his men, but it was too late now.

He tilted his head as he studied her. "Why have you left him? Or has he had enough and sent you away?"

She didn't answer. She would say nothing of what had happened with Madoc to this man.

"You expect me to believe you're just off on a little jaunt with the family, after only being married a month or so?"

"I don't care what you believe. And if you have nothing to tell me about my husband after all, then at least let me be with my parents."

"Very well, don't tell me why you've left him. It doesn't matter anyway."

"How long do you intend to keep us here?"

"Until I get a ransom, as you so cleverly suggested."

"If things are as you suggested and he sent me away, you can't expect that he'll pay a ransom for me."

"Aye, that's true," Trefor mused, running his hand over his chin in a way that reminded her more of Lloyd than her husband.

Was that why she wasn't afraid? Why no feeling

of panic clutched at her heart? Because he was so much like the men of Llanpowell?

Whatever the reason, she wasn't frightened. She was angry.

"Then I'll just tell Madoc you've decided to stay with me, for our mutual pleasure."

She started to stand. "You disgusting lout! How dare you?"

"Sit down, my lady."

She didn't.

"Sit *down,* my lady."

"Or what? You'll force me to?"

"Aye, I will."

"Proving you're just the sort of spoiled, childish brat Madoc said you were."

"That's good, coming from him. But it's no wonder you believe that when you've been told a pack of lies about me."

"You didn't come to your wedding drunk after spending the night with a whore and bragging about it?"

Trefor flushed. "I was drunk and a fool, but Madoc took advantage of it, so he got the woman I loved and the land and castle that should have been mine—just as he'd always wanted."

"What of Gwendolyn, whom you claimed to have loved?" she demanded. "Was she supposed to believe that you loved her after the way you humiliated her?"

Madoc's eyes would have blazed with anger; Trefor's gaze grew as cold as snow on a frozen river. "If she'd loved me as she said she did, she would never have married Madoc. She would have forgiven me."

"As you've forgiven your brother?" she countered.

The Welshman scowled. "You know only his side, my lady, not mine."

"Very well," she said, sitting down again. "I shall listen to your side."

He hesitated a moment, then threw himself onto the bench opposite her. "Did Madoc tell you why I got drunk? Did he explain why I went with that whore, to you or anyone?

"No, he didn't," he said, answering his own question, "although he knows. I got drunk because I saw the oh-so-very-*honorable* Madoc kissing Gwendolyn—and she was kissing him back. I went with another woman because they'd both betrayed me. I was going to announce their duplicity to everybody gathered for the wedding, but first I got drunk and slept with a whore. Why not? Why not go with another woman after what they'd done?"

He smiled at her with cold satisfaction. "The *honorable* Madoc left that out, didn't he? He didn't tell our father, either, or anyone else, so that all the disgrace fell on me. That way, he got Gwendolyn, and our father disinherited me."

"If what you say is true," Roslynn said slowly, not willing to accept what he said at face value, "and Gwendolyn betrayed you, too, perhaps it was just as well you didn't marry her. But you could have confronted them when you saw them. If not then, you could have gone to your father yourself and called off the wedding. You could have behaved with honor and then you would have had Llanpowell at least."

Trefor sniffed with derisive scorn. "You don't understand at all, do you? I *loved* Gwendolyn, and I loved my brother, too. So when I saw them and realized how they'd betrayed me, I couldn't *think*. They'd broken my heart, as well as my trust." He regarded her with skeptical disdain. "I'm forgetting the Normans don't understand love."

"*I* understand, more than you can imagine," she replied, beginning to feel a little sympathy for him, despite what he had done. "I understand making mistakes in the name of love. I've done so myself, made terrible errors that affected my family because I loved, or thought I did. But it was *I* who paid the heaviest price. I didn't try to assuage my wounded pride by hurting anyone else. That's why I did as

John commanded and came here to marry your brother. I wanted to spare my family more trouble and shame. Yet you act like a child, stealing your brother's sheep."

Trefor's gaze hardened to ice. "He's lied about that, too. I've done nothing but seek justice and reparation. He stole from me first, and I've few enough sheep as it is, so I took back an equal number. That's all I've done since. If that's not the truth, why hasn't he sought justice from his good friend, King John?"

"Because he doesn't want to be responsible for your death if you're convicted," she replied, wondering what the truth really was. She couldn't believe Madoc could be so petty and vindictive, so greedy and ambitious. Madoc was hot-tempered and brash, he certainly felt anger toward his brother, but he wasn't a thief.

Yet she was also beginning to believe that Trefor had some justification for his bitter resentment.

Perhaps the truth lay somewhere in between, hidden beneath misunderstandings and hurt feelings. "If what you say is true, why haven't you accused your brother in a court of law?"

"Because Madoc has Llanpowell and so is more powerful than me. They'd surely take his word over mine."

Roslynn had seen enough of kings and courts to

realize that Trefor might have good cause for that conviction.

"What of the black ram?" she asked. "What ram of yours had Madoc stolen and killed?"

"He stole more than that on my wedding day—he stole the woman I loved," Trefor retorted.

He rose and pulled Roslynn to her feet, the coldness in his eyes replaced by the heat of angry lust. "By God, I ought to make him suffer the way he's made me."

Panic came, and fear, but it fled just as quickly, overcome by the certainty that even if Madoc wasn't here, he could still protect her. "What do you think Madoc will do to you if you do?"

"It might be worth it to find out," Trefor growled as he pulled her close.

Never again!

It wasn't fear and panic rushing through her now. It was anger and pride. She was Lady Roslynn of Llanpowell, and she would fight to protect her honor.

She grabbed for his sword, simultaneously twisting away and pulling it from the sheath so quickly that Trefor didn't realize what she'd done until she had the tip of his own sword against his chest.

"I'll kill you," she warned. "Let us go, or by all the saints in heaven, I'll run you through!"

Although he held out his arms in surrender, he

didn't look afraid. He looked…respectful. "I don't doubt it," he said, "but you seem to think I should be afraid to die. I'm not, since Gwendolyn has gone before me."

He began to lower his arms. "And I have no difficulty letting you go, as I never planned to keep you, or your parents, or their men, or harm you, either. I'm no murderer. I didn't even come after you on purpose. I was headed south on other business. Meeting you was just a coincidence and it was only to annoy Madoc I brought you here when I realized who you were. I see now that was a mistake."

"Yes, it was," she said, still keeping the heavy sword pointed at him.

"I give you my word, which is as valuable to me as Madoc's is to him, that you and your party will be safe here," Trefor said. "You're my guests, and tomorrow you'll be free to go, which is what I always intended. It's too dark to travel now. And I promise no harm will come to you and I'll never touch you again." His arms fell to his sides. "Although if you tell Madoc, I suppose my days are numbered."

She finally lowered the sword. "He may very well want to kill you *if* I tell him what you did."

Trefor's unusual eyes widened. "You might not?"

"I *should*," she replied. "Except that Madoc and his men will surely attack Pontyrmwr and innocent men may die. Whatever happened between the two of you and Gwendolyn, that's a poor reason for other men to lose their lives."

Trefor slowly shook his head. "By God, Madoc's a fool indeed if he's sent you away. If you were my wife…"

Roslynn blinked as he seemed to shift and sway. So did the stone walls of the keep. The sword grew too heavy to hold, then fell from her hands as all around her went black.

MADOC STOOD on the outer wall walk facing the road leading to his castle, scarcely believing the evidence of his own eyes. Yet it was true—a soldier bearing the banner of Lord James de Briston was leading a cortege coming toward Llanpowell, and there was the wagon that had taken Roslynn away from him. The cortege was not moving quickly, which meant they must not have been attacked or otherwise in danger, so what else could this return mean but that Roslynn had decided to come back to him?

"Open the gates!" he shouted as he ran to a nearby ladder and skittered down it as if he were part monkey, a creature he'd seen once at a fair.

He dashed to the gate and came to a stumbling halt, only then realizing how he must look to the guards—the lord of Llanpowell as excited as a boy because his wife had changed her mind.

He didn't care what Roslynn made of his enthusiasm, but there were his garrison and household, her parents and the men of their escort to consider. It would be better to meet his wife and her family formally in the courtyard and save the true expression of his joy and relief for when he and Roslynn were alone.

Resolved to be more dignified, he started for the inner gate at a more leisurely pace, straightening his tunic as he went.

It seemed that word of Roslynn's return had already reached the household by the time he got to the yard, for Uncle Lloyd was already waiting, hopping from foot to foot like an overeager boy.

"It's true, isn't it?" he cried when he saw Madoc. "She's coming back. I knew it was only a little fit of temper—but I didn't think she'd change her mind so quick. A mite stubborn, I thought, but look you, here she comes!"

"Aye, here she comes," Madoc replied, trying to act calm, wondering if he was fooling anyone. He hadn't slept at all last night, mentally replaying over and over all the things he'd said and done wrong, and not only where Roslynn was concerned.

"You're not going to be stubborn, too, are you?"

Uncle Lloyd asked anxiously, sliding him a wary glance. "She's had time to calm down and think it over and come to her senses. You ought to be gracious and generous and come to yours."

Worried Roslynn might still be upset with him, he considered warning his uncle that all might not be completely well between them yet, even though he was prepared to do all he could to make it so. "You don't know what we fought about."

Uncle Lloyd blushed. "Well, no, I don't, but it's not so serious you can't make up, is it? Look you, Madoc, she's coming back to you. For a proud woman, that's no small concession."

Feeling a little more hopeful, Madoc permitted himself a small smile. "Aye, and so of course I'll be magnanimous and welcome her back with open arms."

And take her to their chamber, take her in his arms and…

Ivor appeared, hurrying from the stables. "What's this I hear?" he asked as he reached Madoc and Lloyd. "Is it true Lady Roslynn and her parents are returning?"

"Aye. They must be in the outer ward already," Lloyd gleefully replied. "What did I tell you? Just a little lovers' spat, that's all."

It had been more serious than that, but if that's

what Lloyd and others believed, Madoc wasn't going to disillusion them. Ivor, however, was more perceptive, and more skeptical.

"Naturally I hoped this breach could be mended," he said slowly, "although I confess I thought it would take longer. She always struck me as a rather stubborn and defiant young woman."

"She is, and so it's no wonder we quarreled. I expect we will again," Madoc replied, even though he wished with all his heart they wouldn't. "However, since she's my wife, I'm sure I can count on you to treat her with all due respect, even when we disagree."

"Naturally, she has my respect," Ivor said, "but I also hope she isn't going to be one of those wives who goes running off to her parents every time you quarrel."

Madoc didn't reply because he wasn't listening. Lord James had just ridden into the courtyard and the wagon was rumbling in behind him.

Madoc meant to stay where he was, as if Roslynn and her parents were visiting dignitaries. He didn't want to act like a besotted lover. Yet in spite of his desire to appear the cool, calm nobleman, his heart's longing propelled him toward the wagon as fast as he could go without breaking into a run.

"Lord James, welcome back to Llanpowell," he

said, managing to at least sound calm, and despite the strained expression on the Norman's face, as if he thought his daughter was making a mistake coming home.

"This was not my choice," the nobleman bluntly replied. "Your brother stopped us on the road south of here and forced us to accompany him to his keep and—"

"Where's Roslynn?" Madoc demanded as a fear unlike anything he'd ever felt swept over him. If his brother had hurt her, if he'd so much as touched her—

"I'm here, Madoc," she called weakly from the wagon.

In two strides, Madoc was beside it and threw open the door.

Roslynn reclined against her mother. She looked pale and exhausted, and another thought came to him, dark and terrible.

If Trefor had dishonored her, he would die before the day was out.

"I'm all right, Madoc," she said, rising to get out of the wagon, until her mother held her back.

"You shouldn't walk," Lady Eloise said to her daughter before addressing Madoc, and her words were like a noose around his heart. "She's bleeding. Help me get her to a bed."

CHAPTER NINETEEN

MORE TERRIFIED than if he faced a hundred foes single-handedly, Madoc leaned into the wagon and lifted Roslynn, unresisting, in his arms. Her silent acquiescence, her listless manner, made him want to wail with dismay. She was too much like Gwendolyn at the last, bleeding and exhausted and dying.

"Gently, gently," Lady Eloise unnecessarily urged as he backed out of the wagon.

Roslynn nestled against him as he carried her to the hall, trailed by her parents and an unnaturally silent Uncle Lloyd.

"Lloyd, see to Lord James's men and I want more men on watch—everywhere," Madoc ordered while silently praying that Roslynn and the child would both be well.

Once in the hall, Madoc shouted for Bron to bring fresh linen and warm water to the bedchamber, and to Lowri to fetch coals for the brazier. To

Rhonwen he called for bread and mulled wine, and sent another servant for the village midwife.

Despite these orders, by the time he got Roslynn to their bed, there was a crowd of anxious servants behind him.

He set Roslynn carefully down and looked into her pale, beloved face, ready to apologize for the actions of his brother, himself, the king, for anything that would make her well again. "Roslynn-fy-rhosyn, I—"

"Leave us," her mother interrupted, taking command as if this were her own household. "My daughter needs to rest."

His pride subdued by his fear for Roslynn's health and her mother's matronly authority, he didn't argue. "I'll send the midwife up to you as soon as she arrives."

While the women clustered around the bed like a flock of worried birds, Madoc slowly left the chamber, his feet heavy.

Uncle Lloyd bustled up to him the moment he entered the hall.

"No need for such dismay, nephew," his uncle excitedly assured him in Welsh. "Her father says it isn't enough to threaten her life or the babe's."

Madoc realized he hadn't seen her father since they'd come into the hall. "Where is Lord James?"

"Seeing to the stabling of his horses," Lloyd replied. "He told me Trefor sent for a physician and midwife both after Roslynn swooned again and Lady Eloise told him she was with child. They were both sure she hasn't lost the child and there's every hope they'll both be fine."

Madoc's surprise that Trefor had sent for such help was quickly consumed by his growing rage. "It's good he took such care, because if anything had happened to Roslynn while she was in Pontyrmwr, I'd attack with all the force I could muster and I'd kill him myself.

"And he'll still have to answer for abducting her," he finished, meaning it. Trefor had gone way too far this time. Roslynn was more precious to him than his sheep, or even his own life.

"Aye, I suppose you're right," Lloyd muttered, thoughtfully stroking his beard.

"Suppose?" Madoc cried. "*Suppose?* What he did was criminal and I intend to make him pay."

"But she's come back safe and sound, and no harm done. And Trefor's still your brother."

"*Now* you'll defend him?" Madoc demanded incredulously, his hands on his hips.

"Well, it's true he's done a bad thing, Madoc. More than one," he hastily added when he saw Madoc's expression. "But he could have let her go without the expense of the physician and midwife."

Madoc didn't give a damn about the cost to Trefor and said so.

"But there's more. Your brother and his men escorted them almost the whole way here, and he sent some of his men on ahead to make sure the road was clear and to fill any ruts. He didn't have to do that, either, Madoc."

"He had no business taking her to Pontyrmwr in the first place," Madoc retorted, not at all ready to ascribe any generous motives to his brother.

If anything had happened to Roslynn because of Trefor's vindictive act, he meant what he'd said— he would hunt Trefor down and kill him.

"All right, never mind that. The physician said that while neither she nor the baby are in danger at present, a long journey is out of the question. The jostling of the wagon or on horseback would be too much. The physician said coming back to Llanpowell would be all right, but that must be the only traveling she does until the baby's born.

"Do you understand what I'm saying, you hot-tempered young fool?" his uncle gently chided. "She can't leave now. She'll have to stay in Llanpowell until after your child is born."

So he would have even more time to make things right between them. But what if the loss of their child was to be the price?

MADOC WAS STILL PACING the dais, Uncle Lloyd had nodded off in his chair and Lord James was sipping an evil-smelling concoction that was supposed to help his cough when Lady Eloise came down to tell them Roslynn was sleeping peacefully and was not to be disturbed.

Madoc nodded his acquiescence to her edict, and offered her and her husband the hospitality of his hall. Then he went to find Ivor.

WHEN IVOR WASN'T in his workroom, Madoc guessed the armory would be the most likely place he would find his steward.

As he crossed the yard toward it, Ivor came around the corner of the stable and immediately hurried to him as fast as his limp would allow.

"By all the saints, Madoc, it's true then?" he exclaimed, gesturing at the wagon that still stood by the gates, although Lord James's horses had been unhitched and taken to the stable. "Your wife and her parents were taken by force to Pontyrmwr but Trefor let them go and they've come back because your wife's unwell?"

"Aye."

Ivor sucked in his breath. "God save us, Madoc, I'm sorry."

"I need to speak with you. In private."

Ivor nodded and together they went to his work-room, not saying a word as they passed through the kitchen. Hywel and the other servants paused in their labors and watched them curiously, until Ivor unlocked the workroom door.

Then Hywel started as if he'd been awakened from his sleep. "What are you all doing?" he cried. "We've a meal to make and guests come back, too!"

The servants immediately went back to work.

Having opened the door, Ivor stood aside to let Madoc precede him, then followed him into the room, closing the door and bolting it. He hurried to strike a flint and light the thick candle on the table.

"Do you think we've got a spy in Llanpowell?" Madoc asked without preamble as he stood in the middle of the room.

"A spy?" Ivor repeated warily.

"Yes. Is it possible somebody in Llanpowell is giving Trefor information? About who's coming and going, or where my patrols will be?"

Ivor quickly recovered. "No, I don't," he firmly replied. "Your garrison and servants are loyal to you, Madoc. I'd wager my life on it."

Madoc would have, too, until today. "You're cer-tain there's no greedy servant, no disgruntled soldier

or anyone else, who'd be willing to sell such information?"

"Aye," Ivor replied, although he appeared and
sounded a little less confident. "Look you, Madoc,
even if someone was tempted, he'd have to realize
what you'd do if he were caught. How could Trefor
afford the amount it would take to make a man run
that risk? The income from Pontyrmwr's barely
enough to hire and feed his mercenaries, let alone
pay for bribes."

That was true, and it was some comfort, although
Madoc noticed Ivor still looked worried.

"If there's someone you suspect of such activity,
even if you have no proof, tell me," he said.

"Of course I would," Ivor replied. He hesitated
a moment, then regarded Madoc with a pleading expression. "Don't you think this business with Trefor
and your wife is rather strange?"

"I never expected him to do anything so bold, not
when they had an escort of Norman soldiers."

"That, too," Ivor agreed. "But it seems surprisingly generous of him to send for a physician and
a midwife he could ill afford to pay."

"No doubt he feared the consequences if anything
had happened to my wife—as well he should."

Ivor's look became almost...pitying. "Perhaps he

had another reason, and I don't mean kindness. And perhaps there was a reason she went to Pontyrmwr."

Madoc's brow furrowed with confusion. "What sort of reason? She was abducted, taken there by force against her will."

"Was she?"

"Of course!" he retorted, aghast at Ivor's implication. "You think Roslynn or her parents would lie to me about that? That she has some sinister motive for meeting with my brother, or her parents do? And if that were so—which I don't believe for a moment—why, then, would they come back?"

"Because she fell ill and couldn't go farther and your home is more comfortable. Or because it serves John to have you two at odds, and this supposed abduction was planned to inflame your conflict. Maybe she was sent here simply to cause disruption, or maybe she had something to tell Trefor.

"What do we *really* know of her, Madoc?" Ivor persisted. "Even now, how well do you truly know your wife?"

Madoc crossed his arms. "I refuse to believe that Roslynn's in league with my brother, or on some surreptitious mission for the king."

Not his Roslynn. Not the woman who had been so warm and loving, so passionate and so determined to be an exemplary chatelaine.

Ivor's expression softened with sympathy. "I'm not saying she'd gladly or even willingly betray your trust, Madoc, but who knows what she might have had to agree to do for the king if it meant she wasn't accused and convicted of treason along with her husband? Or to show her gratitude." His gaze faltered. "Although I've hesitated to say it, I'm not the only one in Llanpowell who wonders… Well, and not doubting your virility, Madoc, but she got with child quickly, didn't she?"

No. He would not believe that, either.

"Gwendolyn got with child quickly, too," he pointed out, his voice as hard as iron, his temper rising.

"No one doubts you're Owain's father, but Gwendolyn wasn't a Norman come from John's court, you see."

It was as if his heart had been turned to stone, until he remembered Roslynn's fervent assertion that the child was his.

No, he would not believe she was lying, that she had looked him in the eye and spoken so sincerely while all the while telling him a monstrous falsehood.

"I will not accuse my wife of adultery," he said firmly. "I believe the child she carries is mine, and so you should say to anyone who claims otherwise."

He thought of another proof of her innocence. "Nor do I think she's guilty of any treachery with

Trefor, although someone else may be. Trefor's always seemed to know where my patrols would be before Roslynn ever came to Llanpowell."

"Very well, Madoc," Ivor said as he leaned back against the table, "but as you don't think she's betrayed you, I don't question the loyalty of any in this household or your garrison. It could be Trefor's managed to steal your sheep when your patrols were elsewhere through luck, or because his men are keeping watch on the border of your estate.

"But if you're certain your wife didn't go willingly with Trefor—"

"I am."

"Then surely the time has come to stop him."

"Aye," Madoc grimly agreed. "The time has come."

"HAVE YOU GONE MAD?" Ioan protested after Madoc went to the barracks and told his men his plan. "You've got to take us with you. You can't ride into Pontyrmwr by yourself. You'll be killed."

Madoc's grim expression didn't change, nor did his mind. If Trefor hadn't let Roslynn, her parents and their men go, if he hadn't sent for a physician and midwife to tend her, if anything serious had happened to his wife or her family, Madoc would have gathered his men and attacked Pontyrmwr without mercy or remorse. He truly would have struck down his brother himself.

However, because Trefor had sent them all back unharmed, he would give his brother one final warning, one last chance to make peace and end this conflict. "I'm going under a flag of truce."

He flicked the white cloth he'd snatched from the kitchen as he'd passed through after leaving Ivor. "I don't think even Trefor's so far from honor that he won't respect it."

"What if you're wrong?" Hugh the Beak demanded. "What then?"

"Then I'm dead," Madoc replied. "Still, I'll not be so sure of his honor that I won't take a dagger in my belt."

"But Madoc—" Ioan began.

"I am the lord of Llanpowell," he interrupted, "and I give the orders here. I go to Pontyrmwr alone, and no one is to follow. Do you understand?"

Ioan and the others reluctantly nodded.

"What do we tell your wife if you don't come back?" Hugh asked quietly.

"That I wish her well and trust that she'll raise a fine child."

CHAPTER TWENTY

THE SUN WAS LOW in the sky when Madoc approached the rough stone wall that surrounded his brother's keep. Ten of Trefor's men followed him, from the first who'd called a challenge to him as he'd ridden down the rocky, muddy road that led to Pontyrmwr, to the last who'd joined the band behind him only a few yards back.

Whether it was the white flag, or his lack of obvious weapons, or because he was Trefor's brother, Madoc wasn't sure, but he'd not been attacked.

Madoc didn't recognize any of the men behind him and didn't think they were even Welsh. Trefor obviously hired mercenaries without caring where they came from, although what he paid them with, Madoc had no idea. Pontyrmwr was not a large estate and wouldn't yield much income, although Trefor could probably have made more of it if he'd spent less time stealing sheep and nursing his grievances.

He passed but one cottage—little more than a

hut, really—with a lone silent woman watching from the door. The few scraggly chickens in the yard barely made a sound as they scratched for food.

Unlike Llanpowell, there were no woods to speak of, only sparse, gnarled trees, gorse, bracken and bog, and he had to fight the dread that scent of muddy, soft ground always roused.

As for the fortress itself, it was barely enough to deserve the name.

Madoc reached the gates in the single outer wall, and they swung open before he could announce his arrival. Through the opening he could see Trefor, his hands on his hips and a scowl on his face, standing in the center of a courtyard that was little bigger than the hall of Llanpowell.

At nearly the same time, rain began to fall. Trefor didn't so much as flinch, and neither did Madoc as he rode into his brother's stronghold—not even when he dismounted and the gates swung shut behind him, meeting with an ominous thud.

"What do you want?" Trefor demanded, drawing Madoc's attention away from his survey of the dilapidated buildings. Besides the round and ancient stone keep, there were a few other buildings of decaying wood that looked cobbled together and haphazardly repaired.

Madoc looked at his brother who had caused so

much trouble and misery, and fought to control his rage, to do what he'd come to do and then get out, never to see his brother again. "I came to thank you for sending my wife and her parents back to me."

Trefor's eyes narrowed. "She's well then?"

"Well enough."

The rain began to fall faster and Trefor swiped his hand over his face before he grudgingly muttered, as courtesy demanded, "You're welcome to my hall."

If it hadn't started to rain, Madoc would have stayed where he was and let all in Pontyrmwr hear what he had to say; under these conditions, and because his brother might think he was afraid if he refused, Madoc inclined his head and followed as his brother led the way into the dingy, smoky keep. The windows were mere arrow loops, and there was no chimney to let out the smoke from the braziers trying to warm the chilly structure.

Inside were more rough men who got to their feet as they entered, hands on the hilts of their swords, suspicion and hatred in their eyes, as well as a few slatternly women who scurried away, including one young woman who had hair the same color as Gwendolyn's. Maybe Trefor had found some consolation for the loss of his intended bride.

Trefor scowled as he threw himself onto a

scarred bench near the largest brazier and sharply gestured for Madoc to sit on an equally battered bench opposite.

He did not sit, and Trefor's frown deepened. "Not so neat and tidy as your hall, no doubt, but I don't have a pretty Norman wife to run my household. Don't have a wife at all, thanks to you."

"That's not my fault," Madoc replied, "and I haven't come to reminisce or listen to your whining. I've come to say that it's a good thing no harm came to my wife because of your actions, or you'd be dead. Come onto my land one more time, Trefor, if you or any of your men set so much as a toe on my estate, we will fight you. It's only because you sent for a physician and midwife that I'm giving you this warning instead of attacking Pontyrmwr now with all the men at my command."

Madoc ignored the muttering of the men around him and the sound of swords being unsheathed as he watched Trefor's lip curl with disdain. "What, *you* come against *me* in open battle? I thought you more likely to run to the Norman king. You're John's lackey, after all."

It took every ounce of self-control Madoc possessed not to throw himself at his brother and knock him to the ground as he'd done before. "I am no man's lackey. I am the lord of Llanpowell."

"You're my little brother," Trefor replied, the knuckles of his hands turning white as he gripped the edge of the bench as if about to launch himself at Madoc. "My jealous, envious little brother, Mumble-mouth, who repaid me for all the attention I paid him, all the lessons I taught, by stealing what was mine. You got Gwendolyn, you got Llanpowell, you even got a son with her, by God, and now a new wife to give you more, while I have nothing but this rotten pile of rubble and a few stinking sheep!"

"I took nothing that was truly yours," Madoc retorted. "You lost Gwendolyn by your own actions, and your estate because of what you did. I had no hand in it."

Trefor rose abruptly. Madoc stood firm, so they were nose to nose.

"I loved Gwen—you never did!" Trefor charged, his usual cold demeanor twisted with the heat of a fury to equal Madoc's. "You only wanted her because she was mine!"

Trefor raised his fist. Madoc tensed, feet planted, waiting for the blow, as he reached for his dagger.

So Roslynn must have waited many times, fearing the fury of a man bigger and stronger and cruel. No wonder, then, she was afraid of him when he was angry. No wonder, then, that she wouldn't ever love him.

Trefor didn't strike. He slowly lowered his fist and shook his head. "I'm not going to hit you, Mumble-mouth. Unlike you, I can control my temper. And I won't make your pretty lady wife a widow for the second time, not when she's with child. You should thank her for saving your life when you get back home. Now get out of my keep and off my land and never come back."

Madoc drew a deep, shuddering breath as he willed his ire to recede.

"And you stay off mine," he warned, "or that day will be your last."

There could never be any reconciliation between them—nor did he want one. Not now, and not ever.

"Treat your wife well, Mumble-mouth, or maybe one day she'll be coming to back to Pontyrmwr and the better man," Trefor jeered as Madoc passed through the gathered men who made way for him.

Madoc paused on the threshold. "While you have neither wife nor son to bear your name."

Then the lord of Llanpowell walked out, leaving his lonely, bitter brother in his dirty, drafty keep.

"HE WENT TO Pontyrmwr alone?" Roslynn whispered, staring at her father with horror.

To think she'd been so happy and relieved to be back at Llanpowell, knowing the bleeding had stopped, especially when Madoc had taken her in his arms, only to wake and discover what he'd done.

"That's what the man Ioan told me," Lord James confirmed. "I gather your husband was most adamant and refused an escort."

"Perhaps things aren't as bad between Madoc and his brother as you think," her mother suggested.

She, too, was in Roslynn's chamber, sitting on the stool by the bed. "His brother treated us well, and did everything he could for you after you swooned again. Maybe Madoc went to thank him."

Roslynn would like to believe that, but knowing Madoc's tempestuous nature, she could not. "How long has he—"

"Long enough to be back again," Madoc himself announced from the doorway.

Thank God! She could swoon again with relief to see him standing hale and hearty before her.

"I assume Lady Roslynn is feeling better?"

He spoke so formally, so coolly, as if she were any other visitor who might have taken ill. Worst of all, though, she couldn't tell what he was feeling. She had always been able to read his emotions, but now it was as if he spoke through a veil.

What could she expect after she had left him? "Much better," she said.

"Good. I would speak with you alone, Roslynn."

Still so cold, so aloof. What had happened to his fiery temper? How had he become so distant, so stern, so remote?

Had that not been what she'd wanted? her conscience chided. A calm demeanor, a manner devoid of anger—but apparently all other emotions, too.

Roslynn nodded her agreement and her parents immediately departed, while Madoc came to stand at the foot of the bed like a grim and silent effigy.

"You went to see Trefor," she said, deciding to speak first if he would not.

"To warn him that if he or his men set foot on my land again, he will rue it, for next time, I *will* act."

She could see his steadfast resolve, heard the finality in his deep voice and knew this threat was genuine. Trefor had finally pushed him too far.

Although Trefor had wronged him more than once, for whatever reason, she hated to think she would bear any responsibility if men of Llanpowell died in such an attack, especially Madoc. "We were treated well, like guests. All of us, our men included."

"If it had been otherwise, my brother would already be dead, and his men with him.

"But I didn't come here to talk about my brother," Madoc continued. "I understand further travel might cause you and the baby harm, so you must stay in Llanpowell."

It was not a request.

Clutching the bedclothes as if they were a rope pulling her from within a deep well, she decided she wouldn't lose this chance to speak to him about his brother, to try to have some good come from the ruin of their marriage. "Trefor says he's taken your sheep only because you stole from him first—that, like you, he seeks only just reparation."

Her husband crossed his powerful arms. "That's a lie, or more of his self-serving excuses. He also calls my marriage to Gwendolyn a theft and my inheritance of Llanpowell a robbery."

She shifted, so she was sitting more upright. "Is it possible that you both have been robbed by someone else and not each other? Isn't it possible that whoever is stealing your livestock is using your feud to mask their thievery? You've both only blamed each other instead of searching for anyone else."

"No one else but Trefor would dare to steal from Llanpowell."

"Will you not at least *consider* the chance that Trefor is innocent and someone else to blame?"

Anger sparked in his eyes, but this time, she was glad to see it. Better the Madoc she knew than this cold stranger.

"Trefor's lying, trying to stir up more trouble between us," Madoc said, "and he's succeeding, if you take his word over mine."

"I don't, but I can believe there's a third party at work, profiting from this feud." She hurried on before Madoc stormed out of the room, as he looked about to do. "Trefor told me something else, that the day before he was to marry Gwendolyn, he saw you kissing her."

Madoc's face reddened and his body tensed. "There is your proof that he's a lying scoundrel. I never kissed Gwendolyn until after the priest blessed our union."

"Did you kiss *anyone* that day?"

"No, or I would—"

Madoc fell silent, and it was as if he'd hardened into a statue of a man stunned.

"By the saints," he whispered in a voice like a ghost's in a sepulchre, his arms dropping to his sides. "There *was* a woman. Her name was Haldis. She was Gwendolyn's cousin."

He felt for the stool and sat heavily. "Trefor thought *she* was Gwendolyn?"

"He also says he told you what he'd seen when he finally arrived at his wedding."

"God, no, he didn't!" Madoc jumped to his feet and stared at her in disbelief. "He just kept saying he knew what I'd done. As far as I knew, I hadn't done anything wrong—and I hadn't! It was just a few kisses in the shadows, because I was young and a little drunk and Haldis looked like Gwendolyn and she let me. He should have known I'd never betray him like that—*never!* How could he even *think* it?"

"Because you loved Gwendolyn. You said so yourself and I daresay he knew it, too. You aren't very good at hiding your feelings, Madoc."

He was too open, too honest. What he felt others saw, good or bad.

"He should have known that on my honor I wouldn't have touched her, not when he loved her and they were to be married," Madoc protested as if she were his judge. "Gwendolyn would never have betrayed him, either. She loved him too much."

"Yet she married you so quickly."

"Aye, because…" He strode away, then returned, his expression a mixture of rage and anguish. "Because he'd shamed her and our families. If only he'd trusted us—or come right out with his suspicion, I could have told him he was mistaken. God help us all, I could have proven it—Bron would have vouched for me, and Uncle Lloyd, too. He saw me with Haldis and started to tease us about getting married next. That's when I left her and went to bed."

"Now that you know the truth, can you not find it in your heart to forgive him?"

To her dismay, Madoc's expression grew as hard as flint, as adamant as iron. "No. He destroyed her happiness, and much of mine, grieved and disgraced our parents, all because he made a mistake and believed us capable of such dishonor."

"Yes, he made a mistake that night and his heart was broken. You made a mistake when you were so quick to take his place—"

"What?" he cried angrily. "Would you blame me still?"

"Could you not have waited even one day? Can you swear to me on the life of your son that there was no rivalry between you, no ambition, that you never saw a chance to gain?"

"No! I did it for Gwendolyn, and my parents and the alliance."

"And because you loved her," she insisted, determined to make him see that if Trefor was to blame, so was he. "Because you wanted her and Trefor himself had given you the chance to have her."

"All right, I wanted her," he retorted. "I thought she was the prettiest, sweetest creature God had ever made. Does that please you, to hear that? I wanted her and I married her—and regretted it the moment the vows were exchanged."

Arms stiff at his sides, he fixed Roslynn with his glare. "I know your first wedding night was hellish.

Now I'll tell you about mine." He pointed at a spot beside her. "She lay there sobbing all night long, aye, and every night thereafter, because she was sorry she'd married me and loved Trefor still. She never loved me and never would. And then she died—with *his* name on her lips.

"So don't ask me to forgive Trefor, because I can't and I won't. I don't care what mistakes he made—others have paid for them, and Gwendolyn is dead."

Madoc crossed his arms and regarded her with a scorn that broke her heart. "Is that why he took you, to make you his advocate? Or was there another, royal hand at work?"

She fought back tears, for she would not let him see her cry. "I am no man's advocate," she said with a coldness to counter the heat of his anger. "And what do you mean, a royal hand? Do you suspect John sent me to your brother, or wanted me to speak to him? Why, when he sent me to you to be your wife?"

"To cause dissension between us, to make us attack each other until we're both destroyed," Madoc said, moving back. "To be our Helen."

"No, he did not. He sent me to be your reward, as Lord Alfred said. I didn't even know you had a brother until after I arrived."

His glowering gaze faltered for a moment.

"Or do you think I'm lying?"

"No," he brusquely replied as he started for the door.

Before he could open it, Lord James burst into the room, followed by his wife. "I don't care if you're her husband or not, you've been here long enough. My daughter is to rest. The physician said so."

"Then she should rest," Madoc said with a stiff bow. "You are both welcome to stay here until Roslynn is fit to travel or the babe is born."

"I must return to my own estate," Lord James replied. "However, my wife will remain until the child comes."

"As you wish." Madoc glanced back at Roslynn, his eyes inscrutable. "For the sake of your health, my lady, I think it would be best if we slept apart."

Her heart broken, her hopes dashed, she saw no reason to disagree. "Yes, I think that would be best for both of us."

CHAPTER TWENTY-ONE

"WELL, THEN, here you are," Lloyd said to Madoc several weeks later, having finally found him at the tanning yards downriver from the castle.

Madoc stood near the lime vats, where the cow-hides were immersed until the hair grew loose and the fat grew white and easily visible. The stench was enough to make Lloyd's eyes water, although not so bad as the offal pits farther away.

The smell didn't seem to bother Madoc. Nothing seemed to bother Madoc these days. Despite the return of his wife and her good health since those worrying early days of her pregnancy, it was as if Madoc was only half-alive, although these should be happy days for everyone in Llanpowell. Trefor had stopped stealing; the price for wool, sheepskin and leather was high; and there was to be another child for the lord of Llanpowell.

"Plenty of wool and parchment this year, eh?" Lloyd noted, warily eyeing his nephew and once more trying to understand what was going on in that heart of his. "Ivor says we'll have some lovely soft leather for the gambesons. Maybe you'd like some for gloves? Or a new girdle for your wife?"

Madoc sighed. He did a lot of that these days, too. "Is there something you wanted, Uncle?"

"No, nothing in particular," Lloyd replied, looking around. "Just thought I'd come see what you were up to. We'll have a good income this year, eh, Madoc? No need to worry we'll be hungry come the winter."

"Aye."

His nephew started walking toward the heap of willow and oak bark used for tanning, and Lloyd trotted after him. "So, March, then, the midwife says. Busy time of year for a babe to be born."

Madoc didn't reply as he peered into the tan vat, where several layers of hides and tanning material lay.

"Lady Roslynn's looking well, thank God. And up to running the household, with her mother's help, of course. I like Lady Eloise. Doesn't interfere or look down her nose. Reminds me of your own mother some days, she does."

Madoc straightened. "I know you hate coming to the tanning yard, Uncle, so I assume there's something important you wish to discuss. Well?"

Lloyd gave his nephew a disgruntled frown. "I

can't stand to see you miserable, that's all, and your wife, too. Whatever you quarreled about before she left, surely to God you've both had plenty of time to calm down and make up. Look you, she came back and she's living under your roof—"

"I won't discuss my marriage, Uncle. Not with you or Ivor or anyone."

Not even if the tension between him and his wife was almost palpable, and like a distemper in the household.

"If you're still at odds, what will happen when the child comes?" Lloyd demanded.

"Roslynn will go home with her parents and take the child with her."

Madoc had spent many lonely hours thinking about the future, which had once seemed so bright. Since Roslynn's return, it had only stretched bleakly before him.

He'd rather she go home with her parents and take their child with her than remain here. If she stayed, the longing for her would surely drive him to despair and rage and perhaps even madness.

Lloyd's face fell. "You can't mean that. Why, I thought when I saw you working on that cradle…"

"The babe needs a cradle. There's nothing more to it than that."

"Then why didn't you have the carpenter make

it? You would if you didn't care, so no more beating about the bushes with me, Madoc ap Gruffydd. You love the woman. I know it, Ivor knows it, everybody in Llanpowell knows it. And she cares for you, too, despite whatever the hell you argued about. I can see it in her eyes when she looks at you when you aren't looking back. Why can't you apologize or make it up to her?"

Madoc turned to him and answered, his voice low but firm, his expression grimly resolute. "I said I won't discuss my marriage with you, or anyone. If you've nothing else to talk about, Uncle, go back to the hall and your *braggot*. We've plenty of that, Ivor says."

Lloyd flushed and spoke as one who washes his hands of a problem. "All right, Madoc, I'm going. But a pity it is, and I won't say otherwise. We all had such hopes for you, and now…well, it's too bad you're too proud and stubborn to make peace with your wife."

Madoc watched Lloyd march doggedly away, muttering under his breath. There was so much his uncle didn't know or understand, and never would.

ON A GRAY DAY late in February, Roslynn settled herself back in her chair and reached for her needle, wincing as she leaned too far forward for comfort. She put her hand to her swollen belly.

"He—or she—is certainly strong!" she said to her mother as the babe kicked.

Lady Eloise generally kept Roslynn company these days. Roslynn saw Madoc only at mealtimes, when he was polite but distant. It often seemed now that the first blissful days of their marriage had been a happy dream.

"That's good," her mother said with a smile as she put away another length of cloth she'd purchased for the baby.

Roslynn had tried to tell her they already had more than enough to dress the child for a year, yet every time her mother went to market, there would be another bit of cloth or trim she would find absolutely necessary to purchase.

"The midwife says it will be another month at least," Roslynn said with a sigh.

"First babies are generally late to arrive, although you were early."

As the time neared for the baby's birth, Roslynn found it difficult not to worry about the delivery, so she changed the subject. "How many baskets of fish did you count?"

Her mother had told her she'd seen the fishmonger arrive and make a delivery to the kitchen.

"Ten," Lady Eloise replied.

"Will you add this delivery to the list, or shall I?"

"I will," her mother said, fetching the piece of parchment where they'd been recording the tally of goods arriving if they noticed a delivery.

Even if she and Madoc were estranged, Roslynn had no intention of letting the steward cheat him, although sometimes goods arrived when they were otherwise occupied, or they didn't realize a merchant had come until the delivery was almost completed. Even so, there were over twenty-five notations Roslynn had managed to check against Ivor's list of payments in his workroom that didn't match.

She had thought of telling Madoc when there were five, but that had not seemed enough to prove that his trusted friend was cheating him.

She had again contemplated approaching him at ten, but that had been close to Christmas, and she had decided to wait until after the festivities, not that there was much merriment at Llanpowell that year, or as much as usual, she suspected. Everyone had seemed anxious and subdued, even Lloyd.

Her father had sent a small wooden chest that had been hers as a child, as well as a little wooden rattle full of dried beans. She had made Madoc a new tunic of the black wool from the ram's fleece that would surely fit him much better than the one he'd been married in, but he hadn't worn it or, she supposed, even tried it on. On Christmas morning, she had found a cradle by their bed, finely carved of oak and made by Madoc himself, so Lloyd had told her at mass later. She would have thanked Madoc, but he had been gone most of the day, although the air was freezing and there was snow upon the ground. By the time Madoc returned, the feast had already started and she'd had no chance to speak to him alone.

"I think we have enough information to tell Madoc of our suspicions," Roslynn said, putting those painful memories aside. "I can't be making too many more visits to Ivor's workroom to check the accounts. I can barely fit through the door now."

"Nor should you be wandering about," her mother added.

Although Roslynn hadn't bled or been ill since her return to Llanpowell, her mother constantly urged caution. Roslynn had heeded her mother's warnings and accepted her help whenever possible to run the household, too. Fortunately, perhaps because Madoc's own mother had been a Norman, Lady Eloise was well liked and respected, and things had gone smoothly, even with Ivor.

Roslynn ignored another twinge, for this was a very active baby and such movements weren't unusual. "Will you go and ask Madoc to come here?"

"Of course." Lady Eloise's mouth turned down

at the corners, as it always did when she was worried. "I'll be happy to stay with you."

"Thank you, but this will be painful for him to hear, so I think it would be better if we're alone."

He might get angry, but she didn't think he'd hurt her when she was so big with child. If he were even capable of hurting her.

Fortunately, although she had never told her parents exactly why she and her husband were no longer intimate, her mother made no protest. Nevertheless, Roslynn was certain her mother wouldn't be far away. She would stay close by, in case her daughter should find it necessary to call for her.

After her mother had gone, Roslynn picked up the little garment she'd been working on.

These days the bedchamber bore few signs that a man had ever shared it with her. Madoc's chest had disappeared before she'd returned from Pontyrmwr, and she'd never ventured to ask where it had gone or where he slept. Since her father had gone back to Briston, she and her mother shared the large bed, made up with her mother's sheets and blankets. The dressing table held some of her hair ribbons and pins, but also needles and thread, and bits of trim for the garments she was making for the baby.

There was a sharp knock before Madoc walked into the room. As always, he seemed to fill it with his presence, but, also as always since her return from Pontyrmwr, it was as if there was a stone wall separating them.

His expression unreadable, Madoc came toward her and picked up the little gown, examining it in the weak winter sunlight. "It's very small."

Roslynn folded her hands over her rounded belly. "I'm sure it will be large enough."

He put down the gown and raised a brow in query. "Your mother says you wanted to speak with me."

She took a deep breath. This wasn't going to be easy, even though she was sure she was right about Ivor and had the evidence to prove it. "Ivor's cheating you, Madoc. He's pretending to pay for more goods than you're receiving and keeping the difference."

She held out the list she and her mother had made over the past few months. "These are the occasions we can be sure about, when my mother or I were able to see the goods being unloaded and keep a count. Then I checked the number we counted against the number Ivor recorded and the amount he paid. As you can see, there are several discrepancies."

Madoc took the list and ran his eyes down the columns of goods and figures.

"I know you think he's your friend and you've trusted him, but he's cheating you. By cheating you, that man steals from our child, too—from his future inheritance, or her dowry, if the baby is a girl."

"Ivor wouldn't steal from me," Madoc said quietly, still staring at the list. "Not Ivor."

"You have the proof in your hands. There are too many differences to be simple mistakes or errors. This is a pattern, repeated over months. He's probably been doing it for years."

Madoc raised his eyes and held out his hand. "I'll deal with this at once. Since you accuse him, I think you should come with me."

She hadn't foreseen this; nevertheless, she wasn't afraid to confront the steward, because she was right and she knew it.

She took Madoc's hand and gripped it hard as she hoisted herself to her feet. It was the first time they had touched since he'd carried her to this chamber after she'd come back from Pontyrmwr, yet just as before, as always, the sensation of his flesh against hers warmed and thrilled her.

And now filled her with regret.

Going slowly for her sake, Madoc led her down the steps to the hall past her waiting mother. Madoc said nothing to Lady Eloise, and Roslynn shook her head slightly so her mother wouldn't ask questions.

Lloyd, seated near the dais, straightened eagerly when he saw them. "Well, now, and holding hands," he began excitedly, only to fall silent when Madoc shot him a censorious look.

Poor man, Roslynn thought, pitying him for his wasted hope. There could be no happy reunion for her and Madoc, now or ever, especially after she had showed him that a man he'd trusted like a brother had betrayed and robbed him. Although she wasn't responsible, a portion of Madoc's anger and distress would always attach to her because she'd been the one to tell him what Ivor had done.

They entered the kitchen where, not surprisingly, all the work ceased as the cook and the servants stopped to stare at them.

"Is Ivor in his chamber?" Madoc asked, his voice loud in the stillness.

"Aye, my lord," Hywel answered.

With a nod, Madoc and Roslynn proceeded to the workroom, leaving speculative whispers in their wake and Hywel complaining about nobles always traipsing through his kitchen. The door was open and Ivor sat at his table, a bag of silver open at his elbow, one of many scrolls unrolled in front of him. A large beeswax candle, the wax running down its side and spluttering in the chilly draft, illuminated the chamber.

Ivor looked up and his lips widened in a smile. "Madoc!" he cried, shoving the scroll away from him as he got to his feet. "And my lady! To what do I owe the honor?"

"I need to see the record of payments you've made to merchants for the past six months," Madoc said, tapping the rolled parchment Roslynn had given him on the top of the table, "and my wife should sit down."

"I'm quite all right," Roslynn said, hoping that Madoc's brusque manner meant he was ready to believe her. "I can be on my feet for a little while."

"I would rather you sit down."

Ivor was obsequiousness itself as he moved his chair closer to her. Since she didn't want to distract Madoc from the business at hand, she did as he wished, and without further protest.

Meanwhile, Ivor collected several scrolls and laid them on the table, glancing from time to time at the scroll Madoc already held.

"Is something amiss, Madoc?" he ventured when he was finished.

"I hope not," Madoc said, his voice controlled, although there was tension beneath.

She could see the strain, too, in the corners of his mouth and the lines of his brow, as he began to compare the lists.

"What's going on, Madoc?" Ivor asked as Madoc studied the records. "What is that other parchment?"

Madoc turned all the parchments so that Ivor could see and compare them himself. "This is my wife's accounting of goods delivered. As you can see, her numbers and yours don't match. You've apparently been paying for more goods than we received."

He regarded Ivor with angry eyes. "Since this has happened several times, I find it hard to believe it's only a mistake."

Ivor flushed and glanced at Roslynn before addressing Madoc. "So *she* says—and I note she alone provides the alleged proof.

"This accusation has nothing to do with your goods and prices, or discrepancies in records, Madoc," he charged. "She makes these allegations and created this false evidence because she's never liked me and she's wanted me gone from the day she arrived. Indeed, she hates me and she wants you to hate me, too."

"I had no reason to mistrust you," Roslynn countered, "until I saw a discrepancy that raised my suspicions that all was not right with the household accounts. If I accuse you of wrongdoing, it's because I have good cause, as this evidence attests."

"I have my lists, too, my lady," he replied. "It's your word and your document against mine. And if you thought I was such a criminal, why wait until now to say so? The first entry you note was months ago."

"Because you were Madoc's trusted friend, so I would not speak until I was certain and had several instances of your calumny. My mother also—"

"Your mother?" Ivor jeered. "Your *Norman* mother? Madoc is to take her word over mine, too?"

"Need I remind you that I'm Madoc's wife and chatelaine of Llanpowell? It is my duty to keep track of expenses—a duty you've sought to make difficult from the beginning. Why, Ivor? If all your dealings were honest and true, why be an obstacle in my path?"

"Aye, that's right—*your* path, as if we were all helpless babes before you came! Well, my fine Norman lady, we were not and we don't need your interference here."

"It was *not* interference. I only sought to fulfill a chatelaine's duties."

"Provided you're the sort of chatelaine who betrays a husband," Ivor charged.

Roslynn blushed, but wouldn't let him silence her. "Wimarc de Werre was a vicious brute and a traitor to the king. I would betray him again if necessary. But I'd never betray Madoc, who is a finer, better man than Wimarc could ever be. Who is the very opposite, in that he sees only the good in people and wants to trust them, where Wimarc saw only fools and dupes.

"Madoc would never strike a woman, and if he is sometimes angry, he doesn't hide it until he lashes out in sudden, unforeseen violence. His rage is brief, of the moment, soon controlled. A woman need never fear him as she must many another man."

Even as she spoke, Roslynn realized the absolute truth of her words, and how wrong she'd been to doubt her husband, who had been standing silently beside her all this time.

Now Ivor was forgotten as she turned to Madoc, whose chest rose and fell as if he found simply breathing difficult. And in his eyes, she saw not anger or dismay, but hope—a wild, tempestuous hope that filled her own heart with joy. She would have embraced him then, except that Ivor was there and she was not finished yet.

"You're a fine one to speak of betrayal, Ivor," she said, forcing her gaze away from Madoc. "How long have you been stealing from the man you call your friend? How many years? And why? To be rich? Because you're jealous? For vengeance, perhaps, because his mother was a Norman and he helped God's anointed Norman king?"

Ivor stared at her, panic beneath the scorn, and true fear in his voice when he spoke. "There is nothing Madoc has or wants that I would steal. He is my friend, my almost brother."

He drew himself up as he faced her still-silent husband. "Tell her, Madoc—or do you believe her and not me? Do you have so little faith in me? Does all my hard work and friendship count for nothing?"

"Where do you go, Ivor?" Madoc asked quietly. "Where do you go for such long stretches of time when no one can find you? I always thought it was to see a woman. I doubt that now."

He took a step toward the steward, who began to tremble. "Perhaps you venture close to Pontyrmwr. Maybe you even meet my brother and tell him of my plans."

"You'd accuse me of that, too?" Ivor cried, backing away. He pointed at Roslynn, who had not considered that Ivor's treachery might be more far-reaching. "If there's a spy in Llanpowell, it's her!"

"Spy? I am no spy!" Roslynn protested, aghast. "If I was a spy, surely I would have eagerly sought Madoc's bed and marriage, not fought against it despite the inclination of my body and my heart. Madoc, you must not believe I had such a motive when I came here."

"No, I don't, for as you say, you were far from encouraging."

"That was her way to inflame your desire!" Ivor exclaimed. "How great a fool are you, not to see it? How do you even know this child she carries is yours?"

"Because I know *her*," Madoc declared. "I know that she's an honorable, honest woman, and that she is no spy for John, or anyone else. But you, Ivor… Who else knew so well where my patrols would be and of how many men?

"How long have you been a canker in my household? From the first, or only after I married Gwendolyn? I saw your face as I said my vows that day, but I dismissed your shock as a natural reaction to what Trefor had done, and the marriage to repair it. But now I believe it was something else I saw—dismay and anguish and despair—because you loved Gwendolyn as much as Trefor did.

"Who was it who told Trefor where I was that night when I was with Haldis? We weren't out in the open, after all. Who else watches the comings and goings in the hall as carefully as you? Was it by your design that Trefor came upon us?

"Did you lie to him, too, and tell him it was Gwendolyn I was with? By God, I can believe you did.

"And then you tried to make trouble between Roslynn and me—and you succeeded. Why? Do you still hate me that much for taking Gwendolyn from you? What else have I ever done to wrong you?"

Ivor, pale and quaking as Madoc walked toward him, opened his mouth as if he would speak, but no sound came out.

"Thank God Roslynn found out the truth," Madoc said, "and had the greatness of heart to tell me, in spite of what you'd done to ruin our happiness. She is no petty, jealous woman to make a false accusation—not like you."

His expression hardened into firm resolve. "For our old friendship's sake, for we *were* friends once, I give you your life and liberty—but you will leave Llanpowell, Ivor, today, and with nothing save the clothes on your back. If you ever come back, I'll have you arrested and charged with theft."

"You mean that," Ivor murmured incredulously, flushing as red as blood. "You will take *her* word over mine? Believe this flimsy, false evidence?"

"I can and I do," Madoc said. "Now go, or face the king's justice—and mine."

Ivor stumbled past him toward the door. "Mark my words, Madoc. You'll rue this day and the day you married that Norman witch."

WHEN HE WAS GONE, Madoc splayed his hands upon the table and bowed his head.

"God save me," he whispered, sick at heart even though he didn't doubt that he'd done the right thing.

As Roslynn had presented the list and told him what she'd suspected, when he'd looked upon it for himself and all the various, nebulous fears and suspicions, memories and half-forgotten impressions had coalesced in his mind and pointed to Ivor, the truth had come upon him like a thunderbolt.

Madoc raised his head to look at his clever, generous, honest Roslynn—to see her grasping the arms of the chair as if she feared she would fall out of it, her face white, her skirts soaking wet and a puddle at her feet.

CHAPTER TWENTY-TWO

A SHORT WHILE LATER, Roslynn lay on a pallet of straw in her hastily prepared bedchamber and clutched her mother's hand. "It's too soon!" she cried in anguish. "The baby can't be coming now!"

"'Tis," the midwife said. The middle-aged, thin, stern woman had been urgently sent for and now stood by the table, stirring something in a cup that was supposed to lessen the pain. "Can't be stopped, so best lie still and try to rest while you can, my lady."

Roslynn's grip tightened as she regarded her mother, desperation in her eyes. "The baby...will it be all right if it comes so early?"

"It might very well be fine," her mother assured her, although the lines of worry around her mouth belied her tone. "You were a fortnight early, and sound of wind and limb."

Another cramping pain seized Roslynn's abdomen, and she let out a low groan as it had its way with her.

"No blood, my lady?" the midwife asked Lady Eloise as she came forward with the brew made of willow bark.

"No." The women exchanged looks.

"What? What is it?" Roslynn demanded, breathless from the pain.

"That's good," her mother said, brushing her cool hand over her daughter's brow.

Another pain came, and Roslynn bucked and twisted, knocking the cup from the midwife's hand.

"Now, now, deary, you must lie still," the woman ordered a little less brusquely. "It could be a long time yet." The midwife addressed Lady Eloise. "We may need some help to hold her."

"I'll be still!" Roslynn cried. She didn't want the servants to see her struggling, or hear her cries of pain. She imagined the looks they would exchange and knew she couldn't bear to see them. They could count enough to realize it hadn't yet been nine months.

And Madoc…what must he be—

She groaned again and bit her lip, fighting not to cry out, to endure the pain, to suffer in silence. Had she not survived Wimarc's fists and kicks and learned how not to cry and hide how much he hurt her?

What if Wimarc had done something to her when he hit her? What if she was suffering and the babe coming too soon because of something he'd done to her?

What if she was dying?

She must tell Madoc she was sorry for many things, but most of all for hurting him. For not being braver and stronger, and for not trusting that he could control himself in his rage. That he had undeservedly paid the price for another man's actions—and so had she. She must tell him she regretted leaving Llanpowell and wanted to stay.

Because she loved him and needed him.

"Mother, fetch Madoc," she pleaded as, like a fist clenching in her stomach, another pain took hold of her. "Please, bring Madoc!"

"I don't let husbands in," the midwife snapped. "They only get in the way. Or swoon, no matter how tough they look. Why, I've seen big strong ones wilt like a—"

"Mother, please!"

"Of course. Whatever you want, Roslynn," Lady Eloise said, getting to her feet. "At once."

The midwife was about to protest, until she got a look at Lady Eloise's face and wisely shut her mouth.

"YOUR FATHER never liked Ivor, you know," Lloyd mused aloud after taking another swig of ale while Madoc paced the dais. "Too clever by half, he used to say. But you liked him and he knew no harm of the boy, so he let it be, although it was no secret the lad had no love for the Normans."

Straining to hear any sound from the chamber above, Madoc took a gulp of wine. Ivor hated the Normans because he blamed them for his early birth and crippled leg. What if his child was crippled because it came too soon? March, the midwife had said. The babe should be born in March, and it was still February.

"Look you," Lloyd went on, gesturing with his mug, "there was Ioan's brother come a good month before his time and he was a fine, big fellow. His sainted mother always said he would have been the death of her if he'd come when he was supposed to. Like giving birth to an ox." Lloyd chortled before he took another swig. "Ah, bless me, but she had a way with her, did Ioan's mother."

"The child is mine," Madoc said, loud enough that everyone in the hall—the soldiers, the servants, Bron bringing more wine, Uncle Lloyd—wouldn't doubt that Madoc had faith in his wife's honor and would claim this child as his own.

"What, nobody saying otherwise, are they?" Lloyd demanded as if truly surprised anyone would doubt it. "Got her with child on your wedding night, I'm sure, bull that you are. So Trefor was conceived.

I had that from your father himself, and you're as like Gruffydd as a son can be."

Footsteps. Coming from the bedchamber. Madoc was at the bottom of the stairwell in an instant.

Lady Eloise, as anxious and worried as he, appeared, and his heart seemed to stop beating. He'd seen that look on the midwife's face when Gwendolyn was dying.

He had lived with guilt and shame and remorse ever since—and he hadn't even loved her. Not really. He had admired her and thought her pretty and special because Trefor adored her. But he had never loved her. He knew that now, for certain.

He loved Roslynn. With all his heart and everything he had. He always would, and if she died…

"Madoc, she's calling for you," Lady Eloise said. "You had best make haste."

"Roslynn—she's not…she's not…"

He couldn't say it. Couldn't even bring himself to truly think it. Not his wonderful, strong Roslynn. If anybody died…if anybody deserved to die, it was him. Not her.

Lady Eloise gave him a gentle, sympathetic smile that let his heart beat again. "My daughter is a strong, healthy young woman. I think she'll come through this, and the child with her. But she wants to see you, and so I think she should."

As Madoc went to hurry past her, Lady Eloise put her hand on his arm to detain him. "There is one advantage to an early labor, my lord. The babe will be smaller. Think of that, and don't show Roslynn your fear. She needs your strength and confidence now."

"Of course," he said firmly, necessity reaching through the fog of dread. This was something he could do for her, and he needed to do something.

When he entered the chamber, he found Roslynn pale and weak on the pallet, her body still large with child, and the strain of laboring on her face. In spite of that, she managed to smile when she saw him and called out his name.

Thrilled and relieved by that smile, he quickly knelt beside her and pressed a kiss upon her sweat-beaded brow. "Roslynn, my rose, my sweet, sweet rose."

"Madoc, I—" She closed her eyes and a little moan of anguish escaped her compressed lips.

"Now she's seen you, you can leave the chamber, my lord," the midwife commanded.

Madoc hadn't noticed the woman hovering nearby.

He remembered her well from Gwendolyn's childbed, with her formidable manner, iron-gray hair covered by a plain linen cloth, narrow frame as straight as a spear and a glare like a general's.

He had obeyed her without question when
Gwendolyn gave birth and he should obey her now.
Nevertheless, he hesitated. If things went badly, he
must tell Roslynn how he felt. "Roslynn, my rose,
I love you. I love you more than my life."

He couldn't tell if she'd heard him as she gripped
his hand like a vise. "Madoc," she gasped while
another pain assaulted her. "Don't go. Stay with
me. Please."

Whether she had heard his heartfelt avowal or
not, if Roslynn wanted him to stay, he was staying,
and nothing the midwife, or Roslynn's mother, or
the king or any army could do could make him go.
"I'll be here, Roslynn."

The midwife opened her mouth, then shook her
head and snapped, "Very well, my lord. Just keep
out of my way."

"She's very arrogant, isn't she?" Roslynn murmured through half-closed eyes. "Nearly as arrogant as the lord of Llanpowell."

His heart seemed to fall to the floor, until he saw
her lips twitch not with a grimace, but another
smile. "The lord who loves me."

"I do, Roslynn, by all the angels above, I do."

"I'm so glad I'm home."

Home. She had called Llanpowell home. Surely
that meant—

Her face twisted with anguish as she gasped and arched.

Madoc looked desperately at the midwife. "Do something!"

"I've done all I can," she replied. "It's between her and the angels now, and the babe to make its way."

Lady Eloise crouched on the other side of the pallet, her face as pale as her daughter's. "It won't be long," she said to them both. "Not long now and then a baby to love and cherish and for me to fuss over. Lord James will be sorry he wasn't here."

Roslynn relaxed a little and opened her eyes. "Madoc, I'm so sorry..." Grimacing like a man losing a limb, she twisted and moaned again.

Gwendolyn had been sorry, too, before she died. *Oh, God, Roslynn mustn't die,* he prayed as he held her hand. She couldn't die. Please, God, he would die in her stead, if that were the price to pay for her life.

"It's me that's sorry," he said fervently. "Sorry for being a stubborn fool. Sorry I frightened you and made you run away."

Her eyes fluttered open and her grip tightened as she spoke, "The baby is yours, Madoc. I swear to you on my life, the baby is yours."

"I never doubted it," he said, even more upset to think she would believe he had harbored such suspicions.

He stroked her pale cheek, her damp hair. "Why, look you, my lady, how you shied away from my slightest touch at first, and you *liked* me," he said, trying to make her smile again, as well as believe he trusted her. "Those jack-a-dandies at the king's court didn't stand a chance getting in your bed."

"Not the slightest chance," she agreed in a weak whisper before another pain took her. She cried out and her grip seemed about to break his hand, but he didn't move. Let her break it if she must.

The midwife was at her feet. She pushed Roslynn's legs so that the bottoms of her soles touched and her knees fell open.

"Let her hold you," she ordered both Madoc and his mother-in-law, although there was no need. "Now, my lady," she commanded Roslynn. "Push. Push hard!"

"LLOYD?"

Lloyd raised his head and blinked, trying to focus on Ioan and not recall the heartrending scream that had shattered the silence a moment ago.

He didn't want to know that Roslynn was dead. He didn't want to see Madoc looking like he'd died, too, although his body didn't know it yet.

Not again.

"Go away," he muttered, before laying his head down again.

Ioan shook him by the shoulder. "Lloyd, that Norman's come back."

"What Norman? That pike Alfred?"

"No, Lady Roslynn's father."

His hand to his aching head, Lloyd sat up. "What? Here? Now?"

Another cry, somewhat muffled, pierced the air and Lloyd wanted to groan himself, especially when Lord James sauntered into the hall as if he'd just come over the hill for a visit.

Until he stopped dead as another scream came from above. Then he blanched and his worried gaze searched the hall. "Where's my daughter?"

"Above in her chamber, having the baby," Lloyd answered.

Lord James stood as still as a tree on a windless day. *"Now?"*

Aching head forgotten, Lloyd jumped to his feet. "Aye. What else do you think? That we're torturing her?"

"I don't…" The Norman closed his mouth and wordlessly shook his head.

Lloyd grabbed the nearly empty wineskin and took it to him. "Have a drink of this and sit down. It could be hours yet."

Lord James mutely obeyed, finishing the wine in one long gulp, which was a pity. Lloyd could have used another drink himself.

Lord James sat on the edge of the nearest bench. "My wife is with her?"

"Of course."

"How long?"

"Since yesterday."

"Sweet Jesu!" Lord James ran his hand over his beard. "And a midwife's there? A good one?"

"Best for miles. And Madoc, too."

"Her *husband* is in the room?"

"We've had no word that she's in danger," Lloyd hurried to assure Lord James, and himself, as well as Ioan and Bron and anybody else lingering in the hall. "Bron, bring us another wineskin. And some bread. And cheese. Pasties and sweetmeats, too. And get the tables set up. It's almost time for the evening—"

A cry like nothing Lloyd had ever heard ripped through the air.

"I must go to my daughter!" Lord James shouted, starting for the stairs.

Not sure what to do, Lloyd hurried after him. If the poor girl was dying...

The two men reached the stairs at the same time and there was a moment's struggle as both tried to go up first, until Lloyd came to his senses and let Roslynn's father precede him.

They had no sooner gotten to the chamber when the door swung open and Madoc appeared. Although he was obviously exhausted, he smiled when he saw the two men, one behind the other and jostling to see inside the room.

"She's well, God be praised," he said with joy and pride. "It was a trial, but she's come through it at last and we have a son. A fine and healthy boy."

As if to confirm it, a babe's lusty cry filled the air and Lady Eloise came up behind him with a precious, squalling bundle in her arms.

"Here he is, James," Lady Eloise said with tears of happiness and relief in her eyes. "Doesn't he look like Roslynn?"

"Aye, a little, I grant you," Lloyd said, peering at the baby's red face over Lord James's shoulder. "But that's Madoc's nose. And his hair. And chin. The ears are like his father's. And that little mouth could be my own."

"Madoc, tell them Mascen is himself," Roslynn called out wearily.

"Daughter!" Lord James cried, starting forward, until the midwife blocked his way.

"No other visitors yet, especially menfolk," she commanded, holding up her work-worn hand. "The lady needs her rest, and the baby, too. Off you go and do what men do at such times. You can see them in the morning.

"You, too, my lord," she said to Madoc, pushing him out of the room.

"Bring the child here, my lady, and yes, I know he has twenty fine fingers and toes. By the saints, you'd think nobody had ever had a baby," the midwife concluded as she steered Lady Eloise back inside the room and slammed the door behind them.

Lloyd rubbed his hands together with glee. "Another boy! Celebrations to come and lasting all night, I'm thinking. Thank God we've got plenty of ale and wine."

Madoc shook his head as he started down the stairs. "You'll have to celebrate without me," he said as Lloyd trotted after him, followed by Lord James. "I've got a promise to keep."

HUGH THE BEAK LOOKED at Ioan as they rode beside each other in the small group of men. It was well past the noon, but instead of being comfortably seated in the hall of Llanpowell, drinking toasts to the lord's newborn son, they were riding south with Madoc, over a road little used, and they had no idea where they were going, or why.

"Are you going to ask him what we're doing?" Hugh quietly asked his companion.

Ioan's frown deepened. "Not wanting to get knocked from my horse, me," he muttered, eyeing their overlord warily. "The man's beyond weary, so it must be something important to send him from Llanpowell today of all days."

"Aye," Hugh agreed. "Thank God he's kept the pace to a walk, or he'd tumble from the saddle before we could get to wherever we're going. But by the saints, how long are we to be riding? And what will we do for food? We left in such a hurry, we didn't bring a morsel or a drop to drink."

Ioan heaved a sigh and nodded. "All right, then, I'll ask—and I hope you appreciate the sacrifice."

He didn't wait for Hugh's response before nudging his horse from the line, up closer to Madoc. "So, my lord," he said, feigning good humor. "Where might we be off to, then?"

"I was wondering how long it would be before you asked," Madoc replied. "We're going to—"

An arrow whizzed past them, nearly hitting Madoc in the head. Crying out in alarm, both men reined in as more arrows flew about them, one striking Ioan in his right arm. With a groan, his hand around the shaft, Ioan fell to the ground.

"Dismount, dismount!" Madoc shouted as he

flung himself from his horse. The moment he was on the ground, he drew his sword, slapped his horse's flank to send the animal galloping from the ambush and, keeping low to the ground, ran to the moaning, writhing Ioan.

"God, not my arm!" his friend muttered through clenched teeth as he clutched the shaft of the arrow protruding from his flesh. "How'll I ever be able to hoist an ale?"

If Ioan could joke, he couldn't be too badly hurt, or so Madoc fervently hoped as he swiftly assessed the situation. The attackers were in the stand of trees to the right, which gave them good cover. The trees were sparser on the other side of the road, but there were some large stones, big enough to protect them from arrows and give his men time to regroup.

"To the rocks!" he shouted.

Grabbing Ioan by his uninjured arm, Madoc dragged his friend toward the nearest boulder sizable enough to hide them.

"Damn, are you trying to pull it off?" Ioan growled, even as he helped by pushing with his feet.

"Don't tempt me. You're too heavy as it is," Madoc replied, panting, as he finally got them both behind the boulder.

"Thank God their aim is terrible," Ioan said as he lay on the ground, his face pale, his lips blue, his hand still holding the shaft while a red stain grew on the sleeve of his shirt.

"Hugh!" Madoc called out, trying to find out where his men were without making himself a target.

"Here, Madoc. And the rest of us, too. Only Ioan was fool enough to get hit."

"There's friendship for you," Ioan grumbled through clenched teeth.

"Stay here," Madoc ordered as he started to crawl toward Hugh and the others, who were about ten feet away.

"Not likely to go anywhere, am I?"

"THEY'VE GOT the high ground," Madoc said to Hugh as they huddled behind a pile of rocks. "That stream we crossed a ways back makes a valley behind the rise. We can go back and follow the stream and come up behind them. It's got a rocky bed, too, so they shouldn't hear us."

"If they're still there by then," Hugh said doubtfully. "Might be they'll move.

"Or even go," he added hopefully.

"I think they're going to wait us out like a siege," Madoc said. "They've got us trapped and they know it."

"We've got nothing for them to steal except our clothes and weapons now that the horses are gone."

"I'm thinking robbery wasn't their plan," Madoc grimly replied, wishing he'd brought more men. That arrow had flown too close to his head to be a warning, or simply make them stop.

"What, murder?" Hugh gasped.

"Aye."

"Trefor, do you think?"

"Maybe, but I hope not." Not now, when he was ready to tell Trefor everything.

As he'd held his newborn son in his arms, he'd realized the time had come for the truth to be known, whatever the cost.

Even if it meant he could lose Roslynn forever.

"So you think they'll just wait us out?" Gwillym asked breathlessly, doing his best to be brave.

"Not if we attack them, as I intend to do."

"What about Ioan?" Hugh asked. "We can't leave him here."

Madoc had little choice, and said so. "We'll come back for him as soon as we can," he promised.

"I'll stay here with him. I'll show myself now and again, so they think we're all still here," Gwillym offered, although that would mean he'd be a target, or the last man left to face certain death if they failed.

"Very well," Madoc said, admiring his courage. "No need to reveal your presence often and don't

take any foolish chances or try to play the hero." He
gave the young man an encouraging grin. "That's
for the lord to do."

CHAPTER TWENTY-THREE

MADOC HELD UP his hand to halt his men at the bottom of the narrow valley made by the swift-running stream. Ignoring the smell of damp, mossy earth as best he could, he pointed up the slope. Just barely visible through the bracken, trees and holly bushes, a rough-looking fellow in a motley assortment of leather and woolen clothing nocked an arrow. His hair was long, greasy and unkempt, his beard likewise and he was more poorly dressed than any of Trefor's men had been.

Maybe these men *were* thieves, not assassins, and desperate enough to attack any travelers, even armed soldiers.

Madoc gestured for Hugh to join him. "See any others?" he whispered as a breeze rustled the leaves overheard.

Hugh shook his head.

"Wait here. The other men, too," Madoc ordered. He went forward on his own, creeping along the streambed, keeping one eye on the wet, slippery ground beneath him while also searching for the rest of the attackers.

At last he came upon a group of them gathered in one spot, their backs to him. Not a wise move, to be so close together.

They probably weren't professional soldiers or killers, and so not likely hired to attack him specifically, Madoc thought with relief as he made his way back to Hugh and his men.

He pointed at Hugh, then the archer above and silently gestured an order. His expression grimly resolute, Hugh slid through the bracken as if part snake, creeping up behind the man. He threw his arm around the archer's neck, dragged him backward and down to the soft ground before the rogue could utter a sound.

When Hugh returned, Madoc led his men toward the main body of the attackers and signaled for his men to fan out, so that there would be no escape when they attacked.

Meanwhile, oblivious to the danger below, the men above continued to shoot. Given the abundance of arrows in the quivers at their belts, they could have kept it up for hours—or until Madoc and his men finally tried to flee.

"Damn them, what kind of women are they,

hiding behind a rock?" a rough voice demanded from the center of the group. "Never liked Madoc, but I never thought he was a coward."

Rhodri.

Madoc recognized the voice, and so did his men. And if Rhodri was here, that meant Trefor—

"Madoc's gone soft, that's what. Besotted by that woman, like I said."

Ivor. That was Ivor Purse Strings.

Madoc stifled a gasp and his men looked equally shocked.

What were Ivor and Rhodri doing here together and attacking them?

Hugh plucked at Madoc's sleeve. "Rhodri's not a patient fellow," he noted under his breath.

Madoc nodded, understanding. If they were to attack first, they should do so at once.

He looked down the line of his men, to see every eye upon him. He raised his sword, sprang to his feet and, uttering the battle cry of his family, made straight for Rhodri and Ivor.

The attackers, crouching, swiveled toward the stream. Those who had arrows at the ready let fly. One of Madoc's men went down, an arrow in his foot.

Madoc didn't stop, nor did any of his other men. Swords held aloft, they charged up the slope, paying no heed to the sharp points of holly and the arrows flying as they attacked.

Madoc met Rhodri first. Rhodri was a good fighter, but Madoc was better. Rhodri swung his sword as a man cut grain, sweeping the blade before him as if it were a scythe. That kept some men at bay and Madoc, too, for a moment, but it also meant that Rhodri left his side exposed too long.

Waiting for the best chance, Madoc hesitated, then moved in, swinging his blade up and into Rhodri's side, the heavy weapon slicing through leather, cloth, skin and bone until, with a scream, Rhodri fell.

Madoc didn't wait to see him die; he was looking for Ivor while his well-trained men made short work of the rest of their enemies, easily running down any who tried to escape.

Ivor couldn't run, and because Madoc had known him from boyhood, he knew where to look for his hiding place. He strode to the nearest thicket of holly, reached in and grabbed a barely visible booted foot. The bush shook as Ivor cursed and kicked and struggled while Madoc pulled him out.

Although Ivor had never learned how to wield a broadsword, he'd been taught to use a dagger, and he was very good. Madoc knew that, too, and so he was ready to parry the slashing movement of Ivor's dagger with his sword. His action sent the dagger flying and before Ivor could turn or get away, Madoc had planted his foot on Ivor's chest.

He put the tip of his sword at his former steward's throat and stared down at him with disgust. "I trusted you, Ivor, as I trusted no one else. I loved you like a brother, even more than my own. This is how you repay that love and loyalty and faith? It sickens me to realize how wrong I was to trust you and to think that if Roslynn hadn't come to Llanpowell, I might never have learned the truth."

"Spare me your whining criticism," Ivor snarled. "I'm sick to death of hearing about your troubles—you, who's always had everything a man could want. Just kill me and be done."

Madoc grimly shook his head as he removed his foot and moved back, keeping his sword pointed at Ivor's throat. "Without a trial? Without letting everyone, including Trefor, hear what you did—what you are? It was these men stealing sheep, wasn't it? Under your orders, or Rhodri's or both. And it was you told them where my patrols would be, wasn't it, so they wouldn't get caught?"

"I fell in with them after you sent me from Llanpowell," Ivor said as he sat up, bracing himself with his hands. "It was that, or starve."

"You expect me to believe Rhodri led them?" Madoc skeptically replied. "Or did he get conveniently, recently cast out of Pontyrmwr, too?"

"Mercy, my lord!" one of the captured attackers cried as Hugh dragged him toward Madoc by the back of his tunic, then threw him on the ground.

The thief, who was as skinny as a whip and pock-marked, raised his head. His desperate eyes darted about as he licked his cracked lips. "Mercy, my lord," he pleaded. "Spare my life and I'll tell you everything! The cripple's our leader, my lord. Him and that other blackguard you killed."

"This man would sell his own mother for a ha'penny, Madoc," Ivor sneered. "You can't believe a word he says."

"Yet here you are with him," Madoc noted, his rage rising now that the fighting was over. "Hugh, tie Ivor's hands. And this man's, too. I want to hear what he has to say."

Regarding Ivor as if he smelled like rotten fish, Hugh did as he was told while Madoc stood by with his sword at the ready. When he was finished, Hugh pushed both men down so they were sitting on the ground.

Madoc sheathed his sword and sat on his haunches, eye to eye with them.

The thief licked his chapped lips and spoke without waiting for Madoc's questions. "He promised us a fortune, my lord, the cripple did. And Rhodri, too. They said if we joined up with them, we'd be rich—but we never saw hardly a coin. They kept it all for themselves, and if any of us complained or talked of leaving and going our own way, the cripple said he'd send you or your brother after us and we'd hang. Or they'd kill us. We was trapped by those slimy bastards and no mistake. It was all their doing, the sheep and the ram, too."

"You might as well save your breath, Guto," Ivor growled. "Nothing you say's going to make any difference. We're as good as dead already."

Ignoring him, the thief got to his knees to plead with Madoc. "It's true, my lord. I wanted to leave off and run away, but I couldn't."

"You will be tried according to the law," the lord of Llanpowell answered.

"Norman law," Ivor muttered.

"Either way, *you* are going to hang," Madoc said to Ivor as he rose, struggling to control his burning rage.

"While you spend your nights with that Norman trollop King John gave you for services rendered."

The thief began to whimper, while Ivor blanched, for Madoc's expression would have struck fear into any man.

"Never speak of my wife again," he commanded. "You aren't worthy enough to kiss the hem of her gown."

Ivor struggled to stand. "Any Welshman's worth ten Normans! And as for her..." He spit onto the ground at Madoc's feet. "That's for her."

Madoc gripped the hilt of his sword. Never had he been more outraged, so keen to kill a man, but even in his anger, he sensed that losing his temper was exactly what Ivor wanted.

"You want me to attack you, don't you, Ivor?" he said as the truth dawned. "A quick death, is that it?"

Although his hand itched to give him what he wanted, Madoc shook his head. "That would be too easy."

"You lust-crazed oaf!" Ivor cried. "You pawn of the Normans! Do you think I'll let you make a public spectacle out of me? That I'll let people mock and tease me on the way to my death? I had enough mockery when we were children and I was better than any of you!"

In the face of Ivor's bitter fury, Madoc grew calm, yet no less determined to bring his former friend to justice. "I was teased, too, Ivor."

"Oh, yes, the son of the lord—teased a little because he was so quiet and mumbled when he talked," Ivor retorted. "That was nothing compared to what they called *me*."

"You were given a position of trust and responsibility."

"I was your bloody *clerk!*" Ivor screamed, spittle flying from his lips. "That's all I was or ever would be, thanks to the Normans! Yet you expect me to be grateful! To lick your boots and kiss your feet and praise you for the crumbs you gave me, until you gave some Norman whore power over me.

"I'll *never* let you display me for ridicule. Not before a court, or anywhere else!"

Then Ivor ran. He ran like one possessed, his head down, his hands tied—straight into the trunk of a massive oak. There was a sickening, terrible crack as he hit it and he tumbled sideways, to lie twitching on the ground.

"Ivor!"

Madoc ran to his side and rolled him onto his back.

Ivor's head lolled like a broken doll's, and his eyes stared up, unseeing. There was a trickle of blood from his nose, and more from a gash in his forehead.

"Oh, Ivor," Madoc whispered as he embraced his friend and held him close. Because once he had trusted Ivor, and they had been like brothers.

MADOC WAS STILL HOLDING Ivor's body when Hugh appeared with the horses, Rhodri's body slung over one of them. "Madoc?"

"Ivor killed himself," he muttered, still too shocked to quite believe it. "He ran…"

Then he remembered he was the lord of Llanpowell, took a deep breath and cleared his throat.

"Ivor killed himself," he repeated, his voice stronger as he lay Ivor on the ground.

Aghast, Hugh crossed himself. So did the four other men of Llanpowell behind him.

"Put his body on a horse," Madoc said, "and take him back to Llanpowell with Ioan. The rest of the men will come with me."

For he had not yet completed his journey and he still had amends to make.

THE SUN WAS SETTING as Trefor of Pontyrmwr stood in the courtyard of his fortress and again watched Madoc ride through the gates.

But this time there was a boy seated in the saddle in front of Madoc, a dark-haired boy about five years old, with features like Madoc, who looked this way and that like a curious little bird.

Striding toward them, Trefor held up his hand. "Far enough, brother. What do you want? I've not set so much as a toe on your land since the shearing feast, memorable occasion that it was."

"I know. That's not what's brought me here."

"Come to gloat, have you, now that you've got another son? I heard all about it. News travels fast in these parts."

"Who told you? Rhodri?"

"Could be. And you brought your other son, too.

Wise of you, brother, for I'll not harm you with Gwendolyn's child here. Otherwise, I'd drag you off that horse and run you through right now."

"You could try. But I haven't come to fight you, or to gloat," Madoc said as he dismounted.

He reached up and lifted Owain from the saddle. With the boy standing wide-eyed and wondering beside him, Madoc went down on one knee and bowed his head. "I've come to beg your forgiveness, Trefor. I've done you a great wrong."

His eyes narrowing as if expecting a trick or feint, Trefor took a step back and reached for his sword.

"I've done Owain a great wrong, too," Madoc admitted, ignoring his brother's action.

He brought the little boy eye to eye with him. "Owain, I've done a despicable, terrible thing. Out of spite and anger and resentment, I sent you away from Llanpowell and I lied to you. I'm not your true father. I've kept you from him."

Madoc got to his feet and turned the boy so that he faced Trefor. "Look closely, Trefor, and you'll see the truth, and the reason I sent your son from Llanpowell."

Trefor's mouth gaped as he stared at them both, but especially at the boy, who looked back at him with equal confusion out of bright blue irises rimmed with black.

"Trefor, Owain is your son, not mine," Madoc said. "Gwendolyn was already with child when we married. I never made love with her, not once. It was only you she loved. Always, you."

Trefor stumbled backward as if Madoc had struck a mortal blow.

Seeing his brother's shock, it was as if five years' worth of guilt and remorse and shame swept over Madoc all at once, and he had never been more sorry—except when he also looked at little Owain.

What would this revelation mean for him? Madoc had wondered all the way here. Yet whatever the future held, whether Owain or Trefor ever forgave him or not, he had no doubt he was doing the right thing—the thing he should have done years ago, just as he'd promised Gwendolyn he would.

"I'm so sorry. I beg forgiveness of you both," he said humbly, contritely, with no pride at all as he remained on bended knee.

Still staring at him with stunned disbelief, Trefor shook his head. "She never told me. If what you say is true, why didn't she tell me?"

"She wasn't sure herself until after we were married. I never touched her, Trefor, on my honor. She was so upset, I didn't even try, not that night or ever, because it was you she loved, not me.

"Roslynn told me what you said about seeing Gwendolyn and me kissing. We didn't. It was Haldis I was with that night, Trefor. Remember Haldis, Gwendolyn's cousin, who looked so much like her? I would never have kissed Gwendolyn knowing she was to be your wife. *Never.* I thought I loved Gwendolyn, but you are my brother and I would never betray you."

"Haldis?" Trefor whispered incredulously. "That was Haldis you were kissing? Oh, sweet Jesu!"

His hands spread wide, Madoc rose and took a step toward his brother. "Gwendolyn was sorry she agreed to marry me from the moment the vows were spoken. She spent our wedding night weeping for you, and every night thereafter. She was never happy except once in all that time."

He glanced back at Owain, standing so silent and still despite what he'd been told. "That was the day she bore your son—the same day she made me promise I would tell you the truth about Owain. She died with your name on her lips, Trefor, still loving you."

Trefor tore his gaze from Madoc to look at his son. "You broke your promise and claimed Owain as your own when he was not? You kept my son from me?"

"Aye, I did, to my shame and regret," Madoc confessed. "I told myself it was to spare *her* shame,

and you, and our family. But it was really to hurt
you because you'd hurt her and she'd hurt me by
loving you. It was cruel vengeance, Trefor, and I
deserve your hate."

Trefor ignored him as he came closer and went
down on one knee to study the wary little face, the
big searching eyes of the boy before him. "My son.
My son. Gwendolyn's and mine."

And then he gathered the boy into his embrace
and held him tight. "Oh, my son!"

The lad twisted and looked back at Madoc. "Da?"

"No, I'm your uncle," Madoc gently corrected.
"This is your da. I am your uncle and this is your
da, who loves you."

"You needn't be afraid. I'll send for your foster
parents to come live with us here," Trefor said, evinc-
ing a wisdom Madoc hadn't expected, but that took
another enormous weight from him. He'd been worried the unfamiliar surroundings and people would
distress the boy if he came to live at Pontyrmwr.

He'd known he need not worry that Trefor would
treat him well.

Trefor rose and, as he faced Madoc again, that
familiar hard look came to his face. Madoc waited
for the denunciations, the anger, the scorn and disgust. For Trefor to strike him with his fist, or draw
his sword.

Yet neither the rage nor blow came. Instead, the rancor dissipated, replaced by sorrow and a remorse that matched his own. "I *should* hate you for what you've done, and once I would have, but you've given me something I never hoped to have—a son with the woman I loved and lost because I was a proud, headstrong fool. I've cursed myself a thousand times since that terrible day I lost her. I cursed you, too, Madoc, but in my heart, I knew I had reacted rashly, foolishly and with dishonor.

"We both made terrible mistakes, Madoc. I should have trusted her—and you. I never should have believed Ivor that night when he said that you were with Gwendolyn and sent me looking for you."

Ivor. Madoc had guessed it was so, but it still hurt to hear it. How deep Ivor's hatred and jealousy and bitterness must have run, even then. "Ivor was our enemy, Trefor—yours and mine."

He glanced at Owain, who was gravely studying Trefor. "Perhaps we could go to your hall? It's too late for us to return to Llanpowell and I have much to tell you."

"Aye, of course, and gladly," Trefor replied. He smiled at his son and the years of bitterness fell from his face, making him look years younger. "You're in luck, Owain. My cook makes the best honey cakes in Wales and I know for a fact she was making some today. Let's go and have some, eh?"

Owain's eyes lit up like candles as he reached for his father's hand.

CHAPTER TWENTY-FOUR

ROSLYNN SMILED at her mother as Lady Eloise bent over the cradle where her grandson rested and cooed a familiar lullaby.

"He's perfect, isn't he?" Roslynn said, quite certain that he was.

"I'm not sure if I would call little Mascen *perfect*," her mother replied, her voice grave but her cheeks dimpling with a smile. "He is the loudest infant I think I've ever heard. I believe he might shout the rafters down before he's done and you'll have cause to wish he was a little quieter."

"No, he's perfect, and Madoc thinks so, too," Roslynn replied, remembering the joy and wonderment in Madoc's eyes when he held his son.

All the pain and fear that she'd endured had been as nothing when the midwife put their son into Madoc's waiting arms.

Lady Eloise reached down and lifted the baby from the cradle. "Unless I'm very wrong, he's about to start crying again. He may also turn out to be the most ravenous baby I've ever encountered, too."

"So he'll grow up big and strong like his father," Roslynn said as she prepared to nurse. "Where is Madoc? Still sleeping in the hall after celebrating all night? They seemed very subdued. I expected the singing to last until dawn, at least."

"I think we need more linen," Lady Eloise replied as she laid the babe in her daughter's arms and backed away. "Can you manage while I fetch it?"

"Yes, of course."

"I won't be a moment," her mother said, before she hurried from the room.

Why such haste? Roslynn wondered, and where *was* Madoc? He had been so happy and so proud, surely he should have come to see her and the baby before now.

She glanced out the window as her son began to suck. It was well past dawn. Madoc must know, after she'd insisted that he stay with her and he'd held their child, and especially when she'd looked at him with all the love she felt, that she would never leave him again. The dread she'd felt about what he might do in the heat of his temper had not been his fault, but the aftermath of her own past. It was *her* emotions that needed to be conquered more than his, for even when he lost his temper, he was never mean or cruel. He would never hurt her. She need never be afraid of Madoc, no matter how angry he became.

Perhaps something had happened to detain him, she told herself. Perhaps he'd had too much wine or *braggot* and was still sleeping somewhere.

Perhaps Trefor had heard of the birth of another son for his brother and done something terrible.

No, that couldn't be, or she would have heard an alarm sounded and men riding out.

In spite of her efforts to comfort herself, Roslynn's hands trembled as she put the baby to her shoulder and began to rub his little back. Madoc must be all right. No harm would befall him. Not today, or for years to come. She would tell him what she had come to realize, and that she'd been wrong. Given how he'd looked at her last night, she believed he would forgive her, and it would be as it was during the best days of their marriage.

As soon as her mother returned, she would ask her to find Madoc and bring him here.

The door opened a crack. "Mother?" she called out eagerly.

It was not her mother. Two heads, one above the other as if they were stacked, appeared—her father and Uncle Lloyd, as curious and shy as little boys.

Surely if Madoc were in trouble, they wouldn't be looking like that. "Have you come to see the baby?"

"Aye, and you," Lloyd said, sidling into the room. "How are you?"

"Well, and very happy."

Her son burped, and she lowered him, to see that his eyes were closed. He was falling asleep already. "Come and see Mascen."

"He's so small," her father said with awe.

"He's the perfect size for a babe," Lloyd corrected with a frown, as if Lord James's observation was a personal insult. "Mind, smaller than if he'd not wanted to make his entrance early and in a dramatic fashion, but Madoc was only a bit bigger when he was born, and he was a fortnight overdue."

"Now that I think of it, Roslynn," Lord James remarked, "you were about that size, and you were early, too." He leaned over to look closely at the baby. "What a fine grandson!"

"My grandnephew's a marvel and no mistake," Lloyd said, pushing Lord James aside. "Look you at those lips—Madoc's exactly, with that little dip in the center. And the nose is just like my brother's was. He'll be even better looking than his father with that nose."

"There's nothing wrong with my husband's nose!" Roslynn laughingly protested.

"Well, not saying there is, am I?" Lloyd replied, "but his father's was better."

"It *is* a very fine nose," Roslynn agreed. "It would be nice if I could compare it to my husband's right now. I hope he didn't drink too much *braggot* and fall ill?"

"No, he's fine, perfectly fine, I'm sure of it, like Mascen," Lloyd said quickly—too quickly.

Roslynn shifted, then winced. "Where *is* Madoc?"

Lloyd and her father exchanged significant looks, and fear crept into her heart. "Is he in danger? Has Trefor come onto our land? Has he been attacked? Or has he gone to Pontyrmwr to fight him?"

The baby started to fuss and Lloyd reached out to take him. "Now see there, you've upset the poor little man, and no reason for it. Your husband's fine."

"It's true," her father assured her. "He just went to get Owain. It's a bit of a ride, so it's not surprising he's not back yet."

Relieved and pleased she was finally going to meet her stepson, and he was going to meet his little brother, Roslynn smiled. "Oh, that's wonderful!"

Lloyd handed back the baby and started toward the door. "We'd best be off. You need your rest, that termagant of a midwife says. She's probably finished eating by now and there'll be hell to pay if she finds us here when she comes back. I'll send Madoc to you the moment he's back. Should be anytime now."

"When did he depart?" she asked. She wanted to be ready to receive Owain, and have the baby clean and fed and ready, too, when they arrived.

"Well, now, yesterday," Lloyd admitted, "but it would take awhile to get there, and he wouldn't be riding home in the dark, especially with a child."

"No, he wouldn't," she replied even as they heard a commotion on the wall walk.

"It's not an attack," Lloyd said at once. "Must be Madoc come home."

A worried look on her face, Lady Eloise hurried into the room, and Roslynn's relief died in an instant.

"What's happened?" Lord James demanded as Roslynn stared at her, too afraid to speak. But, oh, please, God, let Madoc be safe, or she would live with regret and remorse for not trusting him sooner all the rest of her life.

"There's no need to frighten Roslynn," Lady Eloise said sharply to her husband. "Ioan and some of the men are back, that's all. Madoc will return soon, too, no doubt."

No doubt, she'd said, those two words bringing not comfort, but more fear. "Mother, where is he?"

"I'm not exactly sure," Lady Eloise reluctantly replied.

"Mother, take Mascen and put him in the cradle

and stay with him. I'm going to find my husband, or someone who can tell me where he is."

The men looked horrified, and Lady Eloise only slightly less so. "You've just had a baby," she said. "You must stay in bed."

"Please send Ioan to me."

"That, um, won't be possible."

More determined than ever, Roslynn held out her son to her mother. "Then take the baby, Mother, and help me dress. Father, Uncle, please wait for me on the stairs. I'll need your help going down the steps— but I *will* find out what's happened to my husband."

SUPPORTED BY her father and Uncle Lloyd, Roslynn stepped into the hall and saw the cot on the dais and a man lying upon it. Sick with fear, she nearly swooned until Ioan turned toward her.

"Be of good cheer, my lady," he called out jovially, although he was as white as freshly washed fleece and there was a piece of bloody linen wrapped around his right arm. "I was the only one got hurt."

"How?" she asked as they made their way slowly toward him. "Where?"

"Sit you down and I'll tell you," he said.

When she had done so, and her father, Uncle Lloyd and several others had gathered round, Ioan proceeded to tell them about Madoc's clever and successful strategy after an ambush, and of Gwillym's bravery in volunteering to stay with the wounded man.

When he was finished, Roslynn began to breathe easily again.

"It was Ivor and Rhodri led the scoundrels?" Lloyd demanded.

"Aye, I'm sorry to say, and both dead, more's the pity," Ioan answered. "A quick death's better than they deserve."

"I knew it!" Lloyd cried, smacking his hands on his knees. "I knew Trefor couldn't be a thief and a blackguard!"

Roslynn stared at him with surprise, for she'd heard Lloyd denounce him more than once. So had they all.

But Trefor, Ivor or Rhodri were much less important to her than her husband.

"If Madoc's well, and you were close to where Owain is fostered, shouldn't they be back by now?"

"We are!"

She had been so intent on Ioan, she hadn't heard the door to the hall open. Yet there stood Madoc, as large as life and smiling, with a small boy beside him and...*Trefor* on his other side?

She rose shakily. The boy was a smaller version of both men in terms of build and coloring, but his eyes were like only one of them. The bright blue rimmed with black was exactly the same as Trefor ap Gruffydd.

Not Madoc's eyes. Trefor's. Was it possible... But that would mean Madoc had lied. And deceived her. And everyone.

"Sit down, my dear," her father commanded.

Before she could, Madoc hurried to her and put his arms around her.

"I lied, Roslynn," he confirmed as he sat and brought her down to rest on his lap, speaking to her as if they were all alone instead of in the hall. "I lied to everyone. Gwendolyn and I were never truly husband and wife, because it was Trefor she loved, always, and after we wed, she couldn't bear my touch. So we both knew whose child she bore, and for pride's sake, we let everyone believe the child was mine."

He took a deep breath and held tight to Roslynn's hand, looking at her with eyes full of remorse. "After Owain was born, when she realized she was dying, Gwendolyn asked me to tell the truth and take Owain to his father, and I promised her I would."

A deep, ragged sigh shook his robust frame. His voice dropped to a whisper, although it was clearly audible in the hushed hall. "I broke that promise. I had a host of excuses, but beneath it all, I wanted to punish Trefor for what had happened.

Roslynn, I've been dishonest and dishonorable. It's been like a thorn in my heart, but no more than I'd earned.

"Even when I realized how much you value honesty and trust, my pride would permit no confession. I was too stubborn and too selfish to tell you. I knew I'd lose you if you learned of my deception. Then I lost you anyway.

"But you came back to me, and when I held our child in my arms, I couldn't deny Trefor his son any longer, or Owain his true father. So I got Owain and went to Pontyrmwr and begged Trefor's forgiveness and received it, too, although I don't deserve it.

"Now you know everything, Roslynn-fy-rhosyn. I have no more secrets. I don't expect you to forgive me, but I wanted you to know the whole truth."

"If Trefor can forgive you, how much easier is it for me?" she replied. "You've wronged *me* very little. It's I who've wronged *you,* by treating you like another Wimarc, when you are nothing like him.

"I believe you, Madoc, when you say this is the last lie. I know that I can trust you, and I was wrong to fear you.

"So I will never leave you again, husband. Not as long as I live, because not only do I trust you and respect you, I love you. With all my heart, I love you."

Madoc's eyes widened, and joy and hope and

happiness shone forth as he clutched her to him as if she were the most precious thing in all the world. "I love you, my rose, my blessed, blessed rose. I will always love you."

Somebody loudly cleared his throat. "To be sure, the lad's the image of Trefor and now things make a hell of a lot more sense," Uncle Lloyd declared.

Still on her husband's lap, her arms entwined about his neck, Roslynn smiled at Trefor standing awkwardly in the hall that had once been his home. "Welcome, Trefor. Welcome! And you, too, Owain," she said to the quiet little boy looking about him with awe. "You are very welcome, too."

Madoc called out to Bron, who started as if she'd been in a stupor. "Bron, take Owain to the kitchen. I think he'd probably like some soup or bread."

"Or honey cakes?" the little lad piped up, his voice clear as the first birdsong of spring.

"Yes, my lord," Bron replied, holding out her hand and giving the little boy an encouraging smile—and his father, too.

"Thank you, Bron," Trefor said. "You haven't changed a bit."

Bron blushed as pink as sweet william as she led the boy away.

"I hope that means there can be peace between you," Roslynn said, "although if you must make amends with land or sheep or money, Madoc, you should."

"I want nothing of his," Trefor said at once.

"Then think of it as coming from Llanpowell," Roslynn replied. "Repayment for past wrongs, and Ivor's, too."

Trefor's lips curved up in a smile, which made him look more like her handsome husband. "Since the lovely lady of Llanpowell puts it that way, very well."

"We'll discuss all that later," Lloyd declared. "First, a drink to celebrate, eh? But no more *braggot* or wine for me. Just good honest ale from now on, and not too much. I must stay on my mettle if I'm to help train Mascen."

Roslynn didn't want to drink anything, or celebrate, except alone with Madoc. "If you'll all excuse me, I think I should rest a bit. Madoc, will you—"

Madoc immediately lifted her in his powerful arms. "I'll not have you swooning on me," he declared. Then he dropped his voice to a whisper. "And there is more I would say to you alone, my lady."

"ROSLYNN!" Lady Eloise cried as Madoc carried Roslynn into their chamber. "What's—?"

"I'm all right. I'm just a little tired and my

brawny husband felt the need to demonstrate his strength," she replied as Madoc, with a glance at the cradle and his sleeping son, set her on the bed.

"Would you leave us, please, Mother?" Roslynn asked. "Father can tell you what's happened, and who our visitors are."

Lady Eloise smiled indulgently. "Of course," she replied, going to the door and closing it quietly behind her.

"What did you want to tell me?" Roslynn asked as her husband leaned over the cradle and grinned at his son.

Madoc left the baby and came to sit beside her, taking her hands in his, his expression gravely serious. "Roslynn, I will give you the same promise I made to my brother today. On my honor—such as it is, after all that I've done—I will never lie to you again, about anything."

She smiled at him, her eyes bright with love, and affection and trust. "I have no need for promises, Madoc ap Gruffydd, lord of Llanpowell. I believe you. I trust you. I love you."

"And there is one thing above all you must always believe, Roslynn-fy-rhosyn," he said as he wrapped his arms about her. "I love you. I love you with all my heart, and I will always be truthful and faithful to you for as long as I live."

"As I love you, Madoc ap Gruffydd, and I will always be truthful and faithful for as long as I live."

"Then I have all that a man could ask for," Madoc murmured as he drew her to him.

"And I am as happy and contented as any woman could ever be," Roslynn whispered as she lifted her face for his kiss. "Madoc-fy-cariad."

He smiled as he caressed her cheek and brushed the pad of his thumb over her lips. "Madoc-my-lover," he repeated. "I like that."

"I asked Bron for the right words."

"Thank God you didn't ask Uncle Lloyd," he said, laughing softly as he held her close.

And little Mascen ap Madoc ap Gruffydd, sheltered and surrounded by their love, slumbered peacefully on.

REQUEST YOUR
FREE BOOKS!

2 FREE NOVELS
FROM THE ROMANCE/SUSPENSE
COLLECTION PLUS 2 FREE GIFTS!

YES! Please send me 2 FREE novels from the Romance/Suspense Collection and my 2 FREE gifts (gifts are worth about $10). After receiving them, if I don't wish to receive any more books, I can return the shipping statement marked "cancel." If I don't cancel, I will receive 4 brand-new novels every month and be billed just $5.49 per book in the U.S. or $5.99 per book in Canada, plus 25¢ shipping and handling per book plus applicable taxes, if any*. That's a savings of at least 20% off the cover price! I understand that accepting the 2 free books and gifts places me under no obligation to buy anything. I can always return a shipment and cancel at any time. Even if I never buy another book from the Reader Service, the two free books and gifts are mine to keep forever.

185 MDN EF5Y   385 MDN EF6C

Name	(PLEASE PRINT)	
Address		Apt. #
City	State/Prov.	Zip/Postal Code

Signature (if under 18, a parent or guardian must sign)

Mail to **The Reader Service:**
IN U.S.A.: P.O. Box 1867, Buffalo, NY 14240-1867
IN CANADA: P.O. Box 609, Fort Erie, Ontario L2A 5X3

Not valid to current subscribers to the Romance Collection,
the Suspense Collection or the Romance/Suspense Collection.

Want to try two free books from another line?
Call 1-800-873-8635 or visit www.morefreebooks.com.

* Terms and prices subject to change without notice. N.Y. residents add applicable sales tax. Canadian residents will be charged applicable provincial taxes and GST. Offer not valid in Quebec. This offer is limited to one order per household. All orders subject to approval. Credit or debit balances in a customer's account(s) may be offset by any other outstanding balance owed by or to the customer. Please allow 4 to 6 weeks for delivery. Offer available while quantities last.

Your Privacy: Harlequin is committed to protecting your privacy. Our Privacy Policy is available online at www.eHarlequin.com or upon request from the Reader Service. From time to time we make our lists of customers available to reputable third parties who may have a product or service of interest to you. If you would prefer we not share your name and address, please check here. ☐

BOB08R

MARGARET MOORE

HQN™

We *are* romance™

www.HQNBooks.com   PHMM0109BL